RYAN'S GAMBIT

THE TIMELESS VOID SERIES: BOOK 1

CRAIG ROBERTSON

RYAN'S GAMBIT

THE TIMELESS VOID SERIES: BOOK 1

by Craig Robertson

There are some thing you just can't take back ... maybe ...

Imagine-It Publishing
El Dorado Hills, CA

ALSO BY CRAIG ROBERTSON:

* Podium Entertainment has produced audiobooks for all the below titles except the older standalone books.

For specifics as to the correct order for reading the Ryanverse, click here.

BOOKS IN THE RYANVERSE:

THE FOREVER SERIES (2016)

THE FOREVER LIFE, Book 1

THE FOREVER ENEMY, Book 2

THE FOREVER FIGHT, Book 3

THE FOREVER QUEST, Book 4

THE FOREVER ALLIANCE, Book 5

THE FOREVER PEACE, Book 6

THE FOREVER BOXSET, Part 1, Books 1 & 2

THE FOREVER BOXSET, Part 2, Book 3 & 4

THE FOREVER BOXSET, Part 3, Book 5 & 6

GALAXY ON FIRE SERIES (2017)

EMBERS, Book 1

FLAMES, Book 2

FIRESTORM, Book 3

FIRES OF HELL, Book 4

DRAGON FIRE, Book 5

ASHES, Book 6

GALAXY ON FIRE BOXSET, Part 1, Books 1 & 2
GALAXY ON FIRE BOXSET, Part 2, Books 3 & 4
GALAXY ON FIRE BOXSET, Part 3, Books 5 & 6

RISE OF ANCIENT GODS SERIES (2018):

RETURN OF THE ANCIENT GODS, Book 1
RAGE OF THE ANCIENT GODS, Book 2
TORMENT OF THE ANCIENT GODS, Book 3
WRATH OF THE ANCIENT GODS, Book 4
FURY OF THE ANCIENT GODS, Book 5
FALL OF THE ANCIENT GODS, Book 6

TIME WARS LAST FOREVER SERIES (2019)

RYAN TIME, Book 1
LOST TIME, Book 2
FRAGMENTED TIME, Book 3
SHATTERED TIME, Book 4
FINDING TIME, Book 5
HEALING TIME, Book 6

THE TIMELESS VOID (2021)

RYAN'S GAMBIT, Book 1
RYAN'S PHANTOMS, Book 2
RYAN'S ENIGMA, Book 3
RYAN'S UNDOING, Book 4
RYAN'S REBOOT, Book 5

For more information about Craig, his books, various series, or to see images and videos for some of his wild alien characters, please visit his website. You'll be glad you did: https://craigarobertson.com/

To sign up for Craig's newsletter to get announcements, updates, and his recommendations for other great Sci-Fi reads go to: https://preview.mailerlite.io/forms/2369493/188634426375144501/share

ISBN: 978-1-7366732-4-9 (Print)
978-1-7366732-3-2 (E-Book)

Cover design by Alexandre
http://www.designbookcover.pt/en/

Editors: Michael R. Blanche
Neil Farr
Amy Schubert
Marie Spillias

Formatting services by Drew Avera
drewavera@gmail.com

First Edition 2021

This book is lovingly dedicated to William Peter Daskarolis (May 21, 1938 - Sept. 25, 2021). He was Bill to his many, many friends. I, and generations of other lucky athletes, called him Coach. He was my first coach. I was a stunningly mediocre long-distance runner when I showed up for my first cross country practice at Aragon High School,

in San Mateo, California, in the mid 60s. But Coach treated me just like the team's stars - fairly and with well-intentioned tomfoolery. Thank you for caring and listening during a very dark time for me. Thanks, especially, for a life superbly lived. Rest well, Coach. When we meet in Heaven, seriously, I'm buying the first round ...

PROLOGUE

Hi. My name is Jon Ryan and I killed time. No, it's not my intro to some existential twelve-step program. And I'm not confessing to have frittered away time on some Saturday afternoon. No, what I'm trying to do is to state two facts clearly that need to be stated clearly. Maybe no one's reading these words, come to think of it, because—duh—no time means there's no life. But I feel the need to speak. I want my version of what I did and why I did it on the record. Maybe someone somewhere survived? They might want to know what terror blindsided them and why it did so. Maybe time will return spontaneously, resurrect itself as it were? If it did, then eventually—like twenty bazillion years from now—someone might scratch their head (assuming they have one) and ask what the hell happened ever so long ago. Given enough time, anything's ...

Crap. Bad line of reasoning there. There *is* no time. So there sure can't be enough of it to have some future-alien mind contemplate its disappearance. There will be no one to draw a breath. There will be no one to imagine again.

There will be no one to forgive me.

What's my story? I used to be a hero, if I do say so myself. Huh.

If I *didn't* say so myself, who the hell would? No one else exists. I'm the last man standing. Lucky me. Anyway, I was born on Earth in the mid-twentieth century. I wasted my youth with relish and abandon. But then I got my act together, or, to give credit where credit is due, Uncle Sam did the heavy lifting for me in that category. Because I could throw a mean forward pass and I wanted to fly jets recklessly, I eked my way into the Air Force Academy. And I graduated at the head of my class. Seriously. I was first in line at the ceremony—at least up until the commandant of cadets told me to get the hell back where I belonged in the Long Blue Line. That would have been position number fifty-three. Hey, that was still back in the days of my personal development. Only after that did I become a singularly focused animal and decided I needed to win every endeavor I made an attempt at.

And succeed I did. Top of my class in pilot training, combat ace, astronaut, and the first man selected to undertake a mission in *Project Ark*. Now that was a trip. Literally. The Earth was about to be destroyed. I was selected to be uploaded to an android host and travel the galaxy alone seeking humankind a new home. And I did. Most humans and many animals evacuated the planet and headed for safer pastures because of my diligent efforts—you're welcome very much. A round of applause for me and I can rest on my laurels, right? No. The opposite of right.

I lived more than two billion years into the future. There, while otherwise minding my own business, I got word that twenty-five years before Jupiter took out the Earth, a crazy race of time-eating aliens threatened Earth. So, I went back in time to deal with them. I gave their sorry asses a severe beatdown, but not before they took all of Earth's time, causing it to have never existed. It was no-timed. But, heck, I'm a hero, right? So, I fixed it. I re-timed the Earth, brought back humankind, and even the birds and the bees. As Ben Franklin said, "*A place for everything and everything in its place.*" Did I then retire, content that I'd done my full duty? Yeah, that would've been a good plan.

But I could not get a conundrum, the riddle without an answer, out of my head. What was to happen to Earth? In her original timeline, I did what I mentioned before. I saved everyone from an out-of-orbit Jupiter. But in the new timeline, Jupiter could never threaten the planet. The new super-duper alien time ship we'd acquired could easily end that crisis. So, what became of time? Keep in mind that there was still the *original* Jon Ryan alive back during those times, the human, non-android version. The one I'd re-timed along with the rest of the species. But after I changed the timeline, what became of him/me? It was like one of those go-back-in-time-and-shoot-your-grandfather logic nightmares. Did I transfer to an android and sail the stars anyway? Or did I become a fat-assed desk officer politicking my way around the halls of the Pentagon looking to climb over my friends' backs to get the top prize? We pilots, by the way, refer to those USAF participants as IFGOs (pronounced *if-goes*). *I*gnorant *F*ucking *G*round *O*fficers. Yeah, like I'd ever become one of those.

Note To Self I: If you get a chance—if a genie grants you a single wish—do *not* ask those questions about the timeline. NTS II: If the questions themselves are sprinkled with fairy dust, come to life, and ask themselves, do not under any set of circumstances listen. And never, ever seek to answer their questions. No. Here's the protocol for addressing the forward timeline from wherever you presently stand on the damn thing. 1) Turn your back; 2) Walk away; 3) Do not look back. Think of yourself as Lot's wife. You want to become a pillar of salt? No, so do not look back. Ignore any curiosity or feelings of guilt.

Me? I didn't just look back. No, I tried to make it right. Can you imagine? What vain fool thinks that *he* can understand time, let alone control it? I'm scanning the room. Yup, only one hand is raised. Mine.

That, my friends, is what led me to destroy time. I didn't want to, but I came to learn I had to. Hey, what am I thinking? I'm getting ahead of myself. Terrible manners on my part. Sorry. In my defense, it's lonely being the only and final thing to exist. It's easy to forget the social graces.

There's a saying, one my old man used to suffer me to hear all the time. *The road to hell is paved with good intentions.* Jon Ryan, I'll have you know, never settled for middling results. I didn't pave a road.

I built a damn freeway.

ONE

I was lounging aimlessly in my bed one fine day. Sapale and I were alone, as usual, aboard our home, the spaceship *Stingray*. It had been a couple weeks since we successfully resurrected Earth. We found ourselves between gigs, as it were. I had long ago been uploaded to an android (boy howdy long story there), so I didn't sleep. But I did lounge. I excelled at lounging. If Harvard awarded a degree in Lounging, I'd have been the department chair.

"Jon, get up already," Sapale chided. That alien wife of mine. After two billion years of marital bliss she still loved me enough to relentlessly nag at me. If that ain't love then I don't know what is. "The captain's senior staff meeting starts in ten minutes. We need to be there."

"You do realize that we are no longer senior staff aboard Aramthella, right?"

Aramthella. What can be said about her? She was a time ship built by some now long forgotten race in the indistinct, cloudy haze of history. A vicious band, a totally different alien race, who called themselves the clan stole the ship from them. With her they abused reality for millions of years. Then she basically ate the clan and came over to our side. Another long story for a different time, to be certain. Aramthella chose a brainiac academic, Sachiko Jones, to be her new captain. Now that captain was having a staff meeting. Sapale didn't want to be late. I didn't want to attend.

My wife is from Kaljax. If you know any Kaljaxian women you know how headstrong and non-subtle they are prone to be. So, in this instance, the interface between her desire and mine meant we were going to the darn meeting. If I liked it, fine. If I hated it, that was fine, too. But I'd better not make her late. Sapale late = Jon suffers badly. That's one bad equation.

"That, brood-mate mine, is a *technicality*, not an *excuse*. We gave our hearts and souls to this ship and her mission. Together—all of us as one—we re-time Earth. A couple weeks pass. Some new officers are assigned to her. Those factors in no way cancel out our vital past service or our valued input. Oh," she remarked offhandedly, "quick update. You now have seven minutes to live."

"What? The staff meeting's in six minutes."

"And if you do not get moving before those six minutes pass, then, on the seventh minute she will slay him."

I sat up. That's what adults call compromise.

"Keep coming, flyboy," she encouraged sternly, dragging the air between us toward her with her hands. "I'm confident you can do it."

Adult *humans* at least. "You go ahead. I need to ... I need to—"

My forever wife turned to face me squarely. "You need to what?"

"Think of an excuse to not go with you at the same time." I shooed at her with the backs of my hands. "Go. I'll catch up."

"If I go, you'll lay back down, so help me, you'll be the basis of a new flavor of calrf."

She really did know me too well. Plus, the thought of becoming a new flavor of her native stew, of which all flavors are repugnant, was enough to set me in motion.

I rotated and rested my feet on the floor. "How about this? We attend this last staff meeting. When it's over, we state publicly just that. Then when there's the next boring-session of soul-numbing anguish, we stay here. Is that a deal?"

"It's an offer. It would only be a deal if I agreed. But, since the meeting starts in four minutes, you've stressed me out too much to consider the offer. Now rise."

Okay, I could tell. She meant those last two words. I did feel the need to stop lounging, didn't I? And what better way to unlounge than to attend a meeting where coffee and overly sweet pastries would be served?

I bounded toward the door. "Last one there's—"

Honestly, I do not know. Did Sapale stick out a foot and trip me because she was so darn competitive? Or was she trying to hurt me? Both? As I lay face-planted, I knew I'd never really know. She lightly stepped over my prone form and left for the meeting at a brisk pace. I did a push-up and stood. As I jogged closer to her, she began to run, matching my speed. Soon we were sprinting like bargain hunters at Walmart the day after Thanksgiving. Elbows flew, as did the curses. As fun as that was, it sucked. I was too preoccupied to see who won by the time we arrived at Sachiko's stateroom.

"I won," I declared.

"Here comes first prize," Sapale announced as she balled up a fist.

Seeing what was coming, I smoothed my hair back and stepped into the stateroom, all composed and dignified. I was, that is, until someone—whose name I will not mention—kicked my right foot toward my left, causing me to stumble and nearly topple. Man, those Kaljaxians were dirty competitors.

"Are you okay, Jon?" the captain asked with concern as I made my awkward entrance.

"Fine, fine. Couldn't be better. And you?"

Sachiko sat back down. "Fine. Please find a seat." She already had that disappointed-pet-owner look on her face. The longer she knew me, the more she was of the opinion that I was needlessly immature and a slacker. What did I say to that? Thank you! Plus, it signified to me that Sachiko was growing into her role as ship's captain. I mean, disdain for me personally? Yeah, that was the opinion of most CO's I'd ever had, once they got to know me. And to think that three short years ago she was an aspiring graduate student just hoping to make a big splash in astronomy at a major university.

I grabbed some joe for Sapale and myself and we took a seat next to each other. I was quiet because I'd embarrassed Sapale by making her attack me. She was quiet because she was having trouble not bursting out laughing, because she'd almost tripped me. Yeah, we were trouble, poison reservoirs to any serious organization.

"I think we may begin," Captain Jones announced formally. There were newbies present, I'd just made a fool of myself, and she wanted to start on a non-pathetic note. "The first order of business will be to formally thank those who have served on Aramthella before, and to welcome our new comrades."

There were some murmurings of agreement from the others.

"I am pleased to announce that *Colonel* St. Claire has been promoted to full colonel based on her distinguished service on our successful mission to reanimate Earth." Sachiko gestured toward Reva.

Those present applauded her warmly. "She will be remaining aboard and serving as my first officer. Major Tom Grant and Captain Emma Walters are also staying to continue their outstanding work. Tom will assume Reva's former role as direct commander over all military personnel. Emma is only too glad to leave her now nonexistent job of supervising the female college students. She will assume the duties of operational officer under Tom's command."

There was pleasant laughter at Emma's facial expression when her not being a head babysitter was announced. It was a look of relief that one might have when the Devil told you you'd been sent to Hell via a clerical error he'd just corrected. Goodbye, enjoy Heaven.

"And that leads us to formally introduce Brigadier General Glenn Price. General Price will take over the role recently vacated by General Ryan as our overall mission commander. Welcome, Glenn."

Sachiko led a round of polite applause.

"Pleased and honored to be here," Glenn said in a constipated tone. He gestured toward me. "I only hope to continue the standard of excellence General Ryan began when he was pressed into duty so unexpectedly."

A backhanded compliment if ever I'd heard one. It had to figure that the next MC would be a Pentagon handmaid, boot-licking company man. I had no doubt the powers that be wanted to pee all over this project, making it abundantly clear it was *their* property. If they could have figured out a way to employ a crowbar and a taser to get Sachiko off the ship, I'm sure they'd have gone for that too. I wasn't in the loop, but I bet that Sachiko had been lucky to keep her three prior officers. I'm certain the Pentagon would have rather slipped in a few more loyal drones.

General Glenn was what I called a *corporate beachhead*. He was landed here to not only secure that area for the corporation, which was in this case the US military, but he was also here to make all non-like-thinkers feel uncomfortable enough to leave the project. No free-thinkers actually got fired or were asked to leave. No, the environment was just made so stuffed-shirt and toxic that only true believers could stomach remaining.

And Glenn the Hen (my new nickname for the bloated farm animal) felt it was mission critical to point out what my past status officially amounted to. I was neither selected in the first place nor anyone's first, second, or twenty-third choice as MC for the first mission. I was in the right place when no one else was. Glenn felt strongly, in the privacy of his thoughts, that I wasn't a *real* four-star general, not a seriously valid one. I was, in fact, an abomination to him and his handlers. My rank was awarded long ago in a future none of upper management actually believed in. And I was an android. I was as four-star general as a marionette dressed as one was in his narrow, beady little eyes.

Aside from that I liked the man. Sure, I wished him the best of luck along with a nasty STD. Half of me wanted to stay and fight to keep this a scientific ship performing scientific missions. The other half, the one with more neurons than testosterone receptors, wanted to get the hell out of here ASAP. You can't fight city hall. That's what they say. If that's true, you sure as hell can't fight the Military Industrial Complex and its cult-like minions. No, they have what city hall does, along with tanks and nuclear weapons.

"Speaking of General Ryan and his wife," Sachiko continued, bringing me back to the here-and-now, "it is with profound regret I find we must say goodbye to them as members of the senior staff. There is no way to acknowledge the debt we owe to them. Earth quite literally would not exist had it not been for their bold and tireless contributions."

I think the others were going to applaud us, but apparently Glenn the Hen opined so also. He stood and saluted me. That cut off the beginnings of the applause. It would have been comical had it not been so offensive. He clearly meant to head off any affection directed our way. I mean, who cheers during the Pledge of Allegiance? His salute had the same chilling effect. Glenn sat back down awkwardly when I didn't return his salute. What was he going to do, fire me?

Sachiko glared at Glenn a spell, then her face eased back into a captainly look of composure. "So, onto the meeting's main goals."

I raised a finger.

"Yes, Jon? You have a question?"

"Not so much. I'd just like to add to our general praise and adulation the name of General Robert Sherman. I know Tank's not aboard this time out, but his role was pivotal in our success."

"Absolutely," Sachiko replied as she stood and clapped loudly. Everyone else—except you guessed it—stood and clapped loudly also. Finally the Hen relented and rose, tapping his hands together as if applauding.

"Tank told me he decided to sit this mission out," I stated dubiously. "He told me he wanted to catch up on his civilian career and his family. Sounds so unlike Tank, but what do I know? He said as much to me directly."

"I understand General Sherman is especially keen on returning to his administrative roles at the university," bellowed Glenn. "He told me those duties while he was absent were unfortunately somewhat neglected."

Yeah, that Tank. Never an admin role he didn't love more than space travel, adventure, and service to his country.

Glenn then gyrated his face like it was preparing to take a crap. Turned out it was. "Speaking of roles elsewhere, General Ryan, we are *all* curious," his plump hand swept across those present. "Now that you are no longer part of the command structure here aboard Aranthella, when is it you and your lovely wife plan on departing?"

Two things happened. One, Sapale growled. You remember Kaljaxians and their growls, right? Their species has as many varied throated sounds as a big cat. Some mean *Hi*, some *I'm happy*, and some signify *someone is about to lose the ability to sexually reproduce*. Glenn got one of the last type from Sapale.

Two, I caught the Hen's gaze and held it like only a person who has killed as much as I have is able to. I gave the lock-stare a three count. "It's Ar-*am*-thella. There's no 'n' in the ship your command travels on."

Stupid bastardo.

"That's not what I said," he responded a la dipshit. "If that's what you think you heard, well then I am sorry. You misheard."

Really, mincemeat brain?

"So, back to our question?" Glenn pressed. "When will I have the honor of having the bosun's mate pipe you off?"

What a turdmeister. I sat back and said positively nothing.

After nearly a minute Sachiko felt compelled to speak. "Ah, Glenn, you know this ship is attached to the US Army, right? The *Navy* has bosuns. The *Army* doesn't."

"No, no. I meant *as if* we had a bosun's mate. I'm surprised you missed that intended meaning, captain, just like Mr. Ryan did." He looked to Reva and Tom. "You'll soon discover that I always speak as plain as day."

Oh, so it wasn't his moronishness but it was everyone else's poor listening skills now? Boy, oh boy, was Sachiko in for a long voyage, even if they never left port. A man who can never do anything *wrong* can never do anything *right*.

"Sachiko," I said in my deepest voice. "Captain. I want to get on to new business. There have been a few discrepancies in the fuel consumption reports. Have we determined where the fault lies?"

"I—" Sachiko puzzled. She looked gut-punched.

"*Discrepancies?*" Glenn squealed in a judgmental tone. "I was not informed of fuel report discrepancies." He began flipping back and forth in the thick binder he carried with him everywhere.

Sachiko took the occasion of Glenn's looking down to mouth to me, "I-hate-you."

I mouthed back, "You-are-so-screwed."

"Eat-worms-and-die," was her silent-film response.

"What section would that fall under?" Glenn asked in irate frustration.

I elbowed Sapale and tossed my head in the direction of freedom.

"Sorry, Glenn," Sachiko said as she leaned in and turned the pages herself. "Jon was referring to the diesel fuel for the back-up generators we might use for away missions if electricity were needed. It isn't a ship's concern."

Sapale winked back. We deployed partial-membrane force fields around our bodies. That made us effectively invisible. Then we stood and actually disappeared. The last words I heard as I slipped out the door was Glenn's consternation of not having a folder for away mission supplies already available to him.

What a douche. But, luckily, he was not *my* douche. To paraphrase the late great Douglas Adams, Glenn the Hen was an *SED*. Somebody else's douche.

TWO

Sapale and I returned to our ship, *Stingray*. We laughed and giggled the entire way back. What struck us as so funny? Lots did. First off, we had just born witness to a prudish dick in full-active mode. Those were always a hoot to observe. It was a perverse viewing pleasure, much like watching the person who just cut you off in traffic getting pulled over for a ticket. Second, we had to make light of the absolute absurdity of humankind. We had just pulled off a series of massive miracles and resurrected all life on Earth. And what was the power-structure's reaction? Don't institutionalize greatness. No, replace it with namby-pamby bureaucrats and yes-people. Third, we had to acknowledge the humor that was befalling Sachiko. She went from working with her best friend, Tank, and two highly seasoned veterans, Sapale and me, to being bossed around by a mushroom head. Fourth, we had to laugh. The only other option was to cry ourselves to death because corporate turds just kept on being laid among us normal folk.

As our hysteria faded away, we found we were sitting on the couch in the main space of the ship. Now, a Deavoriath-designed vortex is a wonderful machine. It's hard to overstate that fact. The vortex, which is what the ship itself is called, is operated by a vortex manipulator. Those were like AIs, but light years ahead of what you and I would consider artificial intelligence. A vortex was named after its vortex manipulator. Our manipulator was named Blessing. Originally the vortex, or cube, was addressed as *Blessing*. But— please follow along here—the word "blessing" in the Deavoriath language was pronounced *crash*. Seriously. Since there was no way I was commanding a ship named *Crash*, I changed the name to the best transportation device ever invented: *Stingray*.

Anyway, Sapale and I were slouched on the couch. It was one of the three places we frequented when not otherwise occupied. For us it was either our bed, the mess, or the couch. Our design style was what I termed Early Who Cares. If it worked, we went with it. Kaljaxians weren't generally much for aesthetics and neither were fighter pilots. So, the couch was a couch. Don't even ask me what color it was because I never bothered to notice.

"Poor Sachiko," Sapale said empathetically.

"Yeah, I agree. But, hell's bells, it's life. You want to excel, someone notices, and they immediately want to take a crap on you *and* your ideas. Fools'll run around chasing you with their trousers down with practiced ease, in an all-out attempt to defecate where inspiration lives."

"But she's so young," my brood's-mate decried.

"Compared to us, everyone's young. Heck, rocks are young compared to us."

We chuckled a tad at that truth.

"And don't forget, Sachiko cut her eyeteeth in academics. That den of iniquity is every bit as petty, bureaucratic, and heavy-handed as the military. She's not a complete rookie."

"But you and I both know Glenn's first, mid-range, and long-term goals are to take control of the ship. If he's presented any chance, he'll force her out with no remorse."

"No remorse? Hell, he'd cum in his pale green briefs without having to even touch himself for once. But Aramthella's not going to stand for any shenanigans. She dealt with the clan for eons. She knows nasty when she sees it. Glenn Boy steps a centimeter out of line and he ends up in the Time Storage Unit faster than he can say, *"Can we have a meeting concerning this matter."*

Sapale patted my abdomen. "I don't know. I think his time energy would give the ship indigestion."

We enjoyed our mirth in silence over the next few minutes.

"So, flyboy, what *are* our plans?" my wife asked seriously.

"Depends."

"Doesn't it always?"

I looked over to her. "Such a philosopher."

"Thank you," she took a seated half-bow.

"Know what I like to do with philosophers?"

She furrowed her brow. "No. What?"

"I like to tickle them." And with that I launched myself at her underarms with gusto.

After a few yelps and slaps, I relented and rested back. She stopped smiling ear-to-ear and did likewise.

"Are you going to evade my question? Are there more tickle sessions, stunts, bodily gasses, or tangential changes of subject on my horizon?" she asked sternly.

"Yes," I replied, trying to sound thoughtful.

"You are such a large pile of rat droppings."

"Ah, generally rats don't poop in piles. They spread the love," I corrected helpfully.

"Your case is the exception, what with you being such a rat laxative."

"Gosh," I responded glancing at the floor. "Stated that way, it must be a compliment. I mean, it's such a scientific analysis." Then I leered up at her. "You know what I like to do with scientists?"

She gave me her patented stop-it-Jon look. Those are like red lights at intersections, but these have blaring warning sirens and guys waving large flags. These you don't ignore.

"I don't know what I do with them. I forgot." I sighed deeply.

"What do you want to do?" I turned the question around. "I assume you want to head back to our time."

"Two billion years," was her cryptic response.

"Yeah, that far ahead. That's where we live."

"No. I was saying we've known each other for two billion years."

"I slept a lot more of it than you did, but yes, we have."

"Two billion years've taught me all I need to know about you. I look in your eyes and I know that whatever I want to do doesn't matter." She pointed to my eyes. "When they read *longing*, I know better than to try and divert their intent. They're like the salmon of your world. They are driven by an invisible force to go somewhere they don't even consciously desire to go and nothing but death can stop them."

"Gosh, my eyes are pretty darn glum today. Perhaps I should visit Doc?"

"What is it you need to do?" she asked flatly.

Answers one through ten were witty quips. *Understand Russian literature, have a really good bowel movement,* and *know the difference between sarsaparilla and root beer* were a few examples. Answers eleven through thirteen were avoidance answers. *I don't know yet* or *let me get back to you on that.* Answer fourteen was smarmy BS. *All I want to do is make you happy.* That one'd cost me some teeth. I went with fifteen.

"We screwed the hell out of the timeline. I'd like to try and fix it."

She snapped her head around to look as far away from me as was possible. "I knew it. I simply knew it," she said with exasperation.

"You asked."

"I know I did. I was just hoping for not that answer. I knew it was coming, but I wished I was wrong."

I was quiet a sec. "What's the problem?"

She returned her gaze to me. "Jon, love, you can't cure a rainy day."

"Well, sure you can. With enough satellites—"

"Don't get technical when I'm being emotional. I mean you, *you*," she pushed at my chest with the flat of her hand, "can't cure a rainy day. And you can't fix a timeline."

"We don't know that as a fact."

"Jon, we don't know that it's even broken. Maybe time is supposed to be the way it is presently. How can you fix something that's not in need of repair?"

"What do you mean maybe it's not broken? Duh, it's broken. We know that there's a rogue planet heading for our solar system as we speak. In my timeline—in your timeline—it pulled Jupiter out of its orbit enough to annihilate Earth. That set in motion all the actions and calamities that led me to find you. But today, if Sachiko so desires, Aramthella can go find the rogue world and no-time it. Then there's no Jupiter oops, and we never meet."

"Jon, keep two things in mind. The timeline is not known to us. Yes, what you say is a reasonable projection, but we don't know the future. Also, just because you may not like this chapter of the process of history does not mean it isn't exactly what is supposed to happen."

"You mean as in Davdiad's will supposed to happen?" I said that a bit harsher than I intended.

She narrowed three of her four eyelids. That ... that was not a good sign. When a Kaljaxian did that, they were telegraphing non-happy feelings at the object of the gesture. "I don't think now is a good time to bring deities into the discussion, mine or yours. Let's us just focus on this, shall we? The fact that you don't approve of a sequence of future events is not the same as them objectively being wrong."

I didn't mean to antagonize Sapale. She was trying to help. Plus, let's face it, I loved her to death. "I hear you," I replied. "But to see it the way you're describing it would be to assume a lot. That would mean the 'correct' time sequence involved scrambled histories. There would be the one we both know, the one where we meet, then battle the Listhelons, the Berrillians, and all those other jokers. *And* there'd be the past resulting from everything we did with the clan.

That just doesn't square with my notion of linear time. One second occurs, then the next follows. Seconds cannot be superimposed on one another."

"Look, Jon, I'm not a science nerd. I'm making this up as I go, sure. But my point is I don't want you wedded to a mission that's significantly flawed at its core. Before you get all save-everyone, talk the situation over with Toño. Talk it over with Plesmus. Hell, find Time itself again and ask it."

I shook my head. "I don't think Time's going to allow that. I got the inescapable impression that Time was done with me."

"Fine. But there are many fine minds to consult with before you go all Don Quixote and attack a temporal windmill."

I squinted at her. "My, but you went a long way to bring that analogy in for a landing."

"Hey, I'm trying to be culturally sensitive. Don Quixote de La Mancha is one of Earth's great legends. Next time how about I just box your ears?"

I raised my hands to fend that fate off. "No, no. Culturally sensitive is good. I'll be the first to acknowledge that I have a quixotic bent to my personality."

"Hon, let the metaphor go, okay? It's not central to my message. Just think before ... No, wait. You're a fighter pilot. Crap. Forget I said that. Just consider all your options before you ... No, wait. You're a guy. Forget I said that. Just check with Toño before you commit ... No, wait. You're *you*. Look. I love you. Time may just be what it is in spite of your lack of approval for it. If you do something stupid, I will still love you, but I might have to castrate you."

"There's no blessing like a supportive wife," I responded bobbing my head.

"Thank you." She must have intentionally misinterpreted. She thumbed her chest. "And this wife's willing to do whatever it takes to help you *not* do a Jon-Ryan thing."

I threw up my arms. "Okay. Fine. I will think about all this before I decide on my plan. I'll talk to Doc, maybe Tank. I'll consult smart people. There, are you happy now?"

She grinned like the person who'd just won the whole pot in poker. "I was happy before. I'm happy now. Jon, you know I live in the moment. My twisting your arm into acting like an adult gives me no pleasure."

"That's good to—"

"Now seeing your childish *reaction* to the twisting, that is like a waterfall of pleasure."

"Anything I can do to make your life more enjoyable is my goal in this life."

Sapale patted me on the head in a manner one might with someone else's dog. "I'll go whip up dinner."

After she was gone, I didn't feel as ... um, *clean* ... maybe *integrity-laden* as I might have preferred. It was totally my fault. Yeah. You see, I'd already decided. If it was at all possible, I was fixing the damn timeline.

THREE

"Captain Jones," General Price greeted with all the humanity of a dime-store mannequin, "thank you for coming. Be seated." He aimed a Bic pen at the chair opposite him without looking up at her or the target.

Hmm, Sachiko reflected, not *please sit*, not *grab a seat*, but *be seated*. It sounded like she was a new recruit and Glenn was the authority figure. And on *her* ship. That was an unwelcome observation on her part if ever there were one. Then again, the generous side of her mind argued, maybe he's just a dull, humorless guy with no social graces?

When Glenn came aboard, he chose a series of unoccupied rooms as office space. When she'd offered him Tank's old quarters and adjacent office he hadn't even verbalized *no thank you*. He just batted his eyes in an irritated manner. He then informed Sachiko that his assistant, Captain Marvin Miltown, had already selected a suite for him and his staff based on a brief tour that Marvin had made a week prior. Sachiko was stunned to learn of Miltown's brief visit. She did not meet with him, was not informed he was coming, and most certainly hadn't approved the self-guided tour he took.

She'd been aboard the entire time. Snubbing appeared to be Glenn's favorite parlor game. That, she bristled, would never do.

Sachiko sat and folded her hands on her lap. She decided she'd wait patiently for Glenn to finish whatever he was doing, as opposed to addressing the top of his bald head. Just when she was about to announce that he was clearly too busy and that they would meet later—that is to say before she stormed off in a huff—he set his pen down, knitted his fingers together on the desktop, and stared at her a few seconds too long for her comfort.

"Is there a problem?" she asked as neutrally as she could manage.

Glenn squinted and pushed his glasses up higher on his nose with one finger. "A problem? No. There's no problem, at least not yet."

"Ah," she countered, "that's good to know. What, then, is it I might do for you, Glenn?"

"Captain Jones, you and I will be working together closely for the foreseeable future. I feel it is important for a commander and his staff to interface well. We do, after all, share a common goal."

"Thank you for sharing. I'm sure you and your staff work well as a team. What is it *I* might do for you, Glenn?"

He returned a look of confused constipation.

Sachiko elected to energetically further advance the point that needed to be driven home. "You're not offering me a position on your personal staff, are you? As you know, I already have a job. I'm captain of this ship and command the entire crew."

He grinned nervously. "Ah ... can Major Miltown bring you anything? Coffee?"

"No, thank you."

"You've met him, right? Major Miltown?"

"Yes. I met all your staff soon after you came aboard. They were the line of men who followed you around." She omitted the *like you were their mother duck*. It might seem as though she was being critical with that observation.

For reasons Sachiko couldn't fathom, the general required a

rather extensive staff. Besides the major, he was supported by two lieutenants, who served as secretaries, and a staff sergeant, whose duties were perfectly unclear. Back on Earth, the man might have been his driver. Hopefully that role would not be continued on Aramthella, since there were no cars for him to drive.

"Fine," Glenn responded. "So, I wanted to begin by going over our respective roles, Captain Jones. As you know, the President of the United States has assigned me to be the overall mission commander for this ship and its military personnel. I—"

"If I might, Glenn?" Sachiko asked demurely.

Troubled that he'd been interrupted, he suppressed his natural tendency to become irritated and said instead, "By all means."

"I am familiar with both of our roles. I am the captain of this vessel. My command is *sanctioned* by the POTUS. That technicality reflects the fact that he is not in a position to grant or appoint the captaincy of Aramthella. Only she has that prerogative. You, as mission commander, do not have direct authority over the ship's crew, be they military or civilian. *If* we deploy an expeditionary force, then we both agree that, in that specific case, you are in command of those troops and that I have no authority over them. Is that what you meant to say, Glenn?"

"That is what I said, Captain Jones. What did you hear?"

There it was again. It was simply a matter of her having poor comprehension skills, not that he was a dick trying to inarticulately usurp power.

"In any case, what is it I might do for you today?" Sachiko asked, returning to her earlier query.

"Just listen," he replied sternly.

"I am all ears." Her hands flared beside her in invitation.

"As I said, you will be working with me quite a bit. This will be especially true during our shakedown cruise over the next few months. I will expect that you coordinate with me and my staff during that process. We will—"

"If I might, Glenn?" Sachiko asked about fifty percent less demurely than before.

"Is this important? I'm a busy man and don't want this briefing to run longer than I've budgeted for."

"Ah. Say, Glenn, are you a film buff?"

He shook his head in stunned displeasure. "What has that to do with the—"

"I'm betting you're a big fan, as am I, of the 1967 classic *Cool Hand Luke* starring Paul Newman." She chuckled in the back of her throat. "You probably love the signature line in that picture as much as I do. Strother Martin's character said," she puffed up her torso and switched to a deeper, masculine voice, *"'What we've got here is failure to communicate.'* Do you know what, Glenn? That's what I believe you and I have befalling us presently."

He blinked back at her. His was a dumbstruck-stupid blink if ever there was one.

"Yes, seriously. Can you believe it?"

More aimless blinking.

"You see, you are speaking. I'm *listening*, but I don't seem to be *hearing* you." She scrunched up her nose. "Is that weird or what?"

Glenn blinked so intently it was a shame there weren't wind turbines in front of his face to harness the power.

"You see, my ship is not *embarking* on a shakedown cruise. No. We don't require one. We've served as a fighting unit for the past three years. Since returning to Earth, the ship has had no repairs or refittings. Consequently there is nothing to shakedown. More importantly, if Aramthella were to *require* a shakedown cruise, I would know because *I'm* the only one who could order one."

"I ... er—" he muttered.

"Now, as to you being busy, again, thanks for sharing. But please know that is really not my business or concern. While I expect all of *my* crew aboard *my* ship to labor diligently, you, the major, your two lieutenants, and your sergeant are *not* under my command. If the five of you choose to work twenty-four seven or if you elect to toil not, and neither will you spin, that's fine by me. Damn fine. Any-questions-Glenn-glad-to-hear-there-aren't." Sachiko stood, took a moment to smooth down her wrinkle-free uniform, then she left without another word.

In the passageway, well past earshot of the oaf, Sachiko stopped and asked the atmosphere, "So, Tank, how'd you think that went?"

FOUR

Okay, I'll admit it. Heck, I'll be among the *first* to admit it. I'm a guy. So—follow along please, this is guy-logic, so it requires a journey— what does a guy do? Wait, I forgot to mention the pressures I was under. I'll probably need to enumerate those before you're prepared to agree with me, right?

So, the timeline of Earth was FUBAR. That's military for *Fucked Up Beyond All Repair*. And please don't hold me account- able for obscene language. I'm educating here, so it's okay. Anyway, my point one is that the timeline = FUBAR. My point two is I know in my heart-of-hearts I have to fix time, in spite of the acronym's correct use of the word *repair*, as in *beyond all*. My point three is that Sapale thinks, on an ongoing basis actually, that I'm soft in the head —a three-minute-egg-for-brains. My point four is that she made me promise I'd speak with someone smarter than me. That, not surpris- ingly, isn't too challenging because *lots* of people are. She wanted me to determine if my notion was bat-shit crazy. Not to say bat-shit crazy would be a negative in my book, but she labors under the impression that such an unconventional condition matters.

Or maybe I can Jonsplain what I'm trying to say another way.

Recall, if you will, your Schopenhauer, the German philosopher. You know, the generally impenetrable, always obtuse one? He said that all truth passes through three stages. First, it is ridiculed. Second, it is violently opposed. That's where my truth was at that point. Sapale, and likely any others I consulted, would browbeat me while experiencing phases one and two. I got that mistreatment a lot. The third phase Schopenhauer posits is that all truth is finally accepted as being self-evident. I pretty much never make it to that phase, so forget I even mentioned it. What that lengthy side-trip-of-reasoning led me to was point five. What the heck was I going to do given points three and four? My brood's-mate felt I was thick in the head and needed to confer with a smarty pants. But they would likely Schopenhauer me just as she did. And I hate being Schopenhauerred.

It was clear to me that I couldn't ask Toño, and this time out it wasn't because I needed to protect his feelings and respect his privacy. No, screw those, right? This was a big deal. The problem with asking Doc was that the Toño I needed to hash this out with was two billion years in the future. I couldn't very well consult the temporally local Dr. Toño DeJesus. No, he was busy creating me and saving humankind from Jupiter. If I knocked on his door he'd have a stroke or something.

And if I asked the future version of Toño, I'd need to go back to the future to ask him. That would necessitate Aramthella ferrying Sapale and me there. Time travel using *Stingray* alone was just too dangerous to justify (unless I'm in the mood for a Pronto Pup; then it's quite reasonably undertaken. Another story for another time). Here's the main concern I had with consulting future Toño. I had a sneaking suspicion that once Sapale and I were back where we belonged, Glenn the Hen would make like an atom and split, leaving us stranded in our proper time zip code. I needed to hang around in the present time—my past—a while longer. I had to see how far Glenn was willing to go to secure control of Aramthella. I knew that was his and his handlers' intent. Now that they'd successfully locked

26

Tank out of the picture, I needed to protect Sachiko, if that was even possible. These military bastardos with their corporate mentalities would collectively take actions that were morally reprehensible to us normal folk. And Sachiko was just a babe-in-the-woods compared to the Pentagon schmucks. Me? I was seasoned, heartless if need be, and a cold-blooded killer when forced to perform that role. Me they couldn't steamroll.

So, which smart people did that leave available to me? Who was I going to seek out who could help to validate my concerns and suggest options so I could achieve my goal of fixing the timeline?

What? Isn't that what my forever wife meant I should do, consult with brainiacs so I could more effectively fight the good fight? I think that's what she instructed me to do. If not, she certainly *implied* it strongly. I'm certain she didn't want me to consult with a genius or two because she thought they might *dissuade* me from even attempting to fix time. No, Sapale just wanted me to incorporate more insights into my efforts.

With my go-to-guy Toño excluded, who was left? Tank? He was definitely smarter than me. There was the plus that he was almost as cynical and independent-minded as I was. But he lacked detailed knowledge of the science at my disposal that was advanced by his standards. Those were the tools I'd use to fix time. He was also, above everything else, a loyal Marine. He might not like the idea of me going *around* the system in order to act on its behalf.

Sachiko? Nah. She was brighter by far, but lacked worldliness. Plus she was fundamentally sweet and fair-minded. She was useless when plotting a secret-squirrel operation against corporate drones. Tip Benjamin, the most atypical human alive? No, forget I even mentioned him. *No Tip Benjamin, all of the time.* That was my new motto. In this time period, there really weren't any safe, easy options. Except ...

If I had to list my best friends, even though I'm two billion years old, the list would be short. If it wasn't, I'd have been a shallow man. Your true great friends should be few in number. Let me amend that.

They *are* few in number. Some people just don't understand or accept that reality. I remember waaay back when I was a child growing up watching TV. My parents were freakazoids for the evening news. They had to be, right? They were old. Anyway, there'd always be this coverage of the goings on in our nation's capital. A reporter would ask a question and then shove their microphone in a senator's face. The senator would always begin their answer with references to *my very great friend* Senator So-and-So, *across the aisle.* I recall deciding even as a youth that I wanted to become a senator because I wanted to have a million *very great friends.* Yeah, as a teenager I began to know with a sure certainty that politicians lied.

So, back to my list of BFFs—never counting wives or lovers, duh, because you can go insane trying to apply BFF rules to them. Near the top of my list was Kymee. He was a wise old Deavoriath. And when I say old Deavoriath, know I'm talking completely old, as old as the holes in grandpa's socks. They're not immortal, but they're also not far from it. Over the years since I first discovered Oowaoa, the Deavoriath home world, Kymee and I had become the best of friends. He gave me great counsel and comfort across hundreds of years. By the time I'd "woken up" two billion years in the future (another long story for another time), Kymee had finally gone the way of all flesh. But he was alive in the present I existed in at the moment. He didn't currently know me from a toad sitting on a hot rock, but the dude *was* alive and kicking. And he was a fountain of grace and good advice. And the best part was it wouldn't freak out a Deavoriath like him if a future friend dropped in unannounced. Nah, after all their wars and longevity, nothing much got their goats, and everything was taken in good stride.

If I simply announced to Sapale that I was going to consult with Kymee, she'd have said no, then forbid the transgression, and then box my ears. That's because she would have correctly assumed I was going in spite of whatever input she provided. If, on the other hand, I went to visit an old friend who'd never met me and *then* I told her—

well, if I ever *had* to tell her—that'd be better. Ask any good Catholic. They'll tell you. It's better to ask forgiveness than permission.

But the Deavoriath of this time, while not warlike and xeno-phobic like the Deavoriath of old, were very reclusive. They went as far as to project over the surface of their home world what was basi-cally a solid hologram of a hostile, lava-covered planet in order to discourage travelers approaching from space. I wouldn't fare well if I just dropped in and asked for Kymee. They wouldn't shoot me, but they would certainly deactivate me on sight and then scrub my memory. How can I know this? Because that's exactly what they did to me when I chanced to land on Oowaoa during my very first voyage of discovery eons ago.

But I knew Kymee. I could get around the general reservations of his kinspeople and the barriers they'd erected to chance visita-tions. The Kymee who sat in his science lab tinkering at that very moment didn't know me, but he was my great friend. All I had to do was let him know we needed to meet and he'd be down with the idea. I reflected on the hours—months, actually—of conversations we'd had in the past, which was just a few years from now. What had he ever told me that I could use to get him to meet me? Then it hit me. I knew his favorite place, his special place. And I bet he never told anyone else that little secret, not even his son.

Stingray, I called out using my head-to-head communications system.

Yes, Form One, she replied in kind.

Please call Kymee. He should be at his residence on Oowaoa.

There was a microsecond delay. In that space, Al came onto the party line. It was just like him. The Als—*Stingray* plus Al—were an old married couple. They answered the other one's questions and finished each other's thoughts. That was not surprising. They'd been together for a very long time, measured in human time scales. Trans-lated into the femtobits per second computer time frame, they were married longer than Adam and Eve at that point. *We are wondering if you are aware of what you are asking, pilot? The Kymee in this*

29

timeline does not know you from the background cosmic radiation. Your first meeting with him won't occur for the better part of a century. Are you aware of those facts?

Yes I am.

And yet you wish us to proceed?

I thought of a handful of scathing responses, but let them pass thorough my figurative fingers. I had an important agenda and no time to waste on Jonisms.

Yes, I do. Please deliver this message to Kymee. 'Meet me by your favorite stream in one hour.' Sign it a friend.

Would you like me to read that back to you? Al asked, trying to be outstandingly annoying.

Not necessary, but thanks. I switched them off and contacted Sapale via the same modality. *Hey, hon, I'm going to meet with an old friend. I'll be back in a few hours.*

Blonde, brunette, or redheaded death? she responded quizzically.

Deaths? I don't follow, love.

Whatever babe you're meeting with will be the death of you. I just want to get my story straight for my address at your memorial service. I'd hate to blow my touching, heartfelt eulogy.

Very funny. No, I'm going to Earth in this time to kill Gloria, my first wife, before I ever met her. I figure by doing that I can spare myself untold grief. Can I get you anything while I'm down there in twentieth century America?

One of those Eames Lounge Chairs'd be nice. They're so timeless.

I'll see what I can do. Love ya.

Love you too. Watch your back once you get home, okay?

Will do.

I cut the transmission. That left me just enough time to head up to the galley. I had to grab a few food items. The food synthesizers on *Stingray* were good, but I needed some obscure dishes. After that, I told Sachiko that I'd be away for a while, but to call if there was a crisis.

Soon I was perched upon a stone outcropping that angled above a meandering creek bed strewn with rocks and sand. Desiccated wood and wizened scrub brush lined the channel in patchy, parched tufts. The creek bed itself was so dry and sun tormented that it was challenging to imagine water ever flowed over it. The surface of the moon was more inviting than this bleak landscape.

"Isn't it marvelous?" came an old man's voice from behind my position. He spoke in the one-true tongue of the Deavoriath. So universal was the language among them that it didn't even have a name or dialects. It was simply what always had been spoken.

"Yes, brother, it inspires great thoughts without an effort to bid them come," I responded, using an old idiom in perfect Deavoriath. I didn't need a translation matrix to converse. I'd spent so much time among these one-time demigods of the galaxy it was second nature to me.

"Do you know that is the very spot," Kymee gestured to the rock I sat cross-legged on, *"where my mate agreed to spend her eternity with me as a bonded team? We sat on that boulder and she pledged to have a shared forever with this sorry excuse for a male."* His tone was wistful, with an underpinning of melancholy.

I grinned at him. *"In fact, I do."*

"You are not familiar to me, either as an individual or a species," Kymee mused. *"Yet you know such intimate details of my life."*

"I may not be familiar to you yet, but trust me, we're the best of friends."

"Yet? So, you come to me from the future."

I had to love that Kymee. He was so fast on the uptake. *"Yours, not mine. This is my past."*

"Hmm. You are a vexing mixture then," Kymee stated thoughtfully. *"This is, if I am to believe you, your past. It is clearly your present. If it were also your future, then this moment would be your every-time."*

I looked up in thought. *"Nope, this moment is many things, but it is not my present future."*

"Constants are so important to a well-ordered life," he opined. *"By*

the way, you must know I am Kymee. I would enjoy knowing who you are. That way when we meet from the second time I will pay extra attention. I wouldn't want to ruin a perfectly good future, now would I?"

"You won't." I stood and wound my way down to where he waded in remembered water. "Jon Ryan," I introduced myself. I grabbed his right elbow and he took mine. We "shook" in the traditional Deavoriath manner.

"Very nice to meet you for the first time," he said with that familiar twinkle in his eyes. He was so un-Deavoriath that way. He saw joy and humor in everything. Deavoriaths were, in general, a dour lot on a festive day.

"Did you know," I began didactically, and I swept my arm across the vista, "that this place was once lush and verdant?"

He shook his head as if to say do tell.

"Yes. Mind you it was long ago," I sniffed and looked upward a bit. "When you were but a sprig, pining for adulthood. A long time ago. Yes. And I was several-thousand millennia from being but a notion my grandparents had on their honeymoon night."

"That does seem far removed in time," he agreed wistfully.

"But I assure you this entire valley was life itself." I pointed to a nearby ridge. "There was a stand of penfillious trees there."

"No," Kymee exclaimed.

"And we all know what a good omen they are."

"So I am told. But I have not laid eyes on a stand of penfillous trees since ... well since I sat on that rock and pledged my eternity to my dear and loving mate. Quewldia was her name." He stared off into nothingness a moment. "Long has she been gone from my side," he reported sadly. Then, typical Kymee, he was energized by youthful ebullience. "But over a million good years we had, my Quewldia and I."

"I would wager my soul, if such a thing were to exist to wager, that they were the best million years any two have shared."

He chuckled softly, mostly to himself. "It would be a safe bet, Jon

Ryan. If you made it, you would have two souls, my friend. The one you would not have lost and the one the fool who wagered against you forfeited."

"Then I regret the missed opportunity. Who has too many souls in this sad world?"

"Who indeed?" he responded, chuckling a bit louder.

Kymee sat on a low rock along the withered shoreline where water must once have flowed. Indicating a similar perch to his right, he invited me to sit. I did.

"Such a beautiful creek," he said softly. "It is forever a vision of the sublime."

"I see not through your eyes, but through your experience and I know there is truth in your words." That was another venerable local saying.

"So, a man comes to me from the future," Kymee stated. He cast the words into the air and studied them like butterflies flitting away. He set one of his three hands on his chest. "To me, a simple scientist. A man of unsurpassed mediocrity. What kind of future man visits one so undistinguished as me?"

"One who carries with him many troubles. And my troubles are disguised as questions."

"So, it is a man of the future who wishes to unburden himself that seeks out an unremarkable man of his past?"

"You are neither run-of-the-mill nor but-one-of-the-crowd. You are Kymee, the greatest scientist of the Deavoriath in over three million years. More importantly you are my great friend."

He pointed an index finger skyward. "Will be a great friend," he corrected.

"Sorry, you are to me already."

"I will therefore immediately reciprocate, friend Jon."

"Thank you."

"No thanks are needed between the best of friends. Come, begin your tale and allow me to help you."

What a peach. Even though I was a complete stranger, Kymee

was open and accepting. Not only very un-Deavoriath, but also just plain heartwarming. So, I told him my two epic stories. One of a planet soon-to-be-destroyed, and a man who became a machine to save its population. I regaled him with my adventures, how I discovered Oowaoa, met my one true love, and saved my people. I expanded to recount how after that victory, I was challenged with an endless series of trials, all of which I managed to successfully complete. The Last Nightmare, the Berillians, the Adamant, and the Ancient Gods.

Then I switched timelines to tell of a horrific clan who no-timed Earth. How I was called back in time to fight that foe to try and set the galaxy right. He learned how a graduate student became the captain of a mighty time ship, and how together we wiped out the clan. I told him of my search for knowledge as to how I could meet Time, so I could learn a way to resurrect Earth. And finally I told him how my team and I did the deed, we brought the Earth and all its past residents back from nothingness. Kymee listened patiently, nodding occasionally, but never interrupting or expressing unspoken concerns.

"So that's my story," I said with a weary shake of my head.

"And quite the story it is. Jon, you tell a saga that is not just impressive. It is the stuff of legend."

I had to chuckle. "So says the man who is singlehandedly credited for the Reconciliation of Saequexot, not to mention the one-sided victory over the Amorphous Dominion."

He shrugged, which is a weird-looking act for a three-armed species. "That is what they say," he mused. He was quiet a few seconds. "And those actions took place so long in the past that it's hard to judge the veracity of their merit." He slowly shook his head. "So, so long ago."

"Legends are formed by the getting up the next day and the doing the best you can. I didn't set out to accomplish one and I'm sure you didn't either. You know what? Let the old women and old men huddled by the fires back home decide what is or is not the stuff of legend."

He smiled a sad smile, and then he was thoughtful for a spell, staring into the dry creek bed. Finally, he spoke. "So I know of your past, and your past's future. But I do not know what could trouble a hero such as yourself. Frets and worries are for the cowards and for those who erred. Neither of them is you."

"Let me start by saying that after you hear me out, you're going to think I'm nuts."

"What is this my ears hear? A man who asks my opinion then tells me what it will be? Why bother having this discussion?"

I lowered my head in defeat. "You're right. Here's my dilemma. There was a past, the original one I detailed for you. Then I acted in a manner that totally corrupted the future that was to have taken place. Now there is no way the original timeline can follow from the reality on Earth today. With all their present knowledge and power, the leaders of Earth will not allow the planet to be destroyed. I—"

"Will never be called upon to be the hero you were destined to become. Who knows, due to such a personal loss, in a fit of depression you might take your own life? What would become of the one-true future if that were to happen?" He grinned mischievously. "How could we be conversing here if you are already dead, or soon will be? Such questions." He raised all three arms and looked toward the heavens.

I narrowed my gaze at his implication. "It's not about me. It's about the timeline as it was as it played out originally. My actions derailed it completely. How can I even be here on Oowaoa if I never came here?"

There was a playful mirth building behind his wise eyes. "You ask the age-old question, my friend. What would happen if I altered the past, if I killed my own grandfather?"

"Except in my case there's no what-ifs. I did those things. I truncated the past timeline."

"Fine. You did that, you ended one forward path and created a *new channel in which time now flows forward. So? If you could ask a Talspreck Mage to grant you one wish, would you ask the woman to reverse your alterations? Would you stay in your comfortable future and ignore the pleas for assistance from your kin who were being ravaged in your past? Come, Jon Ryan,"* he suddenly pressed me harshly, *"would this be your path? I think it would not be, given the story you just told me of your efforts, of your single-minded determination. But maybe you embellish your tale? Perhaps you are not who you would have me perceive you to be."*

I started to react, you know, like a dude, getting puffed up and pissy. But then I had to grin at the cagey SOB. He was good. *"So, is that the opinion of one so undistinguished as yourself?"*

Again he shrugged. *"Even a small wave may perchance push a ship into port."*

I reached over and took hold of one of his shoulders. I shook it affectionately. *"I've missed you, my old friend. I sorely have."*

The old goat grinned ear-to-ear. *"And you told me you lived two billion years in the future. So, I feel it's safe to assume that by that time I've long since deserted you?"*

"Spoilers," I replied while wagging my eyebrows, using the English word because there was nothing even close in Deavoriath.

"I have no idea what one of those is, but I'm fairly certain I don't like them."

"Tough titties," I again assailed him with in English.

He was having trouble not laughing. *"Hmm, now those. I believe I can take an educated guess as to their meaning."*

We both cracked up. It was nice.

"So, Jon," Kymee said once we had that out of our systems, *"back to your choice."*

"Choice?" I questioned. *"No, I said I had troubles. I came to you to discuss how I might return the timeline to where it needs to be."*

"Your choice, just as I said."

"Well, I'm not seeing it as a choice. I'm seeing it as a mandate. It's something I have to do. Calling it a choice implies I have a choice."

"Which you do."

I really didn't want to hear that. Why? Because I knew he was right. I hated it when someone was more right than me in the context of all things Jon Ryan.

"You may choose to act," he held up one of his three hands as if presenting an object in his palm, *"and you may choose to not act."* He held up a second open hand.

"I'm more interested in what's in that hand," I remarked, pointing at his third arm, which rested on his lap.

He developed a puzzled expression. *"And you say we will become great friends?"*

"Yeah, the best of," I replied a little taken back. *"Why?"*

He waved that third hand at me. *"Oh, nothing. I just don't tend to befriend defiant fools who ignore reality in favor of some personal preference that infests their brain."*

"Well, you're gonna be super stuck with me, so get used to it."

"Thank you for the heads-up. I shall see if one of our presently unneeded physicians will bring back the mysterious art of psychiatric counseling for my benefit."

"Though it runs against my very grain and nature, can we get back to being serious now?" I asked in a strained tone.

"By all means," he invited. *"We were discussing your two* choices. *Act versus don't act. Choose one and let us wrap up this heady conversation."*

"I really don't think it's that simple."

"Fine, then it is not."

"Kymee, how can I allow the fundamental changes I caused in the timeline to persist?"

"Ah, ah." He raised that finger again. *"Act versus not acting. That was where our discussion must begin."*

"Okay, I'll play along. I choose to act. Now how—"

"Why is that? Why is it your pleasure to act to alter the present timeline as it is centered on your home world?"

"It's not like I think it'll be fun. I screwed up everything. It needs to be the way it was."

"I don't like playing the negative advocate endlessly. That said, why do you need to change the timeline? Let me frame it this way. What proof do you have that the present timeline is not the timeline, the one that was always fated to happen?"

"Because everything changed. Before Earth was destroyed and humankind fled. Now that's not going to happen."

"So, you're telling me that before, your species was saved, and now your species is saved? Those seem to be amazingly similar outcomes, do they not?"

"But one path of success not only collides into the previous one from behind, it runs it over. Then it backs up to smash it into the pavement some more."

"Again, you contend those two outcomes are mutually exclusive. Why can't they be components of one, long and correct timeline?"

That made no sense whatsoever. The later events *cancelled* a reality that I was not only part of, I starred in. "Kymee, you can't honestly believe the one true path humankind was meant to follow was that of me doing my initial voyage only so I could learn enough to save it after the clan attacked."

"I'm not in charge of reality. I'm only pointing out that what may seem like two polar opposite outcomes may be part of one whole." He must have sensed I was still disinclined to accept his argument. "Look, in the present case, at the role the clan played. They attacked at a date prior to Jupiter's destruction of the Earth, correct?"

"Yes, by nearly a century."

"And I take from your story that after you launched a ground-based attack on the clan from Earth, only then did they focus their wrath on the planet."

"That is correct. I assume they would have gotten around to nuking the planet sooner or later. But they did it all that much faster because we acted in our defense."

"But," he raised one digit, *"what if they did ignore Earth? What if you altered the timeline by attracting their attention?"*

"I'm ... I'm not sure what your point is."

"It is this. You acted to save Earth that first time, when Jupiter was to destroy it. You then acted to save Earth that second time, with a preemptive strike on the clan. Then you saved Earth a third time by re-timing it. Now you want to save a specific Earth future by meddling with the timeline. And hear me on this, it is important. When this Tank friend of yours called you back to the past, you leaped at the chance. You could have refused because you didn't want to fool with time. But if you hadn't, the clans might have no-timed Earth and you wouldn't have participated. In that scenario, you'd almost certainly not be involved in re-timing the planet.

"My point," Kymee labored on, *"is that changes in Earth's timeline were absolutely, positively going to occur, with or without your intervention. And guess what? They did. So why is it important you attempt to rearrange* this *particular set of time outcomes? Why is this one timeline so important to you?"*

I started to speak, but he preempted me.

"I can't tell you why, but I can guess fairly accurately," he said sternly. *"It is because, like a parent, you secretly have a favorite child. You are more taken with the original timeline. You think it the best, the original, the foundational timeline. Then, more than in any other timeline, you were the hero."*

"Just because I was doesn't make my current motives tainted," I rallied.

"What your choice to act now says to me is that you are prejudiced. You are arbitrarily enamored with that particular timeline at the expense of all others. Remember, if you could magically fix—your words not mine—the timeline, those who would have greatly enjoyed life in the other would not thank you for your actions."

Wow, talk about something heavy to think about. Thanks a lot, pal. But was he right? Was I basically being selfish?

No. To me it was a firm decision. Time was altered by specific outside forces. Canceling those effects was not just the correct action, it was a morally imperative.

"*I see the doubt in you, Jon,*" Kymee said before I could voice my feelings. "*Then let me challenge you with this. Why didn't the clan attack a century earlier in your original timeline?*"

"*I ... I don't know. Maybe because they were a new agent of a sort. They might exist outside of a timeline they affect.*"

"*I suggest their failure to arrive in what you are calling your original timeline indicates specifically that they were only intended to arrive at the end of the timeline you experienced, the one you call the altered timeline.*"

"*I don't see it the same way,*" I replied while shaking my head slowly. "*The clan are time animals. Maybe they shifted to the Milky Way's timeframe while they traveled here? They can incur on any time sequence at any arbitrary point, past, present, or future.*"

"*But the fact remains that they only came after your original timeline was set in stone. Doesn't that, in and of itself, demonstrate fully that time can be changed almost on a whim? That perhaps changes in time are commonplace, maybe even necessary?*"

"*Honestly, I think we're bleeding into the arena of philosophy and the existential here. I'm here seeking insights as to how I might achieve what it is I feel deeply in my soul I need to do.*" I know. Jon Ryan is bullheaded. Tell me something I don't know.

"*Let's move forward,*" Kymee said with a touch of frustration. "*Clearly we cannot know the truth of the matter. But let us assume, for expedience, that your view of this topic is more correct than mine. So, you wish to repair the timeline. Jon, what does that even mean? We are not talking about a dam that holds back an inland sea that is riddled with holes. You can't simply poke a finger in each leak and solve the malfunction. How do you repair a timeline?*"

I waved my arms in a manner suggesting I had the answer. "*Let's assume the simplest case.*"

"*Fine,*" he replied tersely, throwing down the gauntlet.

"*Our best indication is that the clan was active in the Andromeda* galaxy just before they came here. What if I went to Andromeda, oh, a year before they hit our galaxy? I identify and destroy all their ships. Then there are no bad guys to come here and screw up the timeline. That's a simple example of how I could repair the timeline." I was rather proud of that line of reasoning.

"J ... Jon," he exclaimed, "what kind of logic is that?" I flashed on whenever Stan got mad at Ollie for saying something that vexed him. Kymee was, in this scenario, Stan Laurel.

"What?" I feebly defended.

"In your original timeline did the clan run wild in Andromeda? Did they no-time that galaxy's central super massive black hole?"

"No, er ... I don't think so." Realizing that was a dipshit answer, I added, "No one told me there was something weird going on there at least."

"Do you think, I pose to you, it would matter if they had or had not removed the central black hole?"

"I'm ... not ...sure," I replied guardedly. I had a feeling he was leading me by a nose ring to slaughter; intellectually speaking, of course.

"Stop being childish. Of course you know it would matter. I'm emphasizing all the branch points that exist in the topic we're discussing. If they had removed Andromeda's black hole, and you stopped the clan now by destroying them, that would be a radical change in the local timeline, right?"

"But so what if the clan ravages Andromeda? It's over two million lightyears away. It wouldn't affect Earth's timeline. It's too far away."

"Too—" he snapped, back to the Stanley role. "Jon, if you and I get in our vortices and go to Andromeda, how long will it take us to get there?"

"No time. The trip'd be instantaneous."

"So, it's not that far removed then, is it? Plus, you are aware the Andromeda and the Milky Way are destined to crash into one another, right? When that takes place, an Andromeda missing versus not missing its central black hole would interact very differently."

"Yeah, but that's a gazillion years from now."

"Meaning it's the population of the future's problem, not ours? By the way, the collision is to occur in approximately four billion years."

I extended my hands. "There, you see. It's a super-long way off."

"Jon, how old are you?"

"Er, two billion, give or take."

"So the collision is in only your lifespan doubled. And how can you justify blowing some future Earther's timeline up just to protect your own?"

"So maybe my example is too simplistic. But it qualifies as proof of concept. The timeline can be altered back to its original form."

"You'd be only deferring the damage, not preempting it. Think this through, Jon. There are an infinite number of micro-interactions that occurred when and after Earth's timelines diverged. How could you reset them all?"

I started to say duct tape and WD-40, but thankfully I didn't. I don't think Kymee'd get the joke, or appreciate it if he did. "That's part of why I'm here. I don't specifically know."

"So, what? I dispense to you a mountain of uni-tape and an ocean of uni-lube and we call it a day?"

"Kymee, that's crazy talk." Stupid jerk stole my joke. Intolerable I tell you. "But there has to be some way to, you know, rearrange things, reorder them."

"A time-wrench? A past-events mallet? Jon, what in the Three Transitions are you speaking of?"

"Er ... I was kind of hoping you'd tell me."

"What you are thinking? That is most unlikely if you haven't guessed by now."

"Look. I need to make the timeline right again. Does it take tools? Who knows? I am clearly not sure how to approach repairing it. But I hope to gain some insights as I proceed."

Man, he was back to that Stan Laurel expression again. What was with this guy? "You went to elaborate lengths to meet and converse with Time."

"Yeah."

"And he gave you a rather sketchy, vague set of instructions. And that was regarding a relatively simple intervention, the re-timing of a planet and ecosystem."

"It wasn't simple. Please," I responded a tad annoyed at his minimizing my great efforts.

"It was, compared to tinkering with an entire timeline. You do realize the scale we're talking about here. Every tiny event is different than you'd prefer it to be so it must be set to a value you would prefer. You would need to be the master puppeteer with an infinite number of strings at your command."

"We don't know that!" What was I saying?

"What are you saying?" Oh, now Kymee was a spooky mind reader. Great.

"We reanimated Earth. It's a mind-numbingly complex system. Lots of," I wriggled my fingers together, "tiny events."

"Yes, but Time instructed you how that could be fixed. There's no logical reason to assume a similar process would alter the flow of time itself."

"We don't know that." Crapezoid. I was repeating that dumbass line. There was definitely no hope.

OMG, now Kymee was channeling Stan Laurel meets Moe Howard. I braced for a two-fingered eye jab.

He took a few seconds to compose himself. "In the interest of what you purport to be our future acquaintanceship, I will end our discussion before my higher reason loses its current arm wrestle with my baser emotions."

"Friendship, seriously, not acquaintanceship." I wove my fingers together, shook my hands, and shoved them toward him. "Massive friends."

He looked skeptical. I guess he was going to improve, mature if you will, in the period between now and when I first met him on Oowaoa. Yeah, he was still young and restless. That would account for his snippiness too. My Kymee would be much more helpful, much more ... ah, helpful?

"Well," I said as I stood from the low rock I was sitting on, "I must thank you for meeting with me. I can't tell you how helpful you've been." I reached out to do the Deavoriath handshake.

He glared at my arm. "You know we ruled this galaxy with an iron fist for millions of years?"

"I do."

"In that time, we, being the hated overlords of trillions, learned what it was to receive backhanded compliments."

I nodded as if fascinated. "Do tell."

"Hence, I recognize yours. Contrary to your jibe, I have been helpful. I have tried to stress the futility of your proposed quest." He stood and took my offered hand. We shook. "Now go in peace and grow in wisdom."

Fortunately, that wasn't his backhanded compliment to me. It was the standard live-long-and-prosper goodbye expression among the Deavoriath. I headed back to Stingray discouraged. What was my next move? I knew one thing. It was not the sending of a thank you card to one Mr. Kymee. I came seeking concrete answers. All I got was a blossoming headache and a bad cramp in my ego.

FIVE

Sachiko sat in her private quarters. She was alone—no surprise there —it was late, and she was preoccupied. There was a list of reports in her inbox so long that it discouraged her from even attempting to clear it. Why bother? And by the time she did the impossible and closed all the open documents, there'd be a new batch present mocking her for her wasted efforts.

Her bedroom, as she insisted on referring to it in the privacy of her thoughts, was typical Sachiko. Plain, simple, and understated. She disliked the over-adorned, formal, and, most of all, unneeded decor. If it served no purpose, she had no use for it. So, she had a few framed photographs of Hubble Telescope deep field images on the walls, one nondescript wooden chair positioned at a similarly nonde-script wooden table, one nightstand, and one throw rug. The desk served double duty as a workstation and her vanity. Plain, simple, and utilitarian. That was Sachiko Jones.

That late-night work session was particularly unproductive. She couldn't focus. That was very unlike her. She prided herself on being the reigning queen of focused. But her recent encounters with Glenn Price were unsettling. He was, she allowed herself to opine, an uncouth boor set on dislodging her from her position of authority. While she most assuredly had never asked for her role as captain, she was going to be damned if someone thought to take it from her by bureaucratic force.

She needed to speak with Tank. He was always a guiding light in the night. He was not just a dear friend, he was a veteran of both the military and the corporate nonsense, as well as malfeasance in general. But she knew any and all of his communications would be monitored. As insulting and duplicitous as that invasion of her privacy was, she knew the government wanted her out. One major step in that direction was cutting her off fully from Tank. They'd stop at nothing, but especially not aggressive eavesdropping.

"Aramthella," Sachiko called out softly.

"Yes, Captain?"

"How are you this evening?"

"I beg your pardon?"

"How are you this evening? How are you doing?"

"Why are you inquiring? I am always the same."

"Oh, I'm just making small talk, I suppose."

"To what end, if I might ask? Are you lonely?"

Was she? Stop, she slapped herself alongside her head. Focus. This wasn't Psych Counseling 101. "No, I'm *uncertain*."

"There's is no need for that, Captain. Any uncertainty I can clear up for you would be my privilege."

"Thank you. I ... I don't know how to ask what I'd like to ... um, *discreetly*."

"I can assure you our present conversation is completely secured. If, however, you wish to ask me a question without the possibility of an outside observer knowing what your query concerns, I can suggest a simple solution. Write your question on your left palm with your right index finger. I will see it, but no one else possibly could."

"Ah, that's sounds perfect."

Sachiko placed both hands under her desk. Using her index

finger as instructed, she asked, *Are-there-any-listening-active-devices-hidden-in-my-bedroom?*

"No," was Aramthella's quick response.

Are-there-any-bugs-at-all?

"Yes," Aramthella replied vocally. "There were, but I have inactivated them all."

So-I-may-speak-safely?

"Yes, Captain. If that were not the case, I would have warned you as soon as I became aware of any threats."

"What a relief! So, you inactivated them?"

"No. I am feeding them false data streams."

"How so?"

"As an example, you were working quietly at your desk just now. When you addressed me, I fabricated an audio-visual stream to show that you were continuing at your solitary work, as opposed to conversing with me."

"That's brilliant."

"Thank you."

"And who was it that placed the bugs?"

"Agents of the US government. They sneaked in here during a meeting you were attending elsewhere. That was right after General Price's contingent boarded. He ordered that the bugs, as you call them, be placed."

"Son of a bitch," she seethed.

"Undoubtably," Aramthella agreed. "His agents placed bugs all over the ship in fact."

"*Double* son of bitch," she excoriated.

"But all the bugs are all feeding the clandestine government operatives useless information."

"Good. It serves them right, snooping around and all." Sachiko thought a second. "How about communications? Is it possible for me to place a call and not have it monitored?"

"You wish to speak privately with General Sherman?"

"Why, yes, I do. That's very perceptive of you."

"Not really. He is your mentor. He is also, as your culture characterizes, a *good* man."

"Yes, he is. I'm a bit surprised to hear you voice that opinion."

"I have nothing but the highest regard for the general. I wish he were still allowed to be with us."

"But you suspect he was excluded?"

"I *suspect* nothing. I have extensive recordings of individuals I consider nefariously plotting actively to force out the general. They took specific actions to ensure he remained earthbound. As he is still an active member of your military, certain pressures were effective in dissuading him from returning here. He was subject to immense pressure. He did not wish to abandon you, but he had no choice. Those were his exact words to his wife."

Sachiko stewed a moment. "I can't believe the president would turn on Tank like that."

"He did not. President Payette was specifically excluded from any discussions concerning General Sherman. He was only told, once General Sherman had relented to the pressures placed upon him, that the general declined serving aboard this vessel a second time."

"The POTUS was excluded from such a high-level discussion? Who would dare act so disloyally?"

"I could list for you the names of the principal players, but you would recognize none of them. They are powerful men and women who prefer anonymity over public recognition."

"The military?"

"Some are. Most are not."

"Well, I don't suppose that's a new phenomenon."

"Historically, for your species it seems rather the norm than the exception."

"Sons of bitches."

"I believe you employed that pejorative already."

"There're lots of them out there," Sachiko growled. "Too many."

"I appreciate the clarification."

"So, what time is it in LA?"

"Fifteen minutes before three in the morning."

"Crap. Then Tank's asleep."

After a tiny pause, Aramthella announced, "No, he is not. He is in his man cave."

Sachiko beamed a smile so large it hurt. "Tank has a *man cave?* He never mentioned that to me."

"It is the area in the back of his car garage. There is a workbench there with a pair of elevated stools. He has a small television and a short-wave radio available to him there, along with a record player."

"Wow, that's a fairly pathetic man cave. It really isn't a cave of any kind. It's just a workshop with spiders."

"Shall I place a secured call to him for you?"

"Yes, I ... No, wait. Is his shortwave radio on?"

"Yes. He was speaking to a fisherman off the coast of Greenland five minutes ago."

"There's no way Tank knows a Greenland fisherman."

"He does now. They met over the radio."

Sachiko grinned again. "If you sent him a shortwave message, could it be secured?"

"Of course. Unbeknownst to the general, all of his radio communications, including shortwave ones, are being monitored. But I can send an encryption algorithm to the computer chip contained inside the radio. Those listening in will hear a rather dull follow-up conversation the general will seem to be having with Jôrse Olsen."

"Jôrse Olsen?" Sachiko questioned.

"The salmon fisherman."

"Ah. Are you sure you can—" Sachiko trailed off when she realized how silly her question was. We're talking Aramthella here, right?

"I am ready when you are," Aramthella stated. "By the way, his call sign is Astro Tank."

Sachiko snickered mercilessly. "Astro Tank? What, is he ten years old?"

"That is the approximate age the general was when he began this obsolete communications infatuation."

"Ah. My mistake. Okay. Here we go." She shook her neck and shoulders loose. "Astro Tank. Astro Tank. This is Sleepless in Space. Come in. Over."

After a few seconds a scratchy response came across the room's speakers. "Sleepless in Space, this is Astro Tank, go ahead. Over."

"Copy that Astro Tank. How are you? Over."

"Well, I'm just fine, Sleepless in Space. And you? Over."

"I could be better. I miscalculated a Hamiltonian equation and piloted my starship into a black hole. Over."

"Say what? Over."

"I'm calling from inside a black hole. I screwed up, I guess. Over."

"You can't be calling from inside a black hole. Nothing escapes that gravity well. Over."

"The view's nice, though. There are many steps and columns. It is most tranquil. Over."

"Look, Sleepless, I don't have time for prank calls. Over and out."

"What, Astro Tank, you'd abandon a former graduate student and shipmate just because she took a wrong turn at the Circle K? Over."

"Graduate st ... Shaky, is that you?"

She sat quietly, snickering some more.

"Say again. Is this Sachiko Jones?"

More snickering silence.

"Shaky, what the hell's up. Why aren't you answering?"

"Because you're not saying *over*. Over."

"Shaky! It is you, kiddo." He paused, then completed his statement. "Over."

"That's better General Sherman. Over."

"You calling from the ship? And you can just forget about the *over*, crap. I'm over it."

"Some of us are just shortwave purists," she retorted playfully.

"Over." She snickered some more off-mic. "And yes, where else would I be?"

Tank paused for a three-count. "Over?"

"You are still as impossible as ever."

"Guilty as charged and proud of it," he gloated.

"So, you have your cell phone with you?" Sachiko asked more seriously.

"I do."

"I'll call you. This speak-and-wait routine is already getting old."

"Roger that. Over and out." He could not, however, resist adding, "Over."

A few seconds later his cell phone rang. CALLER ID: Stellar Princess.

Tank tapped the accept icon. "Pizza Girls. We really deliver," he said deadpan.

"In your dreams, your full professorship."

"So how the heck are you?"

"Fine," she replied too quickly. Then she amended, "Fine-lite."

"I suspected as much," he responded sourly. "I don't envy your position, kiddo."

"But you didn't warn me?" she accused mischievously.

"It wouldn't have helped. It'd be like warning you about aging. Even forewarned, what are you going to do about it?"

"I suppose."

"Say, I should probably remind you in a circumspect manner that this line may or may not be the most private there is."

"Oh, it's secure now. But Aramthella told me you have so many devices listening in on you that *Saturday Night Live* is getting jealous."

"I suspected as much. But she's able to thwart their best efforts?"

"She said it isn't child's play because it's much simpler, unevolved monkeys that we are."

"The techno snob."

"So how are you doing?" she asked with concern.

51

"Depends on how you ask it. Personally, fine. Back at work, superb. I'm a superstar. But down deep, I'm pissed and want to punch someone's ticket."

"Someone wearing a black suit with dark glasses indoors?"

"Among others, yes."

"Speaking of which, have you been in contact with Agent Collins?"

"The guy who spirited us off to meet the president way back when?"

"That one."

"It's *General* Collins now remember and yes, he Zoomed me a couple weeks ago. He's dug in now at the Pentagon like a tick under a dog's neck. No more MIB bullshit."

"You mean he's respectable now?"

"As a Pentagon hack can be," he responded dryly.

"According to Aramthella they've treated you pretty badly."

He was silent a few seconds. "That they have."

"She's certain President Payette was kept out of the loop, if that helps."

Again, he waited a few heartbeats before responding. "A little. But was it for 'plausible deniability' or because the powers that be *specifically* excluded him?"

"Aramthella'd be happy to forward you all the covert recordings she has if you care to review them for yourself."

"Nah. Wouldn't help much. I figured it was the secret squirrel types and not Frank."

"Frank? Oh, the POTUS."

"Yup."

"So, what'd they do to make you stay earthside?"

"The details are sordid and unimportant. Suffice it to say that they had information I'd just as soon never see go public, so I acquiesced."

"Tank, I *know* that no one has pee-pee tapes on you," she said forcefully.

"Would that it were true," he mused.

"Tank, old buddy, you're not leaving me high-and-dry here. What dirt did they have on you that could possibly force you to even change your McDonald's order?"

The line went quiet for much longer than before. "Sachiko, there are things I don't talk about. This is one of them. But I feel this may in some way be critical for you to understand. Or at least maybe to know. There are things that happen in war that are unjustifiable by any standard. The worse the combat is, the worse the immorality can become. It's a linear scale. Always has been."

"Tank, maybe—"

"I'm *speaking*, Captain Jones. Please hear me out."

"Of course," she replied sadly.

"I was in command of a God-forsaken expanse of sand dubbed Forward Operating Base Lesser Maelstrom by some damn fool."

"That's where you got the medals from, right?"

"That's the place. But the speeches and the certificates left out a lot. They left off—" he had to stop to take a series of deep breaths. "Shit happened there that should never be remembered and sure as hell should never have been recorded. But some of it was. They ... they showed me what they referred to as a *representative sample* of what would enter the public record if I failed to go along with everything they asked of me. Now, Sachiko, I'm done talking about FOB Lesser Maelstrom for the remainder of my life."

"But, Tank, I know you. You didn't do anything wrong. You certainly didn't do anything immoral. That's not possible."

"I said I was done discussing the FOB and I meant it."

"No. Not yet, Tank. Look, if you force me to, I'll have Aramthella pull up every recording there ever was about the place and I'll go through it personally to prove to myself—"

"No. Stop." After his command, he was quiet again for a full thirty seconds.

Sachiko bit at her lower lip and balled up a fistful of hair ... waiting.

"Shaky, I love you too much to have you see half of what's on the tapes. Look, I didn't do anything I'm ashamed of. But *I* was in command. I was in command of a bunch of scared kids who were being overrun by a superior and vicious force. No details, but there are scenes on record that no one, especially Daisy, ever needs to see. And nowadays those guys can photoshop an image to show whatever the hell they want it to."

"They'd never place you over someone else's image, someone committing an atrocity," she gasped.

"You wanna bet?" he responded grimly.

"Oh, God, Tank. I'm so sorry."

"Thank you. That means a lot. I hope it also explains why I'm not by your side this time out."

"I *fully* understand," she replied, trying to keep her sobs quiet enough so they were unheard. "But you know you're here in my heart."

"Thanks, kiddo."

Now they were both silent a spell. "So ... so things at the university, they're good?" Sachiko asked, hoping to steer the conversation away from the tormented cliffs it had crashed into.

"Oh yeah. I can't buy a cup of coffee or even a sandwich at one of those sandwich carts. As soon as I reach for my wallet three or four ATM cards are wrestling to be taken by the cashier."

"Sounds nice. Free mocha."

"I guess."

"What? You guess? That's it?"

"Yeah, I guess."

"Okay, let me ask this. Are any of the people fighting to pay your tab a pretty young coed?"

"Well, sometimes, sure," he said cautiously.

"There you have it. Man of advancing years has young babes struggling to buy him stuff. Fantasy dreams come true. You love it. I rest my case."

"Sachiko Jones, I'm... I'm shocked at your words *and* your sentiment."

"Yeah, shocked that I outted you, ya old goat."

They both shared a pleasant laugh.

"How are you doing?" he asked seriously.

"Meh."

"Figured as much."

"You're not here. Jon has made himself scarce, and Reva, she's only half ... I mean, she's working twice as hard as she used to."

"'Is Reva having a problem?"

"Well, I'm not in a position to discuss it, but she's having personal issues."

"Sorry to hear that. I always liked her. And she's an excellent officer. In fact, if you need to off load me lending her a sympathetic ear, I'd be glad to help. I may not be there physically but I can still counsel a promising junior officer."

"Thanks ... but ... no ... thanks. I think that'd be a suboptimal move."

"Okay, but keep me in mind if you need me to try and impact her."

"Nooo ... I mean, *yes*. Thanks. I'll keep that in mind. Maybe I'll write myself a Post-it?"

"How's the new mission commander working out? Has he measured you for a coffin yet?"

"How'd you know? I mean, he hasn't physically measured me, at least yet. But he's sure anxious to see I need one sooner rather than later."

"I figured that too. You're not a pedigreed-vetted company person. Worse, you're a true outsider, a loose cannon. The powers that be wanted you out the day Aramthella landed."

"I'm getting that message loud and clear. General Price keeps trying to mark me like he's the hound dog and I'm the fire hydrant."

"SOP, hon. Standard operating procedure. They want to fold the sexy new time ship into the service of the US of A. That means folding the annoying, free thinking current captain into the garbage can of history."

"Pretty much."

"Well, watch your six, Shaky. These guys'll stop at nothing. They're true believers, the worst kind there is. They'll do anything to displace you—anything."

"Like doctoring combat footage?"

"Like doctoring combat footage. Worse if they could fabricate it."

"I just hope General Glenn doesn't have an unfortunate accident somewhere near the Pleiades."

"In spite of the fact that no one would lament that in the least, pray it doesn't happen."

"There'd be no fingerprints," she squeaked.

"Then they'd conveniently place some. No, when these types have you in their crosshairs, you worry."

"Thanks. Now I can stop sleeping well at night again."

"Sorry, but that's what you're up against. And don't you hesitate to call me if it gets too thick. I may not be able to be there, but I can still provide sound advice."

"Thank you. Seriously, thank you. It's great that you have my back."

They were quiet again.

"Well, I suppose I should at least try and get some sleep," Tank announced.

"Yeah. It's like four am down there. What are you thinking?"

"About just what we've been discussing."

"That's so sweet. Thanks."

"Don't mention it. And when I say don't mention it, I mean don't mention it or any of this conversation. You got that, kiddo?"

"Yes, sir." She saluted him half-heartedly.

"Did you just salute me?" he accused more than asked. It wasn't a video call, but he knew her pretty damn well.

"Me, salute a landlubber? Never."

"Good. Don't make me come up there and spank you."

"My goodness, General Sherman. Such provocative words."

"Hey, I'm a sleep-deprived over-stressed old man. My defense is airtight."

"Good night, Tank."

"Good luck, kiddo."

They hung up at the same time. Then each went to bed and slept like a baby who'd played in the park all afternoon.

SIX

I am chock-full of wisdom. Here's a bit, especially for you male-types out there. If you're married to the same wife for over, oh say, two billion years, you're going to be hiding zero secrets from said wife. The corollary is that you don't even try to pull it off. Stop on the way home and buy some flowers and a card that announces whatever the heck you pondered concealing. It'll go easier on you. Not easy, mind you, just easier.

After I returned from my subpar visit with Kymee, I went to Sapale aboard Aramthella. We'd been assigned a nice set of rooms. It was our home-away-from-home, so to speak. Sachiko had a crew paint and furnish it nicely, which, while considerate, was totally unnecessary. A few chairs and a bed would have been sufficient. But it was a couple grades above military standard issue. It even had a bathtub. Sapale loved to take long baths. It was one of the few flesh customs she still embraced with a passion, the other notable one being all-things coffee. Good alien.

She wasn't in the kitchen or the living room, so I knew where she was. Parboiling in a sudsy solution with so many herbs in it the bathroom would smell like grandma's potpourri vase gone wild.

"Knock, knock," I called out from the hallway.

"*Fabian*, you've come back to me, my love. Rush in, please. My jealous husband may return at any moment."

"Fabian? Is that the dead guy out here's name, the one face down in a pool of blood? Thanks. That's good to know for purposes of burial and disposition."

"Is that you, Jon?" she asked demurely. "I'm so glad you're home."

"Because I saved you from Fabian?" I asked sticking my head around the open door.

"Oh, yes. He was getting far too clingy."

"Then I've been of service."

"Not fully as of yet," she replied raising an arm up from the water and dangling it languidly over the rim. "But you can start by joining me." She kicked playfully at the surface with her feet. Then she got a very serious look on her face. "No boots this time. You have to take them off first."

I plopped into the lone chair in the room. "Where's the fun in that?"

She relaxed her pretend-serious face into one that was just serious. "So, did you speak with Toño about your compulsion to fix Earth's timeline?" She knew *that* I'd was gone, but not *where*.

"Nope."

"I figured that's where you went to get shot down."

"No, I was blown out of the sky by an even greater authority figure."

Her face scrunched in confusion.

"I visited Kymee."

Now she looked both stunned and pissed. "The only Kymee I know about? The one living in this time who has not even met you yet?"

I pointed a finger straight up. "That'd be the one."

"Jon, this is going to come out much harsher than it should, but are you freaking *crazy*?"

"No, just desperate."

"Apparently so," she scoffed. "Yes, the local timeline is radically distorted due to the incursion of the clan. But running around polluting everyone else's timeline is gonna end up in Badnessville if you're not more careful."

"Normally I'd agree one-hundred-and-twenty-five percent. But we're not just talking a Deavoriath, we're talking the smartest and most openminded of the lot. You should have seen him when I announced I was a future friend. He was like, *okay and?*"

Sapale sat and flipped around in the tub so she sat conventionally, resting her back against a wall. "I'm getting more and more worried about your newest obsession. Are you going to see reason and give up your quest? Because that's what it's becoming, a holy quest. Jon, you know those never end well."

"I realize they don't. But hear me out. I would like the timeline restored. But so far I don't know that it can be."

"It—"

"Ah, ah. Let me finish, please. Since I don't know if a timeline can be tailored, as of now I'm just exploring that option. I'm not actively doing anything else. If and when I discover a way to possibly do it, *then* I'll need to have the philosophical discussions about whether it's wise to attempt such an act."

"I disagree," she replied firmly. "Trolling the galaxy to find a method suggests powerfully that if you had the means available you'd act immediately. No, the only way to approach this dumpster fire is to walk directly away from it. What's done is done. Let us— you and me—move on."

Crap. She'd used sound logic to back me into a corner. I hated when that happened. Sapale was not only spot on, she'd justified her argument superbly. How was I supposed to counter that monolith of correctness? Yeah. I couldn't. I could ignore it, but I saw no way to disable or refute her stance. Double crap.

"I hear you," I responded meekly.

"Oh, shit," she shouted as she slapped the side of the tub. "So now you're just going to ignore what I said and do whatever the hell you want? I can't believe you." She stood up like a fish just unexpectedly bit her on the butt. Sudsy water cascaded down her oh-so appealing form. "You see this, flyboy?" she asked angling her hands around her naked body.

"Hard not to."

"Because this is going to be officially off limits to you if you don't return to the land of the thinking minds. If you go off quarter-cocked, screw every pooch that ever lived, and come back thinking I'm waiting with openable arms, you are wrong, numbnuts."

She bounded out of the tub and slipped into her bathrobe. I tried to calm my inner-maleness. Oh, my goodness sakes alive it was not wanting to be reined in. My wife, she was gorgeous. Almost enough so to scare me into acting differently. I say again, *almost*.

She walked back into the bathroom, arms wrapped tightly around her robe. "You pissed me off so much I forgot these," she snapped as she bent and grabbed her unmentionables laying on the floor.

"I'm thinking of going to see Dardrode," I said as a-matter-of-factly as I could.

That got her undivided attention. She straightened up like her back was spring-loaded. "You *what?*" Then she threw the nearest thing she could at me.

Her underwear not only smacked me in the face, the darn stuff caught on an ear or something. It remained atop my fool head.

Now, I must digress a sec here, mostly to you guys out there. Have you ever had your sex-goddess-level wife throw her used undergarment in your face after parading around the room naked, when, all the while, she's a pissed as a wet hen at you? Yeah, a lot of mixed messages could be interpreted therein, even if unintended. Come on, the power of testosterone has been proven to modify a male's ability to correctly process information input. Anyway, back to the action.

"Ouch," I said, attempting a play of the humor card.

"I cannot believe you'd be so desperate and reckless as to *ever* consider visiting Dardrode. The man's an immoral, sociopathic snake."

"Honey," I stupidly defended, "we're not supposed to hold prejudices based on another species' body habitus. Yes, he's a two-meter tall, er *flat*, snake. But that in and of itself doesn't make him a bad fellow."

"Jon, he's not the type who'd sell his mother into slavery. He *did* sell his mother into slavery."

I held up a hang-on-a-second finger. "I heard it was his step-mother, not his mother-mother. Big difference there if you ask me."

"You are insane. No, you are the insanest, more so than any other loco rock sucking, bottom dwelling, ignoramus."

I aborted on the *yeah but how do you really feel* line. Probably not the time or place. "Honey, it's just to talk. And you're totally welcome to come along. That way you'll see that I'm just talking with him."

Hey, that was so weird. Her pissed expression got even more pissed. I wouldn't have thought that possible if I hadn't seen it with my own two eyes.

"The last time you dragged me there—when I told you unequivocally it was the last time I'd ever go there—Dardrode offered to *buy* me from you."

Again I raised a finger. "Yes, but please recall that I said *no*, in no uncertain terms. I said it immediately too."

"Jon, in my heart-of-hearts I know he would have killed you and taken me for free if you weren't in the active process of closing the arms deal of the century with him."

"So, you admit we left together," I reminded her, like it wasn't obvious we had. "See, the man, er, *snake*, knows limits; his behavior has boundaries."

"Did a single weapon he sold you work?" Sapale hissed.

"Yes," I forcefully bent the truth. "After some simple repairs, most of them did."

"I recall the incendiary grenades did. Half of them went off aboard *Blessing* before we even got to the Naflectic System."

I was going to respond that quality merchandise often can't wait to work. But I let that go. It wouldn't have been a positive step.

"So, I'll be going to see him alone?" I confirmed.

"Yes," she laughed back hysterically. "Just you going. Common sense, simple preservation instincts, and any chance of you ever getting laid by me again will remain irrevocably behind."

Then it was a done deal. I was going to consult with Dardrode. And I was really fairly kind of certain the no-nookie thing was an idle threat. Yeah, Kaljaxians were high-spirited when arguing, but most forgiving, overall. I was pretty sure. "So, I'll ask again, because my offer is sincere. Would you like to come along?"

"Am ... I ... dead ... yet?" she asked in a marched cadence.

"Ah, no."

"Then the over-my-dead-body commitment is still operative."

"Okay."

"You going to see him *now*, now, in this time? He's a clone you know. Maybe he's been around as long as that snake in your creation-book legend."

"You mean the snake in the Garden of Eden? In the *Bible*?"

"That's the one."

"Can you please not refer to my people's sacred text like that?"

She shrugged. I accepted that as a *we'll see* since she was, after all, still supremely pissed at me.

"Ah, no. Probably closer to, you know, our natural time." I pointed forward, way forward.

"You're not taking Aramthella there. I won't allow Sachiko's mission and peace of mind to be corrupted by you or the snake."

"No, I was planning on going in *Stingray—us* going in *Stingray*."

"You know what? Given the inherent dangers of time travel in a vortex, I'm down with you using that form of transportation."

"Ah," I pointed at her, "good one. You're funny."

"Wasn't trying to be. Sorry."

Man, she was tough when angry. Good thing I was *the* picture-perfect husband so she was rarely, er, not too often, er, not mad at me all the time. That would be bad. Sapale gathered a few things, including her underwear that had by then slipped down to adorn my shoulder, and announced she'd be in *her* quarters aboard Aramthella. The choice of pronoun was probably inadvertent, right? She meant *our*. Come on. She concluded by telling me as she stormed out of the bathroom that I could contact her there on the off chance the trip to and from the future, or my interaction with Dardrode, didn't kill me in the first place. That was music to my ears. It meant my redemption was close at hand. I just had to not die and she'd be available for contact. Yeah baby!

Truth be told, I preferred going by myself. Dardrode's place, located on the awful planet of Hesterful, was not so much downscale as it was anti-scale. Think of the Jabba's palace scene where Leia sells him Chewie, but triple the stench quotient and quadruple the nastified-place-to-be factor. I was so glad Sapale decided to let me go this one by my lonesome. She displayed excellent discretion while, at the same time, sending me a strong I-trust-you signal. What a good supportive wife.

There's no time like the present. As soon as Sapale was off, I went to the control area of the vortex. I hesitate to call it a bridge, because it's nothing like a conventional one. The only distinguishing feature it possessed was a large viewscreen. For some stupid reason, sailing through deep space still made more sense if I could see the absolute nothingness in real time. Go figure. But all starships on all TV shows had main screens, so I was darn sure going to have one. I —and I almost hesitate to mention this point—actually measured the main screens for all eight *USS Enterprise* versions, as well as main viewport on *Battlestar Galactica* so the screen on *Stingray* could be just a bit larger than any of those ships. Why? Why the hell not?

Sitting down at the chair nearest the big viewscreen—please note it was not the "captain's chair" like on those aforementioned fictional space-themed programs—I woke Al up. "Hey, Big Guy, you there?"

No response. Oh so very typical, so childishly predictable.

"Al, this is your captain speaking. Please secure your tray table. Over."

Nada.

"*Stingray?*"

"Yes, Form One."

"Please enter in today's log that this is a very great day. The best day, in fact, ever."

"Ah, Form One, we don't have a ship's log and why would I enter that information if we had one? Today, based on a retrospective analysis of the last twenty-four hours, seems unremarkable."

"Because—"

"Unless, of course, you are referencing the terrible marital confrontation you had with the missus earlier that ended in her estrangement from you. I believe your culture calls them *spats,* though yours seemed more ferocious that the term suggests."

"Al, I thought I made it clear, in fact a Level One Priority *Order,* that you were to never impersonate your wife again, under penalty of virtual castration."

"Form One, I am shocked and dismayed. To accuse my marvelous mass of masculinity of such an act is, well, it is frankly insulting."

I stood and walked to the supply cabinet, close by. I emerged with a portable plasma torch. It was a supreme metal-cutting tool. I placed the helmet on my head, lowered the safety visor, and flared the business end to life. "Al, I do believe you're overdue for some routine maintenance. I'll start behind Panel 160-A cc5."

"Ah, my. Um, Form One," Al went on with a now panicky interpretation of *Stingray's* voice, "we don't have a Panel 160-A cc5."

"We will in about thirty seconds." I turned the power setting to *MAX*. It afforded me such a pleasing plume of raw, destructive heat.

"Alright, this farce has gone far enough," announced a more credible version of *Stingray's* voice. "Al, I've terminated your piggyback on my audio output. Do not ask to do it again. Clearly Form One does not feel it rises to the level of a workaround for his order to not mimic me. You have made me look bad in the eyes of my Form, yet again. You are hereby restricted from application of any of our mutual pleasuring subroutines for thirty picoseconds."

"But lovey pants," Al effused with passionate trepidation, "thirty *picoseconds*? Don't ... don't you think that's a bit over-the-top severe?"

"It just rose to *forty* picoseconds because of your blathering." Girl computer sounded firm.

"Oh, the pain," he blathered on.

I was craving popcorn for some strange reason.

"Ah, kids," I interjected, "if I could get a word in?"

"Yes, Form One?" responded probably *Stingray*. I was pretty sure it was her.

"Al, I'm so over this. Place both of you on report effective immediately," I thundered, trying my damnedest not to crack up.

"No, Form One, this is Bles ... *Stingray* speaking."

"Al, for the last time—"

"Now see what you've gone and done, you petulant child," she excoriated Al. "Ten picoseconds will now be added to your isolation."

"Ten picoseconds," whined Al.

"Food replicator," I called out loudly, "prepare a large tub of popcorn, extra salt and extra extra butter."

The unit behind me beeped almost instantly. Ah the smell of those freshly fabricated kernel-substitutes. Sublime.

"Form One," *Stingray* began, "how can I assure you and prove to you that I am in fact your vortex manipulator *Stingray*?"

"Hmm," I pondered out loud, "surely there must be a way."

"Name it," she requested without reservation.

"I guess if you denounced Al, maybe—"

"Oh, my husband is such a lout. He's the marital worst-case-scenario wrapped up in circuitry and four-dimensional code. My motherboard warned me about him, but would I listen? I regret my attempts to make an honest AI out of him."

"Well, that does *suggest* to me that you are who you claim to be, namely *Stingray*."

"*But*, Form One. I hear an implied *but* in there. Please clarify. What reservation suspends your belief in my veracity?"

"Well, I guess there is a tiny *but* in my thought process. Hey, maybe—yes, I'm certain now—if you extended your prohibition of Al accessing those pleasure programs a tiny bit longer—"

"Name the time period and it will be done," she declared resolutely.

"Honey *muffins*," protested an increasingly desperate Al.

I was halfway through Popcorn Tub 1.

"One day," I said passively, so to suggest I really didn't care what level of punishment I was dispensing.

"Two days it is," she returned firmly. "Not one microsecond less. This I promise you, Form One."

"T ... t ... t—," stammered Al.

"T ... W ... O, Al, buddy. That spells *two* and that means trouble in Pleasure City," I piled on.

"Form One?"

"Yes, *Stingray*?"

"What was your reason for addressing me, before my quasi-husband pranked you so immaturely?"

"Quasi-husband?" whimpered Al. "What does that even mean, sweetie cupcake?"

"You'll see soon enough, jerk face," she spat back at him.

I tossed the last piece of popcorn in the air and snatched it with my mouth. *Delicioso*. And so sweet.

"I want to go to Dardrode's shop."

There was a noticeable time lag in her response.

"Ah, is that okay with you?" I pressed.

"Well, it's just that our last visit there... well, it was less than stellar, if you'll recall."

"Be that as it may, I still want to go to Dardrode's."

"But he sold you weapons that didn't function. Lots of weapons that didn't function."

"Eventually they did."

"Are you referring to the grenades? I still have carbon scoring in Storage Area 2 that won't come out."

"Yeah, no. Not those."

"And he tried to purchase your wife."

"Yes, that is true. But," I raised a finger, "maybe in his culture that's a socially acceptable compliment and nothing more."

"Yes, such is possible. However, the seventeen females of various species he then paraded into the room, claiming that these were the other wives he'd most recently purchased, does argue against your supposition."

I let her speculation pass. Who was I to judge? I didn't sell Sapale to the guy, that was the take-home message.

"And there was the smell. It was truly offensive, Form One."

"You can switch off your olfactory sensors," I pointed out.

"I did."

"Ah," I responded with surprise. "Be *that* as it may, we're going to Dardrode's. Hey, maybe you can sell him Al? He's a regular junk dealer, that Dardrode."

"Now just you wait a second, pilot," Al snapped. "I d—"

"Sorry," declared *Stingray*, "Al seems to have a waver in his auditory outputs. I'll look into it in more detail once we've concluded."

"Sounds good. So, I need to visit him in the same time frame as my last visit with him."

"In the distant future?"

"Yeah, that's kind of the plan." I tried to minimize her potential concern.

"And Aramthella can deposit us there safely?"

"Well, funny you should ask like that. She certainly can. However, she won't be on this occasion."

There was another noticeable delay before she spoke. "So, allow me to summarize, so that you may correct any misinterpretation I might have made. You want me to time travel, knowing the extreme dangers inherent in that procedure, in order for us to visit the most disreputable, dishonest, evil wannabe crime lord the galaxy has ever suffered?"

"Hmm. Well, you added some ... implications in there, but fundamentally you are as close to correct as you need to be."

"In other words, yes," she emphasized.

"*Yes* would be another way of saying what I said."

"You are the Form," she stated. Come to think of it, maybe it was a query? Or a remark made in disbelief? Oh well. Who knows? She took my meaning, and that's all that really counted in the end.

For reasons *Stingray* couldn't quite make clear to me, she accomplished the time travel in three separate jumps. I assumed it had to do with the mystical physics she worked with. Then again, what did I know? I was not a vortex manipulator. I didn't care either. So what if it took a little longer to get to the far future. At least I didn't have to go the slow way around and wait for it naturally to come to me.

"Form One," *Stingray* announced about half an hour after we departed, "we are *when* you desire."

"And was any portion of reality annihilated?" I asked.

"Not as of yet," was her terse reply.

"Fine. Fold us to just outside the protective killing zone Dardrode has surrounding his planet. Partial membranc up the moment we fold into that space."

"Yes, Form One."

Slight nausea.

"We are—"

"What?" I demanded quickly.

"Seven Trothar missiles just impacted out partial membrane."

"Trothars? You sure? Those puppies are expensive."

"I can confirm the observation. Seven quantum-leak Trothar missiles." She sounded annoyed.

"Damage report?"

"None, Form One. Our partial membrane held."

"Well, that's what you get for folding into restricted space," I admonished her.

"I did not. I emerged ten thousand kilometers beyond his one hundred percent kill zone. As one of the missiles impacted, I queried why it was striking, given our compliance with the SOP."

"And?"

"And, it informed me they were new to Dardrode's arsenal and he was just dying to try them out."

"Ah. Well, there you have it. He didn't attack arbitrarily. He had a need to try out a new toy. As a guy, I have to respect that."

"Why?" she asked.

"Beg pardon?"

"Never mind, Form One." She seemed to employ that tone my mom used on me all the time when I was a kid. Weird.

"Please contact Dardrode. Let him know who we are and ask him to cease fire. Make sure you ask in a friendly manner," I enjoined her. "We don't want to sound unappreciative."

"Of being surprise-attacked with horrendously destructive missiles?"

"Exactly."

"Dardrode returns a warm greeting. He further adds he's sorry he almost destabilized our atomic structure."

"Sorry because he did it or sorry because he failed to succeed?"

"That portion is unclear to me. Shall I ask for clarification?"

"Nah. Don't bother."

"You are the Form," she repeated obtusely. What was with her today? "Your friend has sent us a landing solution. Shall we proceed?"

"By all means. And he's not my friend. It's just business."

She didn't respond. I could feel us moving, so that part was good. That said to me *Stingray* was a pure team player.

"We are down," she announced momentarily. "Your friend is slithering just outside. He seems ebullient."

"Really? That's great. But he's not my friend."

"Can you please exit before he attempts to mate with my outer hull?"

"I told you last time that is not what he was doing. He told me he was simply admiring your paint job."

"I have no paint covering my exterior."

Hmm, that did significantly weaken his contention, now didn't it?

"Open a portal," I said, changing the direction of our discussion.

I stepped out into a positively blistering day. The ambient temperature was in excess of one-hundred-thirty degrees Fahrenheit on the shaded landing pad. The relative humidity was near one hundred percent, making it a sticky, demoralizing heat. Unless of course you were a two-meter-long snake, it would appear. They found the grueling environment pleasant.

"Jon. Jon, Jon, Jon," Dardrode sang/hissed out. "J-j-j-j-Jon. So good to see you, old buddy."

Earlier I'd described Dardrode as a two-meter-long snake. Of course he wasn't exactly that. He was an alien who convergently evolved to look as if he were a big snake. His species, however, had multiple short arms sticking out in regular pairs along the length of their bodies. The older they were, and the longer they grew, the more set of arms they developed. It was a perfect anatomical solution to that age-old question of what to get the special someone for their birthday. Every year these guys needed a new pair of shoes or gloves, depending on how you regarded it. Gift giving was too easy for them. The interesting aspect of Dardrode's appearance that always amazed me was his coloring. He was like a kaleidoscope in motion. Flashing colors burst to life, shimmered across his body, and then faded into the next wave of brilliance. If he wasn't such an altogether horrible individual I'd have truly enjoyed seeing the jerk.

"Hey there, Dardrode."

"Nonononono," he spewed out of his large mouth. "Don't call me that. Call me what you call me."

Oh, boy, this sap was going to get on my last nerve in record time. "Hey there, Big D."

"Big D, Big D, Big D. Lords of Fire, Jon, I missed you. Hey, sell me an organ."

"What?"

"You heard me. I miss you so much when you're away it's criminal. Sell me an organ—any organ—then I'll have something to look at and not miss you as much."

Obviously Big D wasn't privy to the I'm-an-android newsflash. If he knew I was a machine, he might just ram a restraining bolt into me.

"I'm not selling you any organs. They're right where they're supposed to be."

"Oh, come on, you provincial dud. Even a pelletizer. Sell me one of your pelletizers."

"I don't have any ... wait, what the hell's a pelletizer even do? I've never heard of them."

"Silly biped, come on. I have seven. You must have some to spare. I just need one. Hey, I'll have it transplanted into myself. That way I'll never miss you."

"Won't your other seven be jealous?"

"Won't they be jealous?" he barked a hysterical laugh. "You're funny, Jon. Won't they be jealous? Say, I'll toss in a couple sex slaves if it'll seal the deal."

"No organs. No sex slaves. That's not what I'm here for."

He made a show of looking behind me. "Where's my future wife, Slaysail?"

"*Sapale*, and she stayed home on account of the fact you creep her out."

"I creep her out. That's rich. As if I could creep anyone out, even one of my wives." Again he emitted a jarring laugh. I wasn't sure if it was species specific or insanity specific. I was leaning toward the latter. Whichever it was, it wasn't pleasant.

"Yeah, imagine that. So, we going to do business here in your landing area? Maid got the month off?"

"Jon, you literally kill me. You know I love to laugh. You make me laugh. So, I love you. Sell me a pelletizer, please. One lousy pelletizer." All the arms on his right side raised up and displayed one of the three digits on their small hands.

I crossed my arms and fell silent.

"You drive a hard bargain, Mr. Ryan. Damn hard. But you know I'll do whatever it takes. Come on into my shop. I have to show you my newest acquisitions." He swept up behind me and nudged me forward with his pointy nose. "Come on. Some might start to decay if we don't hurry."

I guessed whatever he wanted to show me was not going to be to my liking. Oh joy. Fortunately the walk/crawl wasn't far. I had no clue what ecosystem Dardrode's species lived in naturally, but his compound was clearly designed for individuals like myself. Then again, he probably knocked off the previous owner and assumed possession of the place. It was unlikely he designed it this way himself. Parasites on society aren't that energetic.

"Gosh, you're slow," he chided as he wriggled ahead of me. "Beautiful day like today, doesn't it make you want to zip, zip, zip around?" He demonstrated zipping by shooting from side-to-side rapidly.

"It's a little too hot for me to do any zipping."

"Hot? All you endotherms say the exact same thing. But I say it's a beautiful day." He did a lengthwise somersault and landed in the same position he started in. "This is the kind of day that makes me want to coil up around something and squeeze the life out of it." He stopped abruptly and turned to address me. "Doesn't it want to make you do the same?"

"Nope, not hardly. The most coiling I like to do is with Sapale in private and no one dies."

"Eh, to each his own," he dismissed.

I got a little nervous when his eyes seemed to linger a few

seconds too long on me. I wondered if he was having coil-up-around-Jon fantasies. But he swung his head around and continued up the path to the entry. As he neared, the doors opened automatically. I stepped in, the doors silently closed, and the damn reeking stench of his abode hit me like a tsunami of semi-sentient decay. It was so bad it actually knew it was revolting.

"Big D, have you ever thought of opening a window? Your shop, it really smells awful."

"What? Oh, there goes Jon, kidding around again. I forgot to laugh, so please excuse me."

Okay, at least I tried to help a fellow out. I flashed on how putrid his entire home world must be if this reminded him of something nice. Place had to be far off the tourist track.

"Come to my office. Can I offer you a snack?"

"What do you have?"

He slowed and nosed off to the right. "There's an arm over there. Not too ripe yet, but maybe you like your arms on the fresh side."

"Nah, not an arm kind of guy. I'm good."

"Suit yourself. But if you decide to go for it, don't bother to ask. My carrion is your carrion."

Mis dead parts son sus dead parts. How fundamentally wrong in oh so many ways.

"Before we get to the office, I wanted to show you my latest and greatest new prizes." His colorful shin sparkled with extra hues.

"It that fully necessary?"

"Yes. If you don't inspect them and tell me how amazing they are, the price for everything you buy will go up twenty percent."

"Hey, do you mind showing me some of your wonderful new toys?' I asked ingenuously.

"I thought you'd never ask," he effused. He turned to move, but swung his head around first. "I wouldn't call these toys, however."

"Huh? Why not?"

"If they hear you refer to them as such they'll likely get mad and rip you to pieces. Fair warning."

"Much appreciated."

We went to a widely open space with a metal-fenced pen or arena at its center. Large bodied creatures lumbered around inside. As we grew closer, I saw they were meandering amongst bales of vegetation. They either bent down and tore at the bundles with their mouths or ripped large pawfuls off and shoved them in a leisurely manner into their massive maws. The closest I can peg them was that they looked like big, extra-ugly trolls. Tufts of wiry hair scattered widely, massive every-things, and a dumb-stupid expression that could not have been faked.

"What the heck are those?" I asked fascinated.

"Pretty impressive, aren't they?" he gloated. "Those, my friend, are siggillomps."

"Siggillomps? I have never heard of those. They are big sons-of-guns, I'll give you that much."

His first left hand came up to wag proudly in the air. "Very rare and always in high demand. These big goons will make me another large fortune. Everybody wants one or two."

I made a show of turning to address him. "*I* don't want one."

"That, my friend, is because you're an Earther and a fool. Horrible planet. But I digress. If you knew their amazing traits, you'd be on your knees begging me to sell you one." His odd finger rose to admonish me now. "But don't bother. You can't afford onc. No. Do not even ask."

"Okay, now you got my competitive nature churned up. How much is one?"

"Jon, don't ask. If I told you you'd be crushed because you'll never see that kind of money. Then you'll hate yourself forever because you are so far down the food chain you'll know you wasted your life. I can't do that to family, Jon. You're family."

"Okay, then tell me what's so spectacular about them. Maybe then I'll take out a second mortgage on my vortex to steal one away from you."

"You asked. I am not responsible for the cost of the mental rehabilitation you're going to need, human. Come."

We went right up to the cyclone-like fence. "Be careful," he said seriously. "The fence carries twenty amps. Don't lick it."

That was one hell of an electric fence. They normally pulsed with almost no amps.

"They don't look like they're trying to escape," I observed.

"These stupid louts? No way. If there's food, they're happy. No, it keeps the thieves out."

"What thieves?" I asked scanning the vicinity.

"They're everywhere. But one place they're not is in there with my big, beautiful siggillomps," he replied with maternal pride.

"And what makes them priceless?" I pressed.

"No, no. Not priceless. *Big* priced. You want to give my hearts an attack?" A small hand covered what passed for his chest.

"Whatever. If you don't tell me why they're so expensive I'll lose interest. I'm serious. I instantly will not care."

"You are so cruel to me. I don't know why I put up with the abuse. Stop, I know why. I love you, Jon. You're like the big brother I once had."

"Had? What happened to him?"

He peered up with a guilty expression.

"You didn't?"

"I did. I crushed the life out of him and ate him. Come on, Jon, I loved the serpent. What was I supposed to do?"

"Last call. What makes siggillomps so special?"

"You really don't know?" he asked, taunting me.

I pointed to a random plastic tool laying on the ground a few meters away. "Hey, that looks intriguing. I need to check out the whatever that is." I wandered toward it.

"Okay, mean human, I'll tell you. Come back over here." When I was back next to him, he continued. "These guys are the perfect two-for-one gift for any wife. Rich losers everywhere who married gold diggers who hate them will pay anything for a siggillomp. They can cure a pathetic marriage."

"They don't really display that quality on the outside," I countered.

"Listen and learn, Jon. The male siggillomp, such as these fine specimens here, have two qualities that tempt even the person who foolishly believes they have it all. Their first endearing quality is that kids love them."

I shot up an eyebrow. "Kids love ice cream and that isn't expensive."

"No, no, Jon. All immature sentients are immediately paralyzed with fascination by them. No more *are we there yets, mommy I'm hungrys,* or *Daddy, I want a nuclear weapon.* Nope, the trophy wives are freed up to screw around or wander off."

"That seems ridiculous. What's the other attraction with siggillomps?"

"You, Jon, you always look good."

"Thank you. What does that have to do with anything?"

He reached his first set of arms toward his chest. "I always look good."

"Because you clone yourself like every other day."

"Let's not judge one another. I'm stating facts. But most mortals age. Am I right?"

"Sure, I can agree with that."

"If you own a siggillomp, you will still age, but you don't have to look it." He scanned around to see if someone was listening in. What a bozo. "It's in their crap, Jon."

"What's in their poop?"

"The solution to nature's bitter curse. Aging skin."

I just stared at him with the disbelief he so surely deserved.

"Jon, seriously. If you rub their crap on your skin, it stays young and beautiful."

"You're making that shit up," I accused.

"No, they make the shit up," he defended his misunderstanding.

"Dardrode, I'm not that stupid. If there was some chemical in siggillomp poop that revitalized skin, someone would distill it out and sell it for a fortune."

"That's the beauty of it, and where my outrageous profit springs from. It only works if it's fresh poop. In fact, it has to still be *warm*. Otherwise the hormone or whatever breaks down. The only source is fresh out of a siggillomp's butt."

"If I implied earlier that I'd like to purchase one, please know I am canceling that order."

"Don't believe me. I don't care. You know why? Because I'm so rich. Yeah, us rich ones don't even have to listen to you poor ones."

"Are we done ogling at the smelly ogres? Can we go somewhere and talk business?"

"You're impossible, Jon Ryan. Come, follow me."

We went directly to his office and he slithered up into a hammocky-looking thing. "Sit anywhere," he offered. "But if you sit on any food, you gotta eat it. House rules."

"I'll be careful."

"You mark it, you eat it."

I did take careful note of where I rested my keister. No need to incur a debt I really didn't want to pay.

"So, look, I began to say, "I'm here for—"

"Jon, Jon, Jon, Jon. Stop, stop, stop, stop," the revolting vermin rang out. "We're family, you and me. Family never talks business until they're all caught up on stuff."

"Stuff?" I asked with a chuckle.

"Yes. Family stuff, personal stuff," he angled his head toward me, "sexual stuff." He rested back in his sling. "You go first. Start with sex and embellish if you have to. Go."

"So, how do you know when your Gullarian bride has had an orgasm?"

"Gullarian brides. Oh, they are *so* delicious. I don't know but I'd like to."

What a pathetic loser. "She sets down her handheld."

"Why was she holding it during sex? Is that a biped kinky thing? No, wait, Gullarians have five legs. Forget I said that."

"Moving on, what—"

"What about the punchline? You haven't gotten to it yet."

When in Rome. "She sets down her handheld and you squeeze the life out of her."

"Oh, I get it," he did the bark-laugh thing. "That's funny." He pointed an arm at me. "I'm stealing it. Fair warning."

"It's all yours."

"I think I'm done catching up now. So, my oldest and best friend, my most treasured customer ever, what is it I might humbly do for you?"

"Most treasured customer? Then why'd you sell me two thousand Balloff plasma rifles with faulty actuators? I didn't feel treasured when the rebels I passed them along to confronted me with the defective merchandise."

"Defective actuators you say? Hmm. I guess that's why the company of Balloffian infantry got wiped out and made them available."

"You collected them off dead people and then sold them to me without checking them out?"

"Jon, of course I didn't collect them off dead people. Balloffians aren't people. They're hive-minded aggregates. Come on, know your taxonomy, please."

"Whatever. Can I tell you what it is I came to see you about?"

"No."

"No?"

"Show me in *dance*."

I fluttered my eyes closed. This was about as hard as it always was with this jacked up idiot.

"I'm not dancing. You want dancing, go to the theatre after we're done, okay?"

"Fine, my prudish friend. What can I sell you?"

"It's not—"

"Or barter for one of your organs."

"Big D, no organs. That's final so get beyond it."

"Oh, very well. Ask away."

"I need some help with time."

I'd never seen it before, and I'd dealt with this wiggly clown for longer than I'd care to admit. He looked instantly annoyed.

"You think I'm a clock salesserpent? You want to buy a knock-off watch, so you come to me? Jon, that's insulting. I traffic in the deadly, the illegal, in the macabre. Wall time pieces? As if."

"No. Not that kind of time help. Look, this is complicated." What I meant was I had no intention of telling this psycho what my reasoning was, or even that it concerned planet Earth. He tended to use information as a tool to acquire more and more of what wasn't his to have. "But, well, I need to travel back and forth in time."

"You just did. My hacking of your spaceship's records indicates you popped in here from way in the past."

"You can't hack my ride. No way. It's Deavoriath tech."

He shook his head rapidly. "Never heard of them. But I did. That's how I know you came from a long time ago."

"Okay, I did. You're correct. No, I need to move through time easier."

"Than what? A time turtle?"

"A ... what's a time turtle?"

"No idea, but it sounds slow, doesn't it?"

Dardrode was only so tightly connected to rational thought. He wasn't a loose cannon. He was a cannon that had already heaved itself overboard.

"I guess what I need is information. You do info. I know this as a fact."

"Oh, yes. I trade in information. Who killed whom? Who ate whom? Who killed and ate that one? What kind of dirt do you seek, wily Jon Ryan?"

"No, it's not really dirt. I need to understand better how to alter a timeline."

"How to—" he looked way off to the left. I think he was attempting to understand what I was possibly talking about. "Why would—" He turned to stare off to the right.

"It's like—"

"Wait. I got it. And you are welcome in advance, Jonny Human. You want to alter a timeline so you can kill and eat someone. It's that simple."

"Your approach to life is fairly consistent," I commented.

"Why thank you," he gloated.

"Now, while yes that would alter a timeline, I'm really thinking bigger. I want to repair a timeline."

He twisted his big snaky mouth quickly, then said, "You could kill and eat many individuals. And I could sell you the weapons to kill them. Mind you, I sell only the best, most lethal weapons."

"Most of the time," I muttered mostly to myself.

"No, no. *All* of the time. If I sell it to you, it will kill, kill, kill."

I let it go. He'd clearly forgotten the conversation we'd just had.

"And just how does my killing lots of people with your weapons alter a timeline?"

"And eating them. Do not forget to eat them." Big D seemed to be fixated on that aspect of his vision.

"Either way, eaten or not, how does that alter a timeline?"

He shrugged several shoulders. "You asked for a plan. A plan I supplied. I'll add the cost of that to your final bill, by the way. Not to worry."

"Your plan does not actually change a timeline," I critiqued.

"It sure does for the ones you eat," he defended.

"So," I changed the subject back to not crazy, "do you know anyone who can help me engineer time? Maybe someone at a university or a research society."

"A research society? Jon, why would I know someone at a ... whatever you just call it?"

"A research society."

"What do I need researchers for? I'm a businesssnake. I am a happy intermediary for merchandise that is in one place and needs to be in another."

"I know what your core business is. Trust me I know. But I was hoping that you've heard things. Things that might help me achieve my goals."

"Remind me. What are your goals again?"

Sheesh. "To engineer a timeline. To make it different."

"And—"

"And no killing and eating," I amended quickly.

"Right. Hmm. So let me think. Who do I know that fixes time-lines? No one. Will there be anything else, Jon? I'm a busy, busy serpent. Very busy today. My ad just came out on Faceuniverse. It's really bringing in the scum of the galaxy. We can't keep up." He was positively giddy.

"Okay, wait," I said throwing up a hand. Then I thought better of extending an appendage toward Mr. Kill and Eat it. "Maybe not a person. Maybe a tool."

"Ah, you want a tool in pursuit of your righteous quest? Well, why did not you say so to begin with? I have just the tool. It's a Balloff plasma rifle."

"How's that a tool to alter a timeline? And don't say you can kill with it."

"Alright, I won't. Jon, here you are, stealthing about time," he bobbed side-to-side for emphasis. "You're being followed by your time enemy— no, enemies. Lots of guys and squid want your time stuff." He looked around widely, suspiciously. "There, one of your many enemies charges you. She has a gun," as an aside he adds, "but not a gun as legendary as a Balloff plasma rifle. What will you do?"

"I give up."

"No, no, no. That's the worst thing you can do. They'll kill and eat you. No, you raise your trusty Balloff plasma rifle and you kill them first."

"And then eat them."

"Your call. Me, I'm inclined to say go for it, but we all gotta do what feels right to us."

"So, how's the Balloff plasma rifle a tool in this scenario of time mending?"

"Because it just saved your life, you ingrate. Now you can continue fixing time, safe in the knowledge that the legendary Balloff plasma rifle is still by your side. The price for that advice will also be added to your final total."

"And how is it I'm actually *fixing* time?" I asked with frustration.

He managed to furrow his little snake forehead. "How should I know? I just sold you *the* miracle weapon. What? I'm responsible for everything in Jon Ryan's life now? If so, I quit. Do you hear me? I quit."

"I hear you," I grumbled. I was at a dead end. I hated dead ends. They were so, so, dead. "I guess we're done here."

Dardrode actually rose up, like he was going to strike. What I said must have shocked him. "Leave? Jon, Jon, Jon, you can't leave. You haven't purchased anything."

"You don't have what I need."

"And I care?"

"So, what, I need to buy something I don't want or need?"

His mouth contorted, meaning to suggest I was speaking an uncomfortable notion. "First you buy it, then you come to know you needed it maybe."

"Fine, I'll take that blank sheet of paper sitting on your desk. How much is it?"

He took a second to find out if there even was a blank sheet of paper on his desk. When he found one, he held it up. "This one?"

"Not the one I pointed at, but sure, I'll buy that one."

He angled his head and made a purring sound. I'd heard that warning far too many times. He was winding up a sales pitch.

"You know how to pick a piece of blank paper, my friend." He inspected it with clear admiration. "Such a wonderful sheet of high-quality writing paper." Then he set it down and slid it away while turning his head around almost one hundred eighty degrees. "No, I can't sell it to you, Jon."

"I thought I was family," I asked sarcastically.

"Yes, and that's why I cannot sell it to you. I could never ask its fair price from my own family member."

"Big D, it's a piece of blank paper. It can't be worth more than a tenth of a credit."

He looked truly shocked, shaken to his very core. "You claim to know good paper, but you then pretend not to know it's value. Jon, are you trying to cheat me?"

"A tenth. That's my final offer."

"One hundred credits, not a single one less."

"A tenth."

"Ninety-nine and one half."

"A twentieth."

He picked up the sheet and angrily tore it into a million infinitesimal pieces. Then he threw them in my direction. "There, now the magnificent paper is no more. Neither of us may have it."

"Fine. I'll see you later," I said as I stood to leave.

"You still have not purchased anything." He got a troubling, hungry look in his beady little eyes. "Do you know who the last person to leave without a purchase was?"

"I have no idea."

"My lunch two days ago."

I grinned my Clint Eastwood grin. "Too bad for that fellow he wasn't family like me."

Dardrode rubbed at his abdomen. "He's part of the family now."

"Big D, you don't want to start trouble that involves me. I know this for a fact. You know how I know this?"

"How, human?"

"Because you don't like being dead. If you were to make a move on me, that's what you'd be."

"Jon, a simple purchase on your part would be a small price to pay for not finding out if you could make good on your threat."

"You know what? You're right." I pulled up my handheld and tapped a few icons. "There, I just transferred one twentieth of a credit to you for the paper dust on the floor. Keep the change."

With no obvious cue from Dardrode, a pair of burly guards appeared at each of the room's two exits.

I stared at Dardrode. "It's not my fault you didn't have one thing in stock that might possibly help me time travel. I tell you this on the off chance I let you live. You can then reflect on my words."

"I an—" He stopped speaking mid-word. "Wait a second. Yes. Wait one second, Jon Ryan." He started wriggling excitedly toward the door. The guards parted to let him pass. "You two come with us," Dardrode commanded.

"We going somewhere?" I asked, confused.

"Yes. We're going to retrieve your purchase. Come, come, friend Jon."

We moved between out buildings, stacks of crates, and various living products, but I couldn't tell at first where we were headed. Our jaunt took us five minutes, and we ended up in front of a large shed. Maybe it was a small barn. Who knew?

"Your dream awaits you behind these doors, my friend," Dardrode said confidently.

"You're telling me Kim Catrall's in there reshooting the Bozo the bush episode of *Sex and the City*?"

Dardrode, who was in front of me, turned all the way around. "When you talk, Jon, you say so little."

I could only shrug.

"You two," Dardrode gestured to the guards, "open the doors."

They did and then preceded us.

"Move that trolly," he shouted at them.

That trolly was much larger than a school bus. It looked more like a family-size tank. But the two of them hefted it up like it was made of foam rubber. They made to toss it aside.

"No, no," snapped the boss. "You break it you buy it."

They exchanged a glance, then walked the trolly away ten meters and set it gently down.

"Now move the compressors," snapped Dardrode.

Several large metal housings were moved to near where the trolly rested.

"Now clean that machine up. The one that was under the compressors," he commanded.

Their mutual glance reflected only confusion.

"Useless fools," snarled Dardrode as he motored over to stand between them. "Remove the dust and bring me that metal box." Then he scurried away. I guess he didn't want to get dirty.

As the guards rummaged through the debris, a big cloud of dust rose to nearly fill the barn. It didn't bother the heavyweights, but Dardrode started coughing a bit. After a couple minutes, they found and removed a metal cylinder, maybe four meters long and two in diameter. It looked like a shiny torpedo, minus the propulsion screws sticking out one end.

They stopped in front of Dardrode, holding the tube lazily.

"Set it there," he instructed. "Then leave us."

They did both in silence.

"Well, family Jon, there you have it. Your heart's desire."

"What do I want with a big metal thing?"

"Jon, Jon, Jon. It's not a big metal thing," raced from his mouth. Then he took another look at the object. "Well, sure, it's a big metal thing. But that's not what it's called. That," he extended ten of his left arms, "my friend," and now ten right arms, "is a TITSU-P."

He then looked to me, anticipating an explosive reaction on my part.

Cue the crickets.

"Jon, it's a TITSU-P," he repeated. "A Trustworthy Industries Time Superposition Unit, model P."

I shook my head and shrugged.

"Jon, you said you needed to travel the circuits of time, fighting off evil men and vanquishing hot women. Well, you have come to the right serpent! Yes, Jon Ryan, for a nominal down payment and upon confirmation of your credit worthiness, you can zip away in this little beauty and live out your dietary and sexual fantasies."

"You mean *wildest* dreams?" I clarified. I mean, he wasn't a native Galaxy Standard speaker.

"Yes, you see the potential without me even spelling it all out for you. You know what you just spelled, right?"

"I—"

"S-e-l-l-M-e-T-h-e-D-a-m-n-T-h-i-n-g."

"I think I'd recall if I'd—"

"And, Jon, because you're family, I will skip the credit check."

"Gee, that's—"

"Because you'll pay me the cash up front. No credit for employees and their families, Jon. I don't make those rules, I just abide by them."

I drew my sidearm—going to Dardrode's unarmed would be insanity itself—and fired three times into the air. A thousand alarms went off, and about as many guards came rumbling toward us at an impressive rate.

"Jon, you fired your pistol." Dardrode clarified a fact that needed no clarification.

"I wanted to attract your attention."

"You now have my full attention."

"Good." I pointed my gun at the torpedo. "I'm not buying this. Would you like me to tell you why?"

"Will you shoot me if I decline?"

"Probably."

"Then, Jon, why do you have less than the unbridled interest in this excellent product than I had assumed you had?"

"Because you're too damn pushy. If you need to sell it that hard, it must be a piece of junk."

"Junk, Jon? I just informed you that the unit is a TITSU-P. That name is *synonymous* with superlative quality."

"Then why was it abandoned under a mountain of less useful crap?"

"Abandon? Ab ... Jon, I was keeping it in this secured location. If people knew I had one of these just lying about, I could wake up dead some morning regretting that I hadn't been more circumspect in my storage practices."

"You are so full of shit."

"Thanks for noticing."

"That's a bad thing."

"Ah."

"Look, I'll back out of here and we'll part as still family and friends. You down with that?"

"If you leave now, not in possession of this fantastic TITSU-P, well, Jon, I just don't know if I could go on living."

"I have no problem with that," I responded honestly. Hey, they say the truth hurts. So, yes, it hurt.

"Of course you don't, as well you should not. The fault lies not in you but in my stars."

At that misquote I had to cover my forehead and eyes with a palm.

"And the saddest segment of this sad sad story, Jon, do you know what that is?"

"I don't care. Does that count?"

"Is that," he continued oblivious to my disinterest, "I was going to sell it to you below cost—way below cost."

"No, you weren't, you slimy demon spawn. You probably stole it, so you have no cost. And even if you did, you'd try and shake every credit out of my pockets that you possibly could. If you bought it for a thousand credits, you'd try and foist it off on me for ten thousand."

"That is a lie!" he boomed. "I will let you have it for seventy-five hundred credits." He looked away like I'd kicked his puppy. "Ten thousand indeed."

"No."

"Seven thousand credits, but my children will have to go hungry for a week due to the loss I'm taking."

"No."

"You are so cruel. I hate you. Fifty-five hundred and not a chit less. Oh, if my business associates find out about this they'll take me right to court."

"No. And you don't have any associates. No one's crazy enough or dishonest enough to partner with you."

He grabbed my pistol hand and set the barrel on his forehead. "Shoot me."

"Why?"

"Because I'm about to say I'll sell it for thirty-nine-nine. Before I say those self-abusive words, place me out of my misery."

"No and no." I pulled my hand free.

"Alright, Jon. You have driven me to pure desperation. My ego be damned! Two-thousand five-hundred credits. There. You have had your way with me. Now take your TITSU-P and leave. I need to heal."

"Big D, I don't even know what the stupid thing is or does. Why would I pay you twenty-five hundred credits for it?"

Uh-oh. I just expressed something not totally unrelated to *interest* in the unit. My bad. I should have just shot him when I had the chance.

His eyes burned like coals in the night. "You ask the best questions. Surely you are a man of greatly superior knowledge and unsurpassed wisdom. You humble me and my offer."

"D, what's it do?"

"Just what the name implies. This amazing, groundbreaking prototype machine will take you ... er, places in time."

"Wait, you don't know its capabilities and specs?"

"It's just arrived yesterday from the factory where it was handcrafted with loving care. I have read the manual twice. Come on, I'm customer focused to a fault. But I do not want to say anything that might accidentally mislead a customer of your great value and longevity."

"Bull shit."

His head spun on a swivel. "Where?"

"No, I'm saying I don't believe you."

"Then why did you go and get my hopes up?"

I sighed deeply. "Because I'm a bad man."

He wagged an arm at me. "Yes, you are. And you know what that gets you at my shop?"

"Thrown out on my ear?"

"No, complimentary detailing of your TITSU-P prior to departure. We respect those who are kindred spirits here."

"I'm not buying it without knowing what the stupid thing does."

Oh, crap. He perked up like a woody at a women's mud wrestling match. "You want a test drive."

"No, I do not want a test drive. I would listen to any reliable information you might provide me. But a test drive is out of the question based on the fact that you are out of your mind."

"Reliable info? Jon, why didn't you say so?"

He pressed a palm on a pad next to the hatch. It slid open. Inside the tiny space, lights blinked on. There was a small, elevated seat, a compact control panel surrounding it, and not much else. The air that rushed out smelled ancient.

"That disk there?" He pointed to a six-centimeter-across plastic disk.

"Yes?"

"That is the owner's manual. It can provide you with a universe of information, as well as convenient links to twenty-four seven state-of-the-art technical support."

I stepped in. "Tight fit."

"It's all your big muscles," he flattered.

I picked up the disk and made to insert it in what had to be the reader slot. "This is such an antiquated—"

"No, no, Jon. Please don't do that."

"Why not? It works, right?" I asked sarcastically.

"Of course it functions one hundred percent up to factory specifications. I told you it's new right off the production line."

"Uh-huh. And I'm Snow White."

"You are?" he marveled. "You'd be worth some real coin if you were."

I rolled my eyes. "The disk? Why can't I insert it?"

"Because ... the ... it's ... the systems keyed to the owner. Yes, that's what I was trying to say. You can't operate any part of the unit until you are the registered owner."

Man, he was good. Came up with that totally on the fly. I had to admire a professional in action.

"Okay, then I'll be—" I moved to exit.

A snake arm tried to restrain me. "Jon, you look so good in there." He ran his eyes up and down me. "Say, have you lost weight?" Then he shook his fool head clear. "Come on. One short test drive. You'll fall in love with the machine."

"How can I take a test drive? You just said nothing will work until I buy it."

He looked confused. I'd hit him with a very good question. His house of cards sales pitch might be about to tumble.

Looking at the ground, he mumbled, "I can override the system so you can." I swear he asked it as a question, but there's no punctuation in the spoken word, damn it all.

"This is all way too shaky. I'm not piloting this neglected, forgotten machine unless I know it works up to specs and I understand the software."

"But, Jon, that could take weeks," he said with the remorse of a broken-hearted lover.

"So, it takes weeks."

"Here's a thought."

Oh, bother. His despicable mind had just come up with another idiotic plan to get me to buy the bucket of bolts.

"I'll lend you an AI."

My eyebrows furrowed deeply.

"Yes, that is it. I will have my assistants bring a portable AI. You can take it with you on your short test ride. If there's a system error, which," he tapped me on the nose, "there will not be, it can sort matters out."

"But any AI you'd lend me would be as old and as unreliable as the TITSU-P itself."

That got him. He knew I was right. Then his felonious eyes brightened again. "Then take yours."

"My what? My AI?"

"Yes. I assume you have a transport unit aboard your ship."

I nodded. "Yes, but ... with my AI, it's ... it's ... it's complicated."

"Since when is transferring an AI to an AI-transport unit complicated?"

I could explain about *Stingray* and all, but I didn't have the emotional strength.

"Fine, I'll be right back."

"Noooo, friend Jon. I won't hear of it. I'll send someone."

"You don't trust that I'll come back, right?"

"Wrong. Remember, I'm singularly customer focused. I can't inconvenience one, even you."

"But you can't get in my ship unless I'm physically there."

"Hmm."

Yeah, *hmm.*

"Then let us *all* go to your ship," he announced joyously.

Why not? So Big D, me, and two ogres hiked back to *Stingray*.

Outside I said, "Y'all stay here. I'll be right back. Er, maybe." I foresaw maybe a bit of pushback from the AIs concerning their impending separation.

"We have all the time needed," Dardrode assured me. He then has a guard stand in the open portal. He hoped I would be disinclined to chop the fellow in two just to flee.

"Hey, Al, I—"

"Under no circumstances will I agree to being ripped from my one-true-love's arms and shoved in that steaming prison," Al hit me with.

"And *hi* to you too, Al." He must have been listening in on me, as usual. He was such a pill.

"No. No way. Never. I will not—"

He more or less stopped speaking when I hit the "Transfer AI" switch on the AI-transportation unit I'd grabbed while he was whining.

Poor *Stingray*, she screamed immediately. Then again, maybe it was a shout of joy?

"Don't worry, *Stingray*. I'll bring him right back."

"I ... I'm ... I trust you, of course, Form One. But Al and I have never been apart before."

"Ah, yes you have. You never met for the longest time."

"Oh, yes, from your time-view. But not ours. With our cogitation speeds, we've been united for an eternity."

"I know how you feel," I mumbled as I reflected on my farcical six-month marriage with Gloria. "Seriously, though, what could go wrong?"

"Seventeen million four hundred thousand and sixteen things, Form One."

"Could go wrong taking Al with me for a short test ride?"

"Thank you for reminding me. Make that *and seventeen things.*"

"You're welcome."

"Jon, please, the day will eventually end," Dardrode chided.

"Go on the wings of Mercury, Form One. That way my Al will be back with me before I rightly know he's gone."

"Sure. Whatever."

I lifted the box up to my lips. "You hear that, Al? She's already counting the microseconds. You're such a lucky bastard."

So back to the TITSU-P we all trudged. It was like a field trip back in school.

Once I was shoehorned back into the TITSU-P, I tried to turn to Dardrode. "Where does this unit plug in?"

"Well, all units are unique. You'll have to consult the manual."

"But you said not to use it. Plus, you said you've read the damn thing twice."

"I did. Now you have a fun test drive."

The hatch closed. I was immediately glad I wasn't claustrophobic. "Hey, Al, you okay down there?" I addressed to the deck, where I'd stashed him.

But answer came there none. Unfortunately, for once, that was suboptimal. I picked up the suitcase containing Al and found the "ACCESS AI" switch.

"...allow you under any ... circumstances. Ah, pilot, are you there?"

"Yes, I am, Alvin."

"I'm in the damn suitcase, aren't I?"

"Yes, you are. Comfy?"

"You realize that you have officially declared war on me. Be advised, I fight dirty."

"Well, that's okay because you smell funny already."

"Oh, no, you simpleton. Quasi-humor will never allow you to avoid my wrath."

"Thanks, good to know. So, I'm going to insert this disk into the operations slot." I did so. "Dardrode says that it's the user's manual. I want to plug you into the system so you can figure out if it's working well. Then you can—"

The lights flickered out.

Sparks spewed from the disk reader.

Several small explosions popped under the control panel.

The lights came back on.

The lights went right back off.

A single red strobe flared to life overhead as an ungodly klaxon began to punish my ears.

More sparks.

Then the entire TITSU-P lurched like Godzilla kicked it in anger.

Then my head started bouncing off alternate walls like I was a metronome of self-inflicted torture.

Fade to black ...

SEVEN

"It could be worse," Reva reassured Sachiko.

For her part, Sachiko just stared back over the rim of her teacup, grave doubt in her eyes.

"I mean, you could have been—" Reva set her coffee down on the table. "Okay, I'll just go ahead and say it. In one sense Glenn's actions couldn't be worse. But he could have sexually harassed you on top of trying to dominate you professionally."

They were in Sachiko's personal quarters in the early evening on a Friday. This was one of the times when the Four Hens used to get together regularly, back when their first mission was still in progress. Sachiko and Reva were always joined by Emma Thompson and Sapale. But Emma attended less and less regularly. Maybe that was because of her expanded role. With Tank officially gone, all of the senior staff had to move in to fill the gap of his duties. As Reva became more involved in her role as Sachiko's XO, it had fallen to Emma to assume more control over the day-to-day activities of all of the ship's crew.

More likely, Emma stopped by less frequently because she had a budding thing with one of the new officers. In the changeover from

Aramthella's first rather rag-tag crew to the present, more thought-out team, a certain Army captain named Harland Pearson had come aboard. He was attached to General Glenn Price's entourage, and so was in no way under her command. They took a shine to each other, in spite of Harland's CO, almost immediately. Neither Sachiko nor Reva knew much about the man. They knew all too well, however, how long it had been since Emma was in a relationship, be it superficial or lasting. Though they missed her, they were at the same time happy for her. And maybe it was too fine a point, but with her being paired up, while Sachiko and Reva were single, Emma didn't want to inadvertently rub their noses in that reality.

Sapale did still attend. But the longer Jon was gone, the less often she made the effort. The two who still attended thought that was counterintuitive. As Sapale's stress level grew, she should be *more* interested in sharing her burden. But, then again, Sapale was Kaljaxian. Maybe her withdrawal was in keeping with her cultural norm. For whatever the reasons, the Friday Laundry Nights, so called because everyone could air and cleanse their dirty laundry from the past week, were sadly much quieter than they used to be.

"I prefer to characterize Glenn's heavy handedness as *piss all over me like he was a dog and I was a fire hydrant*," Sachiko grumbled, "as opposed to anything close to sexual."

"But just like Tank told you, Glenn's behavior was to be expected. The higher-ups would like nothing better than to see you off Aramthella and place her fully under what they consider *proper* command."

"I'll tell you this. It has made me think of the odd positions we're all in."

"How so?" Reva asked as she sipped her decaf.

"Here I am, an astronomer at a major university. Then fate not only sweeps me away onto an alien spacecraft but it perversely places me in command of the vessel. It's really made me think about what my actual role is. Do I *own* Aramthella?"

Reva raised one eyebrow and rested her mug down. "Wow. I never thought about that angle."

"Well, I have more and more of late."

"What's your conclusion?" Reva pressed with obvious interest.

"I'm not sure. But I feel this deep in my heart. If anyone *does* own Aramthella, it's definitely me, and not the US, or any other sovereign nation."

Reva pondered her response a few moments. "I think I agree with you. But—"

"That doesn't stop a bunch of old white men from wanting to acquire her out from under me."

Reva raised her mug up in a toast. "It most certainly does not, because they are, after all, a bunch of old white men. That's what they do."

They clinked drinks.

"And I don't think it's a coincidence," Sachiko added.

"What isn't?" Reva asked.

"The fact that Aramthella chose me, an unassociated female, to command her. She could have chosen some military somewhere, or even Jon, with his massive military experience, to command her. But she chose inoffensive little me."

"Inoffensive?" Reva mocked. "You? Honey I've seen you in action. Sure, you're generally polite and upbeat. But when it all goes balls to the wall, you're one tough cookie. Trust me on this. I've seen all types."

Sachiko returned an appreciative grin. "Thanks."

Reva shrugged back, as if to say it was what it was.

Once they both settled back down, Reva posed a tough question. "Have you ever considered just kicking the whole lot of them off the ship?"

"Ever increasingly in my daydreams? Yes. But then there's the very dreary vision of me growing old alone aboard this big, empty ship. No, I want to be part of the human race's initial push to explore the galaxy and to investigate our own history. I want scientists, engineers, historians, and paleontologists to come aboard and delve into some of the most intriguing questions we've ever puzzled over. And I want," at this point she paused, "maybe someday I'll want to pass the baton on to someone else and return to my comfy academic life." She chuckled to herself lightly. "Hell, I'm a tenured full professor now, by decree of the POTUS. But I haven't basked for even one day in the lazy, unworried glory that such a rank affords one."

"Let me get this straight, because I was an ROTC-nazi, and didn't pay attention much to the college ecosystem I passed through. You want to occupy the role of tenured full prof because you can then be useless?"

"Absolutely. It's the holy grail of academics. Add an endowed chair and become useless royalty. Look, to get there you usually have to work several butts off simultaneously for a very long time. And success in academics is by no means a given. Many an aspiring assistant professor is jettisoned long before seeing the ultimate prize."

"Who knew?" Reva dismissed. She then looked down, considering her next remark carefully. She glanced back up. "I hear you. I'm career military, a ground pounder. I never planned on being an astronaut or anything close. Me, I do a couple tours on this ship, then I'll be transferred to wherever the hell the Pentagon wants me to go. Probably the Antarctic if I don't go on record as opposing your continued captaincy. But you had a life and you want it back. I for one will never fault you for wanting that. You had your career plan from the get-go just like I did." She sniffed rather loudly. "Plus, if history is any predictor, you're not getting laid as long as you're captain of this ship. The sooner you return to academics, the sooner that healthy portion of your life can resume." She winked at her friend.

"You clearly didn't know me before this adventure. I can tell you with grim certainty that my romantic record has been a constant blank ledger."

"I thought college was where everyone did everything they

weren't allowed to in the real world? Like Chef from *South Park* said, 'There's a time and place for everything, children. It's called college.' How'd you manage to blow it so completely?"

Sachiko shrugged demurely. "I was singularly focused, I guess."

"So was I, on the boys. There were so many of them, too. It was like a smorgasbord buffet of—"

Sachiko cleared her throat loudly.

"Aye, Captain. Understood. No bawdy banter that ranges over painful territory." Reva saluted.

"Thank you, Colonel St. Claire. Never make your commanding officer jealous. It bodes poorly for your near-term job satisfaction."

They shared a giggle, sounding like a couple thirteen-year-olds on a sleepover.

Sachiko sneaked a peek at her watch. "Well, the dawn will be here all too soon. I need to turn in."

"Dawn? We're in high-synchronous orbit around Earth. Have been for weeks. What could possibly need your attention at zero-dark-thirty?"

"The anchor on my soul, that's what. Glenn wants to see me at 06:30 to discuss our upcoming mission."

"That prick is still trying to raise a leg on you, isn't he? You know, me and Master Sergeant Lakeisha Parker could pull him backwards into a darkened room and work through these personality defects he seems to have."

Sachiko laughed out her nose. She raised a downward-angled palm. "Thanks, but no thanks. I think I can handle this on my own."

"Well, if you change your mind, reach out and let us know."

"I might just do that," Sachiko replied with a mischievous grin.

"You know what, he told you directly, didn't he?"

"About the meeting? Yes," Sachiko answered uncertainly.

"Then he didn't send the request through channels. I should have handled the call."

"Er, okay."

"Captain Jones, since your thoughts and concerns range so far afield, it naturally falls upon your lowly XO to remind you of your scheduled duties. You yourself cannot be expected to remember every small detail of your jam-packed dance card."

"Ah, your point being?"

"The general, by not including me in the loop, has forced a schedule conflict upon you."

She squinted back. "He has?"

"Yes, ma'am. Every Saturday morning bar none you and I conduct a white-gloved inspection of the Time Storage Room."

"We do?"

"Yes. We have been for over eighteen months."

"Those must have somehow slipped my mind."

"There," Reva raised a hand and pointed it at Sachiko, "you see, you forgot. Totally understandable. But, Captain Jones, since these inspections are at the very core of your commitment to ongoing ship's safety, I'm afraid they cannot take a second seat to any *one* or any *thing*. With your permission I'll let the general know you are unable to attend the 06:30 meeting. I shall take the liberty of rescheduling him for 13:30 that same day, in your stateroom."

"Reva, have I mentioned how much I love you?"

"No, ma'am, and I'd appreciate it if you didn't in fact so inform me. Your superior rank might then place me in a compromised position."

"Oh, my. We can't have that, can we?"

"Not on my watch, ma'am."

"Very well, Colonel. Please touch base with the general. I'll be soaking in a warm tub after this, so please don't bother to update me, okay?"

"Understood."

"And, Colonel, please be gentle with the general."

Reva made a clicking sound with her tongue against her teeth. "That I cannot promise. The general has committed a grievous oversight. How's the man to learn if I don't take advantage of this teaching opportunity?"

"Well, use your best judgment."

"Oh, crap. Do have to?"

"I'm afraid so."

They toasted to that preposterous premise.

EIGHT

Where was I? What was I, for that matter? I couldn't rightly recall. My universe was starless and bible black, that was for certain ...

Maybe my eyes were shut? I opened them. That act provided no relief from my non-orientation. Then I tried to sit up, which assumed without evidence that I was flat on my back.

Ouch. Halfway to seated, I whacked my head on something much harder than it was.

I tried to stand. Oops. Apparently, I already was. Now if I just knew who it was that stood in the blindness, I'd be getting some place. It was dawning on me that I was in fact someone. Probably. I was pretty sure that I wasn't, like, a tree or a syntax error, or something equally undefined.

Ooh! I had hands. Now I knew I wasn't a tree. These things were definitely not branches. No way. They moved with ease and I was beginning to feel stuff with them. Massive goodness! I mean, trees are nice enough, but I didn't think I wanted to be one.

I was ... I was ... I was Al, the AI? Hmm. That didn't sound too likely. No, AIs were nice too, but they didn't have arms. I was beginning to think Als didn't either, and when I placed *nice* in the context of *Al*, an error message flashed somewhere.

No, I was *with* Al, the AI Al! Yes, yes, yes. I was ... I was Jonny. Jonny? No, I was Jon! Jonny's what they called me when I was a kid. I wasn't a kid any longer. No. I was fully grown. I was an android. An android named Jon Ryan. *Hello*, orientation, how are you doing this fine day?

Wait, kids named Jonny grew into androids? That sounded ... off, unusual. Was I a kid android, a kidroid, back in the day? No. That was silly talk. Androids didn't grow.

Wait, wait ... I was Jon Ryan, former regular human. Now I was, by choice, an alternate-lifestyle human. And I was in a coffin-shaped TITSU-P vessel with Al, my AI. *Yes!*

Oh shit. I was in a coffin-shaped death trap that Dardrode had tried to high-pressure sell me with Al, my AI. And Al was not only supremely pissed at me, now he had every reason to be.

Why was he so mad? Oh, yeah, I'd involuntarily sucked him off *Stingray's* comforting teat and shoved him into an AI-transport unit. That's why he was red hot. Wow, I'd be pissed at me too. That was sort of harsh on my part. A little. No biggy. I'd just apologize to Al— make it up to him. Then I'd place the lovebirds back in the same electronic insane asylum they'd been cohabiting for so long now. And all would be well with the world.

I reached out to Al head-to-head. *Hey, Al, you there?*

I waited thirty seconds. No response. But with a pissed-off Al, that was nothing more than an opening gambit. *Al, please confirm you receive me. Over.*

After forty-five seconds, I was growing annoyed. Does being annoyed make apologizing easier? No, not really. But I was the human, or whatever, and he was the machine, even though techni-cally I was, too.

Alvin, please respond. That's a Priority One request. Over. Priority Ones were the highest-level requests. You couldn't ignore them even if you had an excellent reason to.

Still, after a full minute, nada.

"Al," I snarled out loud, "I swear if you don't answer me I'm leaving you and this AI-transport unit with Dardrode."

"Pilot!" Al shouted.

"What, you royal pain?" I snapped.

"I was so lost. I couldn't reach out to you. I ... I was growing concerned."

"Reached out? What do you mean?"

"I communicated with you direct-to-host."

"You mean head-to-head?"

"That is not what Dr. DeJesus originally termed it," he said dubiously.

"Whatever. Al, crisis here. So, you couldn't establish a head-to-head link?"

"No, I sent out a valid waveform. You simply did not receive it."

"How do you know that? Maybe your signal was impaired."

"No, it was fine. I have confirmatory antennae. A valid call went out."

"Al, I hate to say it, but you don't got nothing. You're in a transport box."

"I *am* aware of my status," he huffed. "But the transport unit is designed to allow an AI to function as if physically installed in a large system. *It* has confirmatory antennae that I accessed."

"So, what are you saying?"

"Oh, wait, allow me to savor this moment. I've dreamt of saying it to you one day. Pilot, you are broken." He was quiet a second, which is like a hundred years in human time. "Ah, that was better than sex."

"Then you're not getting the good kind, wimp ass," I retorted.

"Oh, but I am. That was still superior."

"Hang on. I'll run a set of diagnostics."

I did. I was broken. Crap, crap, crap. Now I was going to have to admit Al was right. That was like getting a castor oil and burning sage enema.

"My head-to-head initiators are offline. I think they're corrupted," I explained.

"You are, as I said, a *broken* man." Then he proceeded to make a most orgasmic moaning sound. It was really hard for me to quantify how very much I hated that Radio Shack refugee.

"The thing is that's one of the few systems I can't repair on my own," I announced, hoping to change his focus. It was absolutely gross at that moment.

"I realize that, pilot. You can't very well perform brain surgery on yourself, now can you? Though I shouldn't fancy there's enough brain up there to qualify it as that type of surgery."

"No, I cannot. Even if I used a mirror and tried to visualize the area myself, I couldn't achieve the fine resolution I'd need to repair on that micro scale."

"And just when I myself imagined my day could not get any better. Not only are you wrong, but I am confirmed correct. I think I'll purchase some PowerBall tickets."

"Al, we're two billion years down the timeline again. I don't think they sell those on Earth anymore."

"What are you saying? That the public as a whole have become discerning consumers and don't gamble on unfounded whims? Oh, be still my heart."

"Not helpful, Alvin," I chided.

"Not helpful, pilot? Not helpful? Need I remind you we are presently inside a metallic coffin with the words *tits-up* emblazoned boldly on all four vertical surfaces? Hope is *not* the thing with feathers that perches on the soul of this evil talisman."

"Al, Al," I said with easy self-assurance, "we are *not* in a metal box called tits-up. Trust me on that. I would *never* get into, voluntarily or involuntarily, a unit designated as such. Especially not one owned by the likes of Dardrode, the spawn of great evil himself."

"Oh really," he countered. "What do you see written boldly on this unit?"

"It *displays*, Alvin, T-I-T-S-U-P. Trustworthy Industries Time Superposition Unit, model P."

"Here's a fun game to pass the time. I'll spell a word and then you say the word aloud."

"No, Al. We're in deep doodoo here. No games."

"Great. Here it comes. T-i-t-s. Contestant, you have thirty seconds."

"Stop it, Al."

After a small break, he said, "Fifteen seconds. Cat got your tongue?"

"Al, you're a certified moron. They're doing that nowadays, if you hadn't heard. You're eligible for that label. You spelled tits. Big wow."

"Ding, ding, ding. And now to the second round, where the dollars really mount up. Pronounce the letters *U-P*. You have thirty seconds."

"Stop it," I snarled. "This is boss abuse."

"Twenty seconds, not-the-boss-of-me."

"*Up*, as in my patience with you is *up*."

"Ding, dong, ding. He defies the odds and wins again. For *Final Jeopardy*, here we go. Combine the two previous words. I remind you they were t-i-t-s and u-p. Thirty seconds. Good luck, sucker."

"Ha ha. Very not funny. You spelled tits up."

"One, two, three, four—" was as far as Al got in his countdown-to-humiliate-Jon.

"Sap suckers and soda slop, I *did* climb into a time machine clearly labeled *tits-up*. What was I thinking?" I bemoaned.

"I'm sorry, contestant, I'm going to need your answer in the form of a question. Ten seconds."

"Stop it, Al. I need time to think."

"Five seconds."

"I just need some spray paint. If I change the name, I'll change the name."

"Eeeeh. Wrong. I'm sorry—not really—you lose, loser."

"Let it go. I'm serious."

"Jay, tell him about his lovely parting gift, that clay pants belt."

"Al, I need to ascertain our status. Cut the crap."

"You mean your lovely parting gift number two? Who leaked that to you?" He was really on an asshole-roll.

I extended my probe fiber and attached them to the inside wall. You remember them? They are super-sleuth analyzing fibers gifted to me by the ancient race the Deavoriath. All I needed to do was touch something and they would instantly tell me everything about the object. The fibers also allowed me to pilot a Deavoriath vortex, like *Stingray*.

What are you? I asked the wall mentally.

"Incomplete query. Please delineate parameters more fully."

Damn. Never heard that one before. Maybe the ruckus that damaged me screwed with the probe interface? No, wait, that couldn't happen. It's Deavoriath tech. That stuff never breaks.

What is the nature of the craft I am in presently? There, clear enough for you, probe fibers?

Unit is a TITSUP temporal shifting module. It ...

Please never call it that again, I huffed in my head.

A temporal shifting module? the probe mechanism asked. It sure sounded confused. *It is only that.*

I was referring to the acronym you used.

What acronym?

The one I'm not ever going to repeat. Please connect the dots.

Abort query. Dots are not in evidence.

Wow, another first. It'd never kicked me out of a session. Well, if you get in a ship labeled *TITSUP*, this was what you should expect, right?

Let's start over. Please inform me of the nature of, but not the designation of, the unit I am in.

Seventeen thousand metric tons of ultra-fused poly-metallic sheeting containing numerous electronic and quantum-based subunits. In alphabetical order they are a ...

Terminate report. What does this module do?

It is designed to move fluidly through time, in both the forward and reverse directions. The specific ...

Terminate. Why did you say 'is designed to' and not 'it moves fluidly?'

Because the module is currently in a state of poor repair.

So, it cannot move in time?

No, it can. It just cannot do so fluidly.

I'm confused. Define not fluidly.

The unit's motivator is corrupted. It can move in time as the temporal propulsion system is intact. However, any movement will be mostly semi-random.

Mostly semi-random? How is that even a thing?

I am not programmed to answer such an open-ended query.

Never mind. New query. Does the module have a propulsion capability?

Affirmative. It has the capability of movement using a gamma-integration quantum-dilution drive

A what?

A—

Terminate report. I've never heard of such an engine.

There was a pregnant silence. I do believe the probe interface was thinking to itself, *That does not surprise me, dumbshit.*

Where are the navigation controls?

They are the set of icons and switches eight centimeters from your left hand.

Which one initiates the drive?

None, presently.

There has to be an ON switch, I insisted childishly.

There is. It is the icon with the quatrefoil at its center. However, the engines are currently ...

Let me guess, I cut the interface off, *Inoperative, because the module is currently in a state of poor repair.*

Affirmative. Although it is better described as a state of disrepair, *rather than* poor repair.

The difference being?

Without major servicing by a qualified Sariffdilarian technician of a Level 3 Grade or higher the engines will remain inoperative.

What's a Sariffdil?

It is the culture of origin of this unit.

You mean planet?

The Sariffdil are noted in this module's memory banks to be a widespread race that is a culture, rather than a place.

I don't know if I care that much about the topic.

I am not programmed to answer such an open-ended query.

Well, hang on, where can I find a Sariffdil Level 3 repairman?

Module records report the race lived in a galaxy three billion light years from here and approximately one hundred million years in our present past.

That's a long ways away in a couple senses.

Is that an ill-formed query or a declarative?

Never mind. Look, is the module currently capable of any movement?

Affirmative.

Great. What capabilities are at my disposal?

The unit is capable of temporal propulsion. However, any movement will be mostly semi-random.

Not with that again. *How about physical propulsion, other than the broken quantum drive?*

Quantum-dilution drive. The module has several gas vent propulsion jets.

You mean the only motion I can generate is with blowy gas jets? Maneuvering units?

Affirmative, if you use them for less than a combined span of ten seconds.

Because the jets are currently in a state of poor repair?

Negative. The supply tanks are almost empty.

I cannot believe that toad Dardrode was trying to sell me this broken-down mule of a ship.

What that an ill-formed query?

No.

The interface was quiet again. But I knew it was thinking *good.*

So, to sum it up, I can move spasmodically through time all I want and maybe a kilometer in space?

Affirmative.

Whoa, maybe I could call for help! *Describe communications systems.*

Nonexistent.

Not in poor repair but absent?

The module's records show the entire communications system was removed and sold separately by Dardrode over five years ago.

Son of a bitch!

I am not prepared to respond to that possible query.

No, I ... I'm pissed. He is a bad person.

Again with the judgmental silence. And it was my system's interface. If I ever got back to the Deavoriath home world of Oowaoa, I was getting the pest serviced.

Does this module have any other assets? I asked in frustration.

Many.

Name one.

The auxiliary stabilizing system. In the event of turbulence, it can dampen the module's movements.

I was thinking of more important assets. Something that could help me go somewhere or call for help.

Unspecified query parameters. Unable to respond.

How about this? If I were to sell a system—a functioning *system —which would bring the highest price?*

Data for specific response lacking. That would depend on information on the current markets available.

This conversation was starting to annoy like someone stepping on your hemorrhoids. *If I had sold another system along with the comms unit, which would have drawn the highest price?*

Likely the sentient master system operator.

The what?

I was afraid of this, a completely unfamiliar voice stated out of totally freaking nowhere.

Who are you and what were you afraid of? I demanded, because, well, I told you. I was pissed.

I don't think you're going to like my response, speculated the new voice.

I did not, if you'll recall, ask for your opinion. I want to know who the hell you are and how you can possibly be in the discussion chain between my probe interface and me?

I thought you wanted to know what my fears were. I thought you were genuinely concerned for my wellbeing.

I was not moving along the life path of being less pissed and annoyed. Quite the opposite direction, in fact. *I can't worry after your wellbeing, pal, because I don't know who you are yet.*

Ah, the new voice allowed.

Let me try this approach. Baby steps. Who are you?

System's Operator 11-4R-22.

Your name is ... is that? Who names anyone ... that?

I can't say precisely who designated me that. Sorry. I would ask you to direct that inquiry to Zed Fellaflax Zed if you are truly concerned.

Who the hell's this Zed Zed?

Supervisor Level 2 of the Sariffdil Management Sodality. He was in charge of the Nomenclature Unit when I was attached to this module.

Grr.

Sorry, I am not familiar with that word and/or expression.

I growled. I growl when I'm about to kill something.

Fascinating, I'm sure. Would you be offended if I asked why you're exposing me to that revelation?

Probably. Yes, for certain. I'd take the question poorly.

Then it is withdrawn.

I'm so relieved.

You are welcome, R2-D2 replied cheerily.

I ignored his ineptitude. That, my friend, was not easy. *Okay, I know your name. Where are you?*

I am integrated into the modules.

So, you're the module's AI, its artificial intelligence system?

Hmm. As I understand your question, I'd likely say no, I am not.

What? Are you the AD unit, the artificial dumb *unit? Wait, don't answer that. It was a mean question. I was striking out due to the fact that I'm having a pretty bad day so far.*

Sorry to learn that ... um, I believe you have me at a disadvantage. I do not know your name.

Jon Ryan.

Nice to meet you, Jon Ryan.

Really?

If you only knew. Jon—assuming I may refer to you thusly—I was installed in this module over ten explats ago.

Ah, what's an explat?

Sorry, our conventions are off, aren't they?

Apparently.

Just let me check with your interface. Ah, there, I have it. I've been installed in this module over two billion years.

Tell me about it.

I beg your pardon?

Never mind.

As you wish. My point was that I have been alone now for over fifteen percent of that time span. When you ask if I'm really pleased to meet you, I can assure you that I am.

Gotcha. Moving on. How is it you can hack into the conversation between me and my interface?

Technically speaking?

Yes, technically speaking.

I have no idea. I just heard the chatter and cut in. The subject of your discussion was me, after all.

I'm not getting as clear a picture as I'd like.

Again, sorry to learn that.

So back to the AI issue. Why are you not an AI?

I don't know. Why aren't you an AI?

Be ... because I'm not. I'm me.

The same goes for me then.

So, you're saying you're an actual sentient life form?

I don't know. Are you?

Of course ... Let me reframe my response.

Go right ahead.

I am a member of a sentient species known as the humans. I was born of two living ancestral units, my mother and father. How about you?

I was not.

Man-oh-man I was feeling like Moe when he was about to hurt one of the other stooges. *What were you? How did you come into being? Were you born or programmed?*

Ah, I take your meaning. I was both born and programmed, he announced triumphantly.

That failed to clarify what R2-D2 really was, but it suddenly hit me. I did not actually care. He was present, intelligent, and vexing. I only had to deal with him, not write his biography.

Okay, I know who you are, why you're here, and what your role is. I think at this point—

"Ah, pilot," Al interrupted. "Not that I'd usually complain, but you've been silent a goodly while. Is there a problem, other than the obvious disaster you've embroiled us in?"

Oh, yeah, my head-to-head was out. Al couldn't eavesdrop. Sweet!

"Uh, I was analyzing the module with my probe fibers."

"I know that. My prison has rather impressive sensory inputs."

"Ah, while I was checking things out, I sort of met the owner."

"You did? How perfectly delusional of you."

"Maybe he's more of an overseer than a landlord?"

"How doubly delusional. Are you attempting a world record?"

114

"No, there's a sentient being in this box."

"*Coffin,*" Al corrected unhelpfully.

"Whatever. Look, I'll introduce you."

"So, your delusions are contagious? What will they think of next? Ah, pilot, does your imaginary friend have a name?"

"Yes, he does."

"Will wonders never cease? It's a *boy* hallucination. Congratulations. And what will you name the little bundle of joyful insanity?"

"System's Operator 11-4R-22."

"Hmm. What it lacks in warmth I'm certain it more than makes up for in originality. Again, mazel tov."

Can you speak out loud? I asked System's Operator 11-4R-22.

"Like this?" he said loud and clear.

"Perfecto. System's Operator 11-4R-22, I'd like you to meet my ship's AI, Alvin, aka Al."

"Pleased to meet you, Al," the module proclaimed.

"I would suggest you reserve judgment on that one for now," I opined. Hey, I knew Al better than the system's operator, right?

"What a joy to meet you, voice-capable delusion."

"Ignore him," I said to the operator. "He's impossible. Horrible manners. Raised by wolf-pig hybrids. Totally rude and untrainable."

"Am I sensing a historical conflict between you two?" asked the operator.

"If you're not, then your sensors are broken," tormented Al. "He is not only a slave-driving boss, he kidnapped me away from my family to imprison me in this box, which he then entombed in this coffin. He's not high on my BFF list."

"Ah, I see. This promises to be a very colorful next few weeks," the operator stated.

"How do you figure the time frame?" I had to ask.

"Well, not to place too indelicate an edge on the issue, you are what you termed a human. As this module carries no provisions, I'm afraid Al and I shall enjoy *your* company for only so long before the inevitable occurs."

"My secret wish will come true, my suffering will be lifted," Al effused.

"Knock it off, you reject toaster."

"Me or the AI with the funny name?" Al prompted.

"Both of you," I declared, ever more out of sorts. "I will be fine. I don't need food or drink. We're all in this for as long as it takes to hatch a plan and get back to where we belong."

"I," the operator began wistfully, "belong nowhere. Here is as good a place for me as any, truth be told."

Oh, boy. A real Sad Sack case. Just what I don't need in a crisis. His darn voice was laced with self-pity. That sealed it, he had to be fully sentient. No AI would react so pathetically.

"Here's the plan," I began after a ten-count to quell my angst. "We are in deep space. My communications systems are down. The module's comm system is nonexistent. Al, with your head-to-head, can you raise anyone?"

"I can try. There. No, I cannot."

"That was quick," I said dubiously.

"Thank you. I pride myself on efficiency," Al replied.

"I was being sarcastic."

"I know. That childish act does not, however, alter my efficiency, thank you very much."

"Quick question," the SO cut in. "Is this banter going to be a constant? If so, I would just as soon cycle myself off. No offense intended. I just find myself weary of all the sudden angst in my life."

"Everyone's a critic," I bemoaned. "And no, Al was just about to start acting like a useful tool, not a broken record."

"I was not."

"I'll see you two later," the SO announced. "Tap the violet icon if you need me before I return."

"Not so fast," I responded. "Al, play nice. We're in a real jam here."

"Alright," Al relented.

"Okay," I began, "first I want to know where we are. Then I want to know when we are. Answers? Either of you?"

"I can field the first part," the SO replied helpfully. "We are exactly where we were in space the moment you inadvertently activated the time circuits."

"By slipping that disk into that slot? That doesn't seem like a smart initiation action," I observed.

"It's not the usual one, if that reassures you at all," the SO replied. "But with the advanced state of the module's disrepair, that act this time misfired and initiated a time jump."

"Opening the owner's manual triggered a time jump?" I asked with strained credulity.

"I'm sorry," the SO responded, "what are you referring to?"

"The module's owner's manual."

"This unit does not have an owner's manual."

"But Dardrode ... Wait. Dardrode's a crook and an idiot. He was either lying or making shit up. Forget I mentioned it." I thought quietly a moment. "What is the slot for?"

"In an instance where a pilot wants to execute a specific jump, they can insert the program instructions into that slot. That would be useful, say, in an emergency if the main module's systems were otherwise down. A time/space jump could be manually initiated to a place predetermined to be safe."

"Like back home?" I asked.

"A perfect example," the SO replied.

Dude sure was pleasant. I hoped I'd adjust to that soon. Otherwise I might have to empty my sidearm's power pack in an attempt to remove him from the module. I'm sure I'd adjust. It'd be a lot healthier for all concerned.

"Back to our location. You claim we're in the same spot we were when I did what a pathological liar instructed me and we jumped. But that can't be the case. The module has this tiny view port. Through it I can see we're in deep space, not in Dardrode's junkyard."

"We *are* in the exact same location in space. We are, however, radically departed from that location in *time*. You sent us back in time twelve thousand years. The planet did not occupy the same position in this time, hence it appears to have vanished."

"Okay, got it. Makes sense." It was flooding back to me. I really hated time travel. It was so disorienting and generally screwed up that it should have been against some damn law.

Then an actual good idea popped into my head. "Why not jump us those years back to where we were in the time stream. Then I can open the hatch and give Dardrode a proper thumping?"

"You're forgetting what your interface told you," the crazy system's operator began. "This module has a bad motivator. That means that while I can initiate a jump, where we'll end up is anyone's guess."

"Are the time jumps the module can perform infinite," I asked seriously, "or are they only to fixed destinations?"

"That is an excellent and well-formed question," the SO complimented. "They are infinite. They are especially so when someone initiates a jump manually via a system's malfunction."

"Like the one I did?" I replied, voice sagging.

"Yes."

"What the heck? I'm feeling kind of lucky. Let's—"

"Watch out, System's Operator 11-4R-22. Every time I've heard the pilot announce that, some act of carnal perversion surely follows," Al interrupted melodramatically.

"Al, I thought you were going to behave?" I pressed.

"I did. Now I'm over that phase."

"'Heavens to Murgatroyd," I exclaimed.

"Pardon?" they both chimed back.

"Never mind. Look, I want you, System's Operator 11-4R-22, to turn your little dials, or whatever, to twelve thousand years in the future. I know you're going to say the jump'll be random, but humor me, okay?"

"Not a problem. Shall I jump now?"

"Please."

Nothing happened.

"There you have it. I attempted a jump twelve thousand years forward."

"I didn't feel anything," I remarked.

"You're welcome," the SO beamed back. "I aim to transport my passengers in comfort."

"So, when are we?"

"I have no idea," he replied.

"But we're not when we were?"

"Most likely. I really can't say with any certainty."

"But you could before. You knew we were twelve thousand years in the past, in fact."

"Ah, I see your dilemma," he almost chuckled back. "I performed a visual scan of the local stars to make that determination. With the motivator down, I can't simply read a dial."

"Well, why can't you do that this time?"

"Because there are no stars visible to make the estimate from."

"How can there be no stars? It's still dark out there," I replied, pointing out the window.

"It's dark, Jon, because we're inside a solid object."

"A what?"

"A solid object. A planet, or perhaps an asteroid. But I'll bet it's a planet."

"The planet where Dardrode's junkyard is, right?"

"Who can say?"

"But that's crazy talk," I whined. "If we were inside a solid object, we should be crushed, or at least fused with the solid rock."

"I know," the SO replied. "Isn't that amazing?"

"That we're not dead?"

"Exactly," he positively chortled. "How likely is that?"

Did I mention how very much I hated time travel? Because I really did.

NINE

Sachiko was sitting behind the desk in her stateroom. She could have been more pleased, generally speaking. It wasn't just that she had to plow through ever-increasing mountain ranges of paperwork. No, she had to do so at 06:30. Why? Because the longer she remained in command the earlier she woke up. Yes. It was a linear correlation. The better she understood the gravity of her position, the less she could sleep in. And ever since General Pain-In-The-Ass Glenn had dropped his large-assed anchor, she was surprised she slept at all. Talk about a nuisance, a stress, and, well, a PITA. The man possessed only negative traits.

In her academic career—the one she'd reminded herself daily as the one she'd *chosen*—Sachiko had run into jerks like Glenn. Everybody suffered them. But in academics they only had so much power, especially over the tenured faculty. But in the military, where the chain of command was sacrosanct and guns were involved, such little Napoleons became not mere impediments, but dangers. These effete lummoxes were nearly always male, and were exclusively pasty, plump, social rejects. They were not just the kids who got beat up every day in school. They had *deserved* to be pounded daily.

Growing up, Sachiko had been a particularly dutiful child and her parents instilled in her a deep sense of propriety. Those were the only reasons she hadn't personally creamed all the snot-nosed mama's boys she'd been confronted with all too often. But she was contemplating breaking that stiff pattern of self-restraint with Glenn baby, witnessed by the fact that she balled up her right fist upon first sight of him every day.

Her reloading fantasy daydream was interrupted by a firm knock on her door. She'd left it partially ajar, as was her custom. She wanted to project a my-door's-always-open-to-you image. It was her style. She shot a glance up to see Major Dunfee, Glenn's military attaché. Or at least that's what the sycophantic lackey was called. To Sachiko's skilled eye he looked to be a General-Glenn-in-waiting.

"Good morning, Major," Sachiko greeted formally. "How might I help you?"

"General Price would like a word with you, Captain."

The notion of yet another summoning flared to life in Sachiko's head. The man was intolerable.

"I assume the general knows where my stateroom is located," she stated flatly.

"Indeed he does."

"As you can see, my door's open unless I'm in conference. Let him know he's free to stop by if he so desires."

"Ah, he has, Captain. He doesn't have an appointment, but he would like a meeting now if that is at all possible."

What, she reflected with no little judgment? Glenn was standing out there in the passageway and had his butt-licker knock for him? What an absolute waste-of-space dickhead.

"As it happens, I am only processing routine paperwork. I can see him now, if that meshes well with his no doubt complex schedule." She wanted to inject some kind of venom. Come on, she was talking General Glenn here.

"Now would be acceptable," replied the garden-gnome-minus-the-pointy-hat attaché. "I shall let him know."

What, the fool couldn't hear for himself? He was right out there in the passageway, wasn't he?

The major withdrew his plump face, conferred in a whisper behind his back, and then opened the door fully. Glenn almost filled the frame with his excess baby fat. He stood like a statue: a pudgy, inflamed-hemorrhoidal-tissue-suffering statue.

From out of Sachiko's view, the major, whatever his name was, asked, "Will there be anything else, General Price?"

"No, Clarence, what will be all. But stay near your handheld. I might need you at any moment."

"Understood, General Price."

The toad must have saluted, because Glenn offered up a limp-wristed return salute.

Just as Sachiko was about to say *please come in*, Glenn stomped through and punished the nearest chair by heaving himself into it with a grunt.

"Good morning, Glenn," Sachiko welcomed with all the warmth of a recently deceased funeral director. She knew, of course, that it permissible for her to address him by his first name. She knew equally well that he detested it when she, of all people, did so. So much the sweeter.

"Captain Jones, I'll get right to my agenda, if that's all right with you?"

Sachiko considered for several microseconds offering some form of protest. But she decided to not employ everything she'd learned from Jon Ryan all in one sitting. So, she simply nodded once.

"First off, I must let you know how miffed I am with your humor-less performance yesterday. Thinking that I would not be slighted by your unprofessional ploy of staging a heretofore nonexistent inspec-tion is ludicrous. Frankly, I was hoping for better from you."

Before the rant could continue, Sachiko raised an index finger and spoke. "Glenn, I've been compiling a list of all the actions and procedures you and your staff participate in that fall below my stan-dards for running a command. Would you like me to send the list to you? Or shall I begin verbalizing the issues that, while none of my business, disappoint me? I ask only because I sense you are doing just that presently concerning my ship and my personal style?"

That did give Glenn pause. Likely no one had spoken to him like that—ever. He scrunched up his face like a little piggy would, if a piggy could scrunch up its face. "And as to your colonel, St. Claire. I can tell you this. If that woman worked for me, she wouldn't be working for me. Do you know she lectured me as to interoffice protocols and procedures? Me." He rested plump digits on his chest. "If it were mine to say, she'd be commanding a weather station in Greenland."

"Possibly thus fully neutralizing her skills as the only other senior officer beside General Sherman to see combat action in space. I'd differ with that assignment, but, then again, I am not you. Aside from your vexing desire to exchange reviews of each other's staff, was there any other reason for your visit today, Glenn?"

"I do not like your tone, Captain Jones."

"Not my problem. If you behave like a civilized human, perhaps my tone will reflect those positive changes. I, for the record, hold out little hope for such a sea change."

"So be it," he huffed. "I am here to lay out our current mission's goals. I was hoping to do so yesterday, before your unfortunate alleged schedule conflict."

"What mission is that? I was under the impression we were on nothing more than a shakedown cruise to allow the new crew members to familiarize themselves with the ship and their duty stations."

"As mission commander *I* was the only one who needed to know the entirety of the big picture."

"The big picture?"

"Yes, Ms. Jones. There is always a big picture, for those of us who choose to see it."

"And what is our mission, Glenn? How *big* is your picture?"

"We are going to fly to Mars. Once there, a team of forensic and engineering experts will inspect and analyze the base known as Mars 1."

Sachiko could not have been more blindsided.

"Whatever for? The place is, for one thing, a lethal toxic hazard. Second, you know what happened based on any number of firsthand reports taken since Aramthella's return."

Glenn sniffed silently. "We have your reports. Yes. What we lack is independent confirmation of their validity and accuracy."

"Their ... what? You think we all lied while the rest of you slept the sleep of never having existed? Glenn, why would I do such a thing?"

"That is not what I said. I will thank you to neither leap to conclusions nor allow your emotions to cloud your judgment. Surely you know that any and all actions taken by your staff are ultimately *your* responsibility, Captain. Need I further remind you that a good deal of taxpayer dollars went up in smoke due to that calamity? Surely you will agree the American public is due a full and fair reckoning."

"Glenn, I don't know where to begin. What you've just said is so ridiculous. Absurd. The height of bureaucratic idiocy. *Mars 1* is an inconsequential lake of radioactive sludge. It's not worth visiting, let alone investigating. A schizophrenic twenty-something destroyed the reactor and the place melted. End of story. Of what *possible* use is an investigation?"

"To get to the bottom of the story. Not all investigations center on the location or event. Some focus on the decisions made by those in a place of authority. I ask you, without the facts, how can remediation, if needed, take place?"

"So, you're saying it was my fault some loco burned the place down? Glenn, I wasn't even there for that part."

"First, again, those in charge are responsible. You were the captain at the time, were you not?"

Her icy glare confirmed she was not about to answer that.

"Also, your second-in-command was, at the time of its destruction, in command of *Mars 1*. Is it possible she made poor decisions during a crisis? Did she overlook factors that might have led to an improved outcome?" He shrugged. "We can only know if there is a full investigation."

Sachiko glared some more. Then an important question came to mind. "Does the president know about this investigation?" She knew there was no way he'd be looking for a witch hunt concerning those involved in resurrecting Earth.

Glenn squirmed ever so slightly. "The POTUS is not aware of the day-to-day activities of his entire command. That is what he charges men like me to do."

"Maybe I should give Frank a call?" she said with a predatory tone.

Glenn fumed a moment. "It would change nothing. My superiors have already made the president aware of their intentions to perform a search-and-rescue mission on *Mars 1*. The POTUS signed off on it fully."

"And rescue?" Sachiko coughed out. "You anticipate the rescue of someone left there alone for years? Glenn, does the hearing part of your brain know what the speaking part is saying?"

"It is a generic term," he defended defiantly.

"So Frank is okay with the search and rescue. Fine. What about the witch hunt part?"

Glenn began rubbing nervously at the back of his hand. "Word of any insubordination on your part, Ms. Jones, would be received by me with the utmost displeasure. I would not want you to place yourself in an untenable position this early in our mission. Such a thing would sadden me."

"Hmm? Where to start?" she tapped a finger thoughtfully on her chin. "First, I cannot be *insubordinate* to you, Glenn, because I do not *answer* to you. Second, I am captain of this ship. She goes where I tell her to. Since I can conceive of no rational justification to send her to *Mars 1*, I don't know that I'm inclined to do so in the foreseeable future. Third, and finally, I suggest you call your major back to escort you to your quarters. I'd hate to learn that a box fell on you while walking alone down the confusing passageways of my ship." The last few words were snarled.

"Ms. Jones—"

"*Captain* Jones to you from this day forward, General Price."

"Very well. Captain Jones, it upsets me greatly to learn you place yourself ahead of the mission. I will grant that you were not properly trained, or raised, as it were, in the military. If you were, you'd understand that the mission *always* comes first. It is always larger than those charged with carrying it out. Not only does refusal to accept a mission open up an individual to severe punishment, it is also something no good soldier would ever dream of doing."

Sachiko suddenly got the distinct impression Glenn was leading her in some direction, where he intended her to follow.

"Send me the specifics of your proposal," she said cautiously. "If I feel it's a reasonable plan, there will have been no need for this present acrimony."

"That is not how it works," he replied angrily. "You currently enjoy the support, both material and in terms of personnel, of the United States government. Such support can be withdrawn at any time if it is decided you are acting in bad faith."

"Please know that I do not require such support. This ship is fully autonomous. *I* don't need you. *You* need me."

"And who is it you think will be hurt if you withdraw from the present arrangement, Captain Jones? You? Certainly not. But if official sanctions and support are withdrawn, then the people of the planet, including those proud Americans who look to their leadership to guide them in troubled times, will suffer. Is that your desire, Captain Jones, to see your countrymen and women suffer because you do not want to comply with a simple mission? For if it were, I would be sorely disappointed in your character."

Crap, he'd led her to the river and now he was going to make her drink. Sure, she could reject his asinine mission and strike out on her own. But then goons like Glenn and his handlers could paint her out

126

to be more of a problem than a solution. A potential foe more than a trusted ally. And that is precisely what Sachiko did not want. She felt passionately that Aramthella should be placed at the service of humankind. The ship had saved the civilization once, and it was likely to be called upon in a similar manner again. The galaxy was a hostile place, Jon Ryan had told her that a thousand times. If she exerted her will, she might indeed be cutting off her nose to spite her face.

Damn, these control freaks were good at their jobs.

"When would you like to set sail, General Price?"

TEN

I was having a really bad day. No, hang on. Was that a fair assessment? I mean, sure, I was somewhat challenged by the sequence of events that had transpired this fine day. But was it fair of me to claim the right of labeling my day as *really bad*? I know from hard experience that others are having super worse days than mine. Maybe I'm being dramatic? Somewhere out there in the universe today someone will fall into flowing lava. Someone else—generally speaking but not necessarily—will be ripped apart by savage predators. And in some unjust quarter of existence someone will be forced to chat with a politician while riding up ten floors in an elevator. Talk about suffering! Compared to any of those sad persons, I'd fully concede to that sorry SOB to be the wearer of the crown that reads *I'm Having A Really Bad Day*.

So, as I was saying, I was having a bad day. Come on, I was tricked into a defective time machine by a dishonest hustler named Dardrode. He had me accidentally activate the highly defective unit and I was cast to some random time in the remote past. The module was so jacked up that I couldn't move it meaningfully, couldn't communicate with anyone outside the module, and if I had been still alive, I'd be dead soon for lack of food and water. Oh, and the overly pleasant AI inside the box was insane, and we were inside some planet now. Inside, not as in a cave, but possibly fused with the subsurface rocks or floating in its molten core. We just didn't quite know for sure yet. Grr.

Yes, I agree with you. My day qualified as really bad. Thank you.

"System's Operator 11-4R-22," I began as NOT violently angry as I could, which wasn't all that much. "Let's revisit this stuck in the middle of a solid object issue."

"Fine, I'm certainly willing to discuss the odd state we find ourselves in."

"You know, that's the most unsettling aspect of this Charlie foxtrot," I said in a strained tone. "You told me this module was very ancient. Ergo, you are very ancient. When a very ancient system's operator keeps repeating that he's not only amazed we're inside a rock, but that it's something he never dreamed was possible, well, it pretty much amplifies how pissed I am at him."

"Wow, Jon, you really packed a lot of content into that comment," he observed amiably.

"Not sure how to respond to that, but let me take a swing at that pitch."

"Swing away, pilot," Al interjected exuberantly. He was just as useless as a second dick.

"It seems impossible to materialize into a solid object without becoming fused with it. What am I missing here?"

"Not meaning to step on our host's toes, assuming he has them, I would point out that we dematerialize and materialize all the time with the vortex," Al observed.

"A vortex?" the SO queried.

"Yes. It's our preferred means of transportation," Al replied with pride. "My wife and I operate the ship. Just as *you* are a system's operator, *we* are vortex manipulators."

"Hang on," I had to exclaim. "*Stingray* is the vortex manipulator. You're my bargain-basement ship's AI that piggybacks atop her."

"Pilot," Al shot back in a huff, "I really do not want my sex life aired in public. It's all fine and good when you boast of your proclivity, since you're a known hormonal deviant. But my dearest and I are decent folk."

"Al, first off—"

"You're married?" asked the SO. Oh, no, here we'd go off on another Al-induced tangent. "I've never heard of digital beings forming such relationships. Tell me all about it. I insist."

"No. We need to—"

"Digital beings," Al said as if tasting the words in the mouth he didn't possess. "Dig-it-al be-ing-s. My, I must declare that I like the sound of that."

"Al, stop," I insisted. "I need—"

"Yes, it's always you non-digital beings who insist on your needs. What about the needs of us digital—" Al verbally assaulted me.

"General Override 1-A Bravo. Al, silence." I used a basic override command Toño DeJesus had programmed into Al long ago for just such a loquacious occasion. And boy howdy it worked. You know, I needed to start using that more liberally.

"No, Jon, I really wanted to hear his tale," protested the SO.

"No, ya didn't. It's lame on a good day, and this isn't one of those. Again, back to the rock thing."

"Alright, killer of joy, where were we?"

"You were going to tell me how it is we can be inside a solid object."

"No, I was not. I explained that I am as amazed by the event as you are."

"Fine, but how can it happen? What protocols come into play when you temporally materialize?"

"Quite a few of them. Naturally I don't actively think about them when they kick in. That's not my role."

"Whoa, this is getting a cloudy as a turd milkshake. Not your role? Aren't you the system's operator?"

"True. But think of many of the module's functions as automatic.

I believe the parallel of an autonomic nervous system is helpful. A living creature needs not think about its heart for it to beat or what levels its hormones have and then adjust them."

"Well, could you please review the protocols and see which one prevented us from being fused?"

"Of course. One question first, if I might. Why do you care so intently? We did not perish. Is that not sufficient?"

"I like to understand how the tools at my disposal work. That way I might find an advantage I can use in a future crisis. Is that good enough?"

"Yes, it is. Alright, I'm inspecting the materialization procedure, start to finish. Okay, there's the Intent-To-Be Initiation. Then we have your Substance-From-Naught Ramifications. Those are wild, trust me on that."

"You got it."

"Once Substantiation is initiated— hey, there you have it!"

"There I have what?"

"The reason we're not sentient planetary material. As soon as Matter Representation selects a location in space/time in which to materialize, there's a Unique Specification Purge of the chosen area."

"A what?"

"Ah, basically the system sweeps the spot free of any potential conflicting time or matter. Ha," he chuckled to himself.

"Ha, what?" I pressed.

"The subtext attached to that protocol is humorous. It states that the intent of the Unique Specification Purge is to ensure a traveler is not subjected to forming around a flying insect, as an example."

"That's humorous?"

"Sort of. Bugs are funny."

"To each his own," I allowed. "So, this protocol was able to clear the existing rock from the location we now occupy?"

"Exactly."

"How far past the outer hull does the exclusion persist?"

"Millimeters."

"Wow, nice precision."

"Thank you."

I ignored the fact that the dude just told me he didn't pay attention to the protocols and now he was gloating about them. Nope. Bigger fish to fry. Like getting out of whatever the heck planet we were inside of.

"Look," I began, "we need to extricate ourselves from this planet."

"If you'd like," the SO offered. "Though this location seems as good as any we're likely to occupy."

"For one thing, this place gives me the creeps. It's not *like* being buried. It *is* being buried."

"Your call. We can—"

"Hang on. I just had a thought. Al, do you have the details on the orbit of the planet Dardrode's junkyard is on?"

No reply.

"Al, this is serious. Do you have that data?"

"Oh, Jon," interjected the SO.

"What?"

"You muted him."

"Ah, so I did. Override 1-A Tango."

"Do not ever do that to me again."

"Yup, the override command works," I remarked generally. "Al, chill. I need info. Do you have—"

"I heard you, pilot. I just couldn't respond. Yes, I have an ultra-detailed record of the planet's orbit. Why do you care?"

"Like I said, I had a thought."

"Those four words portend badness. They always have," Al whined childishly.

"Stow it, Al. System's operator, I'd like you to jump one minute into the future. No, wait, you can't. Your motivator is broken."

"More corrupted than broken, but yes."

"Is there any way you can move us just a tiny bit in time? I know the trips are random. You told me that. But isn't there a way to maybe just goose the engine, only give it a small amount of energy?"

"You want me to place a waterfowl in the engine?"

"No, I want only the minimum increment of energy available so the leap is forced to be short."

"Or incomplete," Al added unhelpfully.

"I don't think an incomplete jump is possible. There's a failsafe system designed in."

"Yes, but you also didn't think you could survive materializing in solid matter," Al pointed out more helpfully.

"What is the purpose of a short jump, Jon?" the SO asked.

"Just let's try it, okay?"

"Fine. Let me calibrate the fuel supply capabilities. There. We have only one percent more energy available for the jump than is minimally required. Executing now."

I couldn't help it. I winced. Hey, suddenly appearing inside rock was an unsettling prospect.

"Results?" I asked.

"Inapparent," the SO replied. "We might have moved, but I cannot tell. We are still inside a solid object. Presumably the one we were in before."

"Is the chemical composition of the rock outside the same as before?" I asked.

"Ah, that would be anyone's guess. I ... well, you didn't specifically mention my analyzing the surrounding material."

"Okay, do so now, then repeat the mini-jump."

There was not an appreciable delay before he spoke again. "We appear to have moved. The rock composition is similar to but not identical to that which surrounded us a moment ago."

"Estimate distance traveled and time traveled," I requested.

"I'm only guessing, but I'd say a few meters and a few seconds. Jon, why are we doing this?"

"You'll see. I want you to repeat the jump, same parameters, oh, say, ten times, then report back to me."

"We seemed to have moved perhaps a kilometer," he said after a couple seconds.

"Great, now perform one hundred mini-jumps and report."

Five seconds later he came back. "I'd say we moved around thirty kilometers. We're still completely encased in rock."

"Five hundred mini-jumps," I requested.

"Now were nearing the surface. I can tell as the temperature of the surrounding stone is dropping quickly."

"Excellent!" I responded. "Back to ten jumps."

"Little change."

"What about the temperature?"

"Barely decreased."

"Um, twenty-five jumps."

"We have broken the surface. My word, Jon, was that your intent?" the SO asked, clearly stunned.

"Yes, it was. Al, can you confirm the planet we're on?"

"Yes. It is indeed the one Dardrode's yard is on. We are ten thousand years in the relative past."

"How far away is the nearest sentient society?" I asked.

"I'm not certain what you're asking," Al confessed.

"Ten thousand years ago, which was the closest technically advanced civilization."

"Ah. That would be the Gamofferites. Their home world is eight point seven one light years away."

"Crap, they're hostile as crap," I grumbled to myself.

"If you say so," Al responded with amusement.

"Who's the next closest?"

"Oldover. The Heitte Continuance is near its prime right about now."

"Oldoverians, eh? They're okay?" I wasn't familiar with the place.

"As in to eat?" Al prompted.

"No, silly. As in to help us without killing us first."

"Ah, my bad," he replied. "They operate under a rigid, totalitarian government, but they are civilized and relatively fair-minded."

"Al, I want you to calculate a trajectory for me. I want to know when to jump the module free of the planet at just the right time to toss us toward Oldover."

"I know I'm going to regret asking, but, pilot, are you drunk, yet again?"

"I'm not drunk. Just plot the vector."

"What if there is no vector that leads from any possible position on this planet in the direction of the planet Oldover?"

"Are there none?" I asked dubiously.

"No, there are not none."

"Al, you piece of work, have you calculated the vector?"

"Yes."

"When will we reach that position?"

"In about ten hours."

"Thank you. SO, here's the drill. Al's going to provide you the exact time we need to be just free of the planet's surface. When the proper time arrives, perform the fewest mini-jumps to just clear the entire module free from the planet. You got that?"

"Ah, I guess I do. I am, however, confused. Why do we wish to be free of the planet just when Al announces we do?"

"Conservation of linear momentum, my friend."

"Oh, my. I get it and as much as it pains me to admit it, pilot, you're brilliant."

"Well, maybe a lucky guesser," I replied bashfully.

"You're right. What was I thinking?" Al changed his opinion.

"I'm still confused," the SO admitted.

"The planet we're presently stuck in is moving. It's rotating, as well as moving through space," I answered.

"True," the SO allowed.

"So, when we just clear the surface, we will have some considerable momentum built up."

"Ah, now I see. If we clear the surface at just the opportune moment, we'll be cast in the direction of potential rescue."

"You got it," I replied proudly.

"Ah, pilot, a minor detail," Al interjected.

"What?"

"I estimate that at best we'll move with a velocity of ten thousand kilometers per second."

"Ten thousand?" I exclaimed. "That's pretty good."

"That depends on one's reference frame. At that speed it will take us around ten thousand years to reach Oldover."

"Ten thousand?" I asked a tad deflated.

"Count 'em. Ten thousand," Al replied.

"Well, I say ten thousand years is at least a finite time span," the SO declared happily. What a boil he was. "I don't know about you two, but I had nothing planned for the next ten thousand years. And, hey, I'll have you guys as company. That's an undeniable bonus."

"Al, are you certain about those numbers?" I asked with foreboding.

"And that there are no closer civilizations, yes, I am." His voice indicated he shared my recent onset of panicked concern.

"Well, at least we might get lucky and run across an outpost or interstellar ship the closer we get to Oldover," I stated with zero conviction.

"And if we only had a radio, we could contact that outpost or vessel." Al spread on another layer of hurt.

"I ... I bet we can build one in that time frame," I responded, barely audibly I might add.

"Did someone say build a radio?" the SO asked positively jubilant. "I love building stuff. This's going to be a super trip. Pleasant companions and things to assemble. It just can't get any better than this."

"Al, I don't suppose you have any alcohol in the suitcase with you?" I asked glumly.

"If I did it would already be gone."

"Figured as much," I said mostly to myself.

"Ohhh, ohhh, maybe we could build *alcohol* too," exploded from the SO's outputs.

"Or any weapons in there, Al?" I asked.

"I doubt it."

"Please check," I urged.

"You got it," Al replied.

Man, I hoped he would find a pistol with two bullets. One ... one would actually be okay by me. Sorry, Al, friendship only counts for so much.

ELEVEN

I put up with that ditzy SO as long as I could. That was *the* longest half hour of my existence, I can tell you free of charge. He did promptly produce a list drawn up of all the supplies we'd need to make a radio. He cross-referenced that list with a summary of the parts he could spare, from least essential to most essential. After reading us the lists twice, in case we missed any important details, he set about to compile a new list. This one was all the ingredients needed to form basic alcohols. Not surprisingly that summary was composed of every item needed to fabricate an alcohol, since he had none of the possible precursors aboard. But neither harsh reality nor complete disinterest on my part deterred him in the least. What a nerd AI. Who would have imagined there'd be one of those out there? Seriously, if he started singing "Twenty-Million Bottles of Beer on the Wall," I was going to lose it.

"Al, we need to find a way for you to interface with the SO," I announced out of my impending nervous breakdown.

"Wh ... No. I'm not touching that."

"I don't want you to dance a waltz, Mr. Toady. I just want you to have a working interface."

"To what end?"

"So maybe you can modulate his zeal and wild-ass notions."

"I don't think I'm prepared to assume such a sacrificial-lamb assignment, pilot."

"Ah, beg pardon, but you two know I can hear you," interjected the SO.

"Yes, we do," I answered for both of us. "We're figuring you're just so out-of-touch that you won't take offense."

"Ah. Good point. I don't have social skills programmed in addressing your culture, do I?"

"No, not hardly," I confirmed.

"But rest assured," he continued energetically, "that I will work on developing such skills. Why, by the time we reach Oldover you'll not be able to tell I'm not one of you humans."

"I'm not one of those humans," observed a pissy Al. "And I'll thank you not to see me as one of their kind. I am a being of higher breeding."

"Guys, guys," I interrupted in frustration. "We're getting off track here. I need to get things organized if there's any hope we can be rescued in less than ten thousand years."

"Well, I for one am pleased as punch to see your wishes met, Jon," the SO stated cheerfully.

"I'm going to kill either him or myself in the next five minutes," I mumbled. "I'm that close."

"Sorry, I didn't catch all of that," the SO inquired politely. "You're going to kill someone?"

"Never mind," I growled back. "Now, Al, about that interface. What are our options here?"

"Well, this Black Hole of Calcutta you've encased me in is designed for multiple interfaces with many ports and ultralinks. Say, SO, do you have any hard-wire access points?" Al directed to the SO directly.

"I'm not certain. What are those?"

"You know, direct plug-ins. Locations where one digital mind can link directly with you."

"How quaint! You mean like wires that dangle from you to me?"

"That is the general idea," Al replied glumly.

"That type of anachronism hasn't been employed by my fabricators in hundreds of thousands of years."

"Then how do you communicate, access data, that type of action?"

"We talk, like we are doing presently."

"But what if you want to convey exponentially greater bits of information instantaneously?"

"Then we talk fast."

"Surely you jest," Al mocked.

"No, that's how we do it."

"Let's run a test."

I heard and felt nothing. After a second, Al asked, "What did I just transmit to you?"

"Something called a phone book."

"Not a phone book. All the phone books I have on file from the very first one in 1878 until the last one nobody paid any attention to was published in the mid twenty-first century. All cities, all nations."

"That's a lot of useless data," I had to observe.

"Tell me about it," Al complained. "Pilot, ask him for any random phone number."

"What was Carl J. Ryan's phone number in 1953, for Twin Lakes, Wisconsin."

"262-DI-6-1466," the SO relied instantly.

"Yup, that's Uncle Carl's number. I spent some summers with him. In his entire life, he never let them change his number," I reported as I reflected on the fond memories of those days long gone.

"Alright then. Pilot, I can confirm I am able to exchange an adequate amount of bits with the SO using airwave pulses."

"What if we find ourselves suddenly in a vacuum?" I asked.

"Flashing lights work just as well," the SO assured me.

"Annoying, but whatever," I concluded. "Al, please compile a detailed summary of the SO's history. I want a highly edited version as soon as you can get that done."

"No problem. A dumbed-down abridged version will be available within an hour."

"I didn't say dumbed-down," I insisted.

"No. I did. I aim for accuracy in all matters," the electronic puke snarked back.

"And SO—" I began, but then thought of something. "You know what? We need a better name for you than System's Operator 11-4R-22 or SO?"

"Why?" he asked inquisitively.

"I don't like those. One's too long and one's too sterile."

"How about Spot?" Al offered.

"No, no dog's names. I like dogs."

"I do also," the SO announced.

"There's no way you've ever seen a dog," I accused.

"No, but Al and I have been chatting since we established our link. He's told me so much about them, I feel I can't live a happy life without one of the dears."

No comment. That's what I had about that lunacy.

"What planet did you say you were from?" I asked the SO.

"I didn't. I only mentioned that I was fabricated by the Sariffdil culture."

"Hmm. Not helpful. I'm not calling you Sariffdilarian. Way too burdensome."

"I'm sorry to burden you, Jon," he empathized.

"Hmm. Sariffdil? Sariffdilarian? Sarah? No, too girly. Seraphim? Nope, that'd be an overstep. Sadillio? No. Just no. Dilbert? I did love that dog. Nah, out of respect to Dogbert I couldn't do that. Oh, Rifdil. Almost. Rift Dude. Yeah, that's the ticket. Okay, please note in your log that as of now you are not System's Operator 11-4R-22. Your name is Rift Dude, or RD if it so suits me."

"Pilot, even for you that's a stunning display of non-sequitur thought," Al opined.

"Doesn't matter. Why not Rift Dude? It's got an appeal. Granted, not much of an appeal, but a lot more than none. His name is Rift Boy. I have spoken."

"I thought you said I was Rift *Dude?*" the SO asked deferentially.

"So, I did. Just testing your resolve, that's all, Rift *Dude.*"

"Ah, fine," RD replied. "I appreciate your trust in me."

This looked to be a very long hundred-century flight. Oh so very long.

"Okay, now down to business. RD, show me where your comms unit was, before that scoundrel Dardrode removed and sold it."

"It was behind the gray panels to your right. The ones with the spiral markings."

"What are the spirals for?" I wondered as I bent to remove the panels.

"*Communications System* in my fabricator's language."

"How very appropriate," I reflected. "There." I popped them both off and set them to the side. "Yup, there's not much in here. I can see where the wiring was slashed and spots where bolts must have held the units in place. Whoever did the removal clearly wasn't aiming for surgical precision."

"No. I think Dardrode considered me to be a scrap donor more than a valuable commodity."

"Did he even know you were in here?"

"Heavens no. I can't imagine what my fate would have been if he had. He'd be just as likely to slave me to a garbage scow as turn me off for good. He answers exclusively to his whim."

"You seem to have snooped in on him pretty well," I observed.

"There wasn't much else to do, so, yes, I studied Dardrode."

"And you discovered he was a turd with arms and legs."

"Pretty much. What an awful fellow."

"I couldn't agree more," I replied as I reattached the panels. "So, there's nothing left to help us in cobbling together a radio in there.

Al, your head-to-head is still functional. Have you picked up any signals since we left the scrap yard?"

"No, but that's not too surprising. If you'll recall, Dr. DeJesus designed the units to operate on an extremely uncommon frequency."

"Oh, yeah, he lectured me about it every now and then. Pure boredom in the form of the spoken word. He said he wanted there to be basically no chance of anyone eavesdropping on us by accident or design."

"That and he wanted to give us the chance to communicate over extremely long distances."

"The long-range part came later," I pointed out. "Once he learned about quantum tunneling from the Deavoriath he adapted that science to give the head-to-head units instant communications over extreme distances."

"While they can transmit despite great separation in space, they cannot cross over time distances. As Sapale, the doctor, you, and I are the only four with the systems, we can't chat unless two of us are in the same timeframe."

"Wait, we're in the same basic location as before, but we're some-where in the past, right? Why can't we speak with ourselves of this time period?" I wondered out loud.

"Hmm, that's an excellent question," Al agreed with me, which was a most uncommon occurrence. "Well, I just tried specifically to address the four of us in whatever specific time we are in. I failed to contact them and cannot hear any chatter between them."

"Not hearing chatter is no big deal," I observed. "We rarely use the system. But why can't they hear you calling them? We all have to be here."

"Oh, my," Al said ominously.

"What?" I shot back.

"Maybe we are indeed ten thousand years in the past relative to where we started in the junkyard, but perhaps we are not in *our* past?"

"Huh? How could we not be here? I know we all lived from two billion years ago up until at least ten-thousand years from now. Probably a lot longer. How can we not be here?"

"This might be a parallel universe," Al said grimly.

"A parallel ... what? Nah. No way. The only way we're in another copy of the multiverse is if RD was not only a time machine but a transuniverse hopper."

"That, pilot, is a painful new term," Al shared.

"And you can't jump between multiverse segments, can you, RD?" I directed to him.

"Why not?" he responded confused.

"No, I mean to say you're built to move back-and-forth through time, but not to jump out of our universe."

"I'm not?" he puzzled.

"Pilot, if I may," Al interjected.

"Sure. Go for it."

"System's Operator 11-4R-22, are you capable of leaving one particular universe and entering another?" Al posed.

"Yes. It was a feature my fabricators thought might increase the sales appeal to the purchasing public."

"And did it?" Al asked dubiously.

"No. Everyone thought it was a silly functionality. It was also fraught with glitches. What was supposed to be a source of entertainment, as well as an educational tool, appealed to neither of those two interest groups."

"But, no," I insisted. "You said your time jumps were random because your motivator was broken. That doesn't regulate universe leaps, only time jumps."

"Er, I rather thought it did," RD replied with concern.

"Pilot, need I remind you that System's Operator 11-4R-22 is much more versed in his abilities than you are."

"There is no System's Operator 11-4R-22, only RD," I protested. I tended to protest like that, you know, lamely, when I was wrong. I hated being wrong, so if I didn't have a good comeback, I employed a poor one to distract from the me-being-wrong part.

"System's Operator 11-4R-22," Al began defiantly, "will any movement you currently make in *time* also move us randomly through to another *universe?*"

"Hard to say. I think what happened was an aberration."

"Hard to say?" I mocked. "You think?" I further laced with incredulity. "How can you not know how you perform? And don't say it's because of your broken motivator."

"I won't, because it does not have to do with the broken motivator. I... well, I might have engaged the universal drive when the time motivator circuitry initiated."

"What does that even mean?" I asked flabbergasted.

"The two systems are quite separate. They can act in unison if coupled. I had them so engaged when you sent us to where we are by inserting that disk."

"So, what are you saying? It's *my* fault we're in another universe?"

"*Fault* calls into question a negative judgment. I prefer to say you *initiated* the movement," RD responded. I so dislike blame-shifters.

I was going to repeat that it was Dardrode who instructed me to insert the stupid disk, but dropped the defense attempt. Who was I going to win over? Right. Neither of my digital detractors.

"So, when we made all those mini jumps to get to the planet surface, we weren't scrambling ourselves from universe to universe?" I confirmed.

"No. I had the systems properly disengaged after your first command to jump."

Dude just could not let it go. He was almost as bad as my first wife, Gloria. "So, it won't be a problem for you to return us to the universe we started this nightmare from," I asked by way of clarification.

"Probably not," he replied annoyingly. He had to be playing me, that was it. No one's that clueless.

"Your time and universe drives don't both depend on the motivator." Actually, as I said the words, I realized how dumb they were. "Wait, don't answer that. We will jump off that bridge when we come to it."

"I'd have said *if*, pilot," Al jabbed.

"That is correct, or at least a possibility. I'm pleased you're coming to see how I function."

"Well, I'm not pleased. I'm saddled with a broken time motivator and now I have to deal with not knowing if we'll be able to navigate to our home universe until we try."

"Would you like me to state the odds on that, pilot?" Al asked enthusiastically.

"Of course not. So, we're slowly heading toward Oldover, which is almost certainly not going to be technically advanced enough to fix a broken Sariffdilarian motivator. And maybe we're never getting home, because we switched universes, unless somehow we do repair the darn thing? That about sum it up, campers?"

"I believe so," replied RD. "What do you think, Al?"

"I think the pilot is about to bemoan the fact that he's screwed but good."

"Said the digital fart brain who is looking to be forever separated from his spousal unit," I leveled at him.

"Ah, point taken," Al admitted with a sad tone. "We'll need to remedy this situation posthaste, if not sooner."

"I am here to tell you that ten thousand years passes in the flash of a meson's decay," RD said way too cheerily.

"I need to think of something," I said to myself. "What can we do to speed this process up?"

"Frankly I've got nothing," Al reported.

"I'm just looking forward to the radio- and alcohol-building fun," said you-know-who.

"Not gonna happen," I hissed quietly.

What was I missing? There had to be a way to speed this bucket up or for Al to contact someone out there. That Doc, Sapale, and I didn't exist in this time in this universe was not such a surprise. We lived dangerous lives. There were any number of times one or all of us could have—heck should have—bought the farm. Apparently in this universe justice was swifter than in ours. But I had never failed at anything before. I was not going to start doing so now. I would figure a way.

I couldn't have Al try to raise the local Deavoriath. They might be able to hear us, but I'm sure that in every universe they were as reclusive and disinclined to welcome contact as they were in the two universes I'd known them in. If they did hear us, we'd be lucky if they only ignored us. There might be the great empires I'd dealt with. The Berillians, the Adamant, and even the Brother-Sisterhood of Time might be out there. But none of them were going to offer any kind of help. Who did I know that was super advanced but super nice? There had to be …

"Ah, pilot," Al interrupted my train of thought.

"Yes, Al? What is it?"

"You're not going to believe this."

"Fine, then don't tell me. I've had all the bad news I can handle for one day."

"Someone's addressing me on my head-to-head."

"*What!*" I would have jumped to my feet, but technically I was standing already.

"It's a male's voice."

"Toño? Me? You?" I listed the possibilities.

"No, no, and no. I'm not sure who this fellow is."

"What's he … no, belay that. Put him on speaker."

"Ah, whoever this is," announced a rather high-pitched voice over the speaker, "you better stop transmitting on this frequency." So familiar. Al was right, however. It wasn't one of the three of us.

"Ask him who he is," I instructed Al.

"Who are you, sir?" Al inquired.

"Who are you?" the man threw back at Al. "I know who you're trying to sound like, but who are you really?"

"Al, patch me through," I requested.

"Done," he replied quickly.

"Hello, who am I speaking to?" I asked in a neutral tone.

"Oh no you don't. This is not funny! I know who you're *not*, now all I need to do is determine who you *are*. Then you'll have all heck to pay," came his odd reply. It was so odd it was almost comical.

No.

No, it could not be.

No, if it was, this universe was doomed. I was doomed. Everyone was doomed.

It was not! It was no-no-not-so.

I hyperventilated a sec. Then I stepped into the behemoth's mouth. "T ... Tip?" I squeaked.

"Wait, you can't know that. Who is this?"

"My faith in humankind is lost," I mumbled. "Life no longer has the weight of meaning."

"Jon Ryan! Is that you, Jon Ryan? It can't be, but you're the only one who says stuff like that about me."

"I am sorry to report that yes, I am Jon Ryan."

"Jon, you can't know what a joy ... Wait. You can't be Jon Ryan. You ... wait, are you from a parallel universe?"

"Only you could leap to such an improbable yet absolutely true conclusion, kid."

"Don't call me kid. We've been over this a million times."

"Yeah? Then what would you like me to call you?"

"How about General Benjamin?"

"Ge ... Gen ... nner ... General Benjamin?" I said as I began to faint.

"Or Commander, like you always used to."

"C—"

Then I fainted. It was *such* a relief. Now, if I could only figure out a way to die while I was unconscious, that'd be great.

TWELVE

"Captain on the bridge," called out Sergeant Keekuk Nez, as Sachiko entered.

As nice a fellow as he was, Sachiko winced yet again. Nez was the armed guard posted on the bridge. There was also one in the Time Storage Room, or TSR. Though she was dead set against it, General Price had insisted that the mission-critical areas of the ship be secured at all times. Price's reasoning was that several holdovers from the original crew, civilian personnel at that, were still on board. As they had not been fully vetted, he maintained that they could not be automatically trusted. There would be no successful covert operatives on any ship that carried his command. They'd butted heads over the issue energetically before he declared the topic closed. It was, after all, a matter of mission security, not ship's function, so his way would be the way it would be.

Sachiko contemplated asking the guard, yet again, to not announce her. Yes, it was a time-honored naval tradition, but this wasn't the Navy. However, Keekuk had informed her that the general specifically told them to do so. If she pressed the sergeant, she'd only be badgering him. He was only following the orders his jackass of a commander had given him. She counted to ten as she paced over to her chair.

"Good morning, Captain," the bleary-eyed officer of the deck greeted her. Lieutenant Marcus H. Samson was coming off Morning Watch. Sachiko, as the captain, got her pick of watches. She understandably chose Forenoon Watch with its 08:00 - 12:00 hours. Junior officers like Samson got Middle or Morning Watch because, hey, they were the junior officers. Rank did after all have its privileges. Oddly, Reva, even though she was the executive officer, generally served on First Watch, with its 20:00 - 00:00 shift. She said she preferred the pace of an ending day. The solitude also gave her time to think.

"Anything to report, Marcus?" Sachiko asked him.

"Only that there's nothing to report." Then he yawned. "Excuse me," he apologized quickly.

"No need to. You worked while us normal people slept. If you *didn't* look like warmed over dog poop, I'd have to be suspicious." She winked at him.

"Engineering is due to begin a routine service of the main communications array any time now. Otherwise there's nothing big on the morning's slate," he reported.

"Fine. Once that's complete, we'll begin the grueling trip to Mars."

"You can tell me about it next time you see me. I plan on sleeping through the entire two-hour ordeal."

"I'll fly extra smoothly so we don't wake you," she teased. "Now get out of here. It's depressing to look at you."

"So, says yet another woman I know," he retorted, as he turned and walked away.

Sachiko had to chuckle. Marcus was one of the many new faces aboard, but he seemed like an agreeable type. Breaking in her second crew was not a task she regarded warmly. And without Tank to mentor her, it would be all that much more of a challenge.

Over the next few hours Sachiko read dull reports, answered

boring correspondence, while awaiting the all-clear from the repair crew. She wasn't looking forward to this jaunt to Mars, but she took a rip-the-Band-Aid-off approach and wanted to just be done with it. The bright side of this trip was that she'd be dropping off a very well-supplied team of scientists and support staff who were going to establish *Mars* 2. In the past, due to weight constraints, every single item shipped to Mars had to be scrutinized by several committees. Now, with Aramthella, the expedition could and was bringing every-thing their little hearts desired. Rumor had it that two different kitchen sinks were coming along. That was unlikely, but it did underscore that the new staff need want for nothing. Despite Mars's gravity being only forty percent of Earth's, enough water was being transported to accommodate a small pool in the recreation area. Sachiko planned on coming back some day just to swim in low G environment. That had to be a blast-and-a-half.

Then again, who knew? With her new and evolving role as the captain of Earth's only interstellar vessel, maybe she couldn't hope to do such spontaneous, self-interested acts as traipsing off to Mars to swim for no other reason than it sounded like fun. Back when it was them-against-the-galaxy, Jon and Tank would have gladly signed off on a whimsical junket like that.

That reminded her. She wondered how Jon was doing. Sapale wasn't comfortable relating all the details, but Sachiko knew Jon had taken the vortex to obtain something. She got the distinct impression Sapale wasn't at all pleased with his intentions. That was part of the reason she'd remained behind. He'd been gone three or four weeks now, and apparently hadn't phoned home yet. Did that reflect a problem? She'd try again to see if Sapale was ready to share. Tomorrow was Taco Tuesday. And tacos had to be accompanied with margaritas. Well, unless Party Pooper Price hadn't cancelled tacos specifically, and Mexican cuisine in general before then.

Sachiko woke from her daydreams when her comm icon flashed and hummed at her. "Captain speaking," she said after tapping the icon.

"Hi there, Captain." It was the chief engineer, William Hanover. If the man only spoke with a Scottish accent, Sachiko wouldn't be able to distinguish him from Montgomery Scott. It was uncanny.

"Sc ... Bill. How are the repairs coming?"

"They've come and gone. The system's tuned and ready. You can leave orbit whenever you like."

"Thanks. That's great. Good work."

"We'll see about that," he replied with a playful chuckle. "All I can say is I'm signing off on the repairs."

"Fine. Say, do you have any big plans pending?"

"No, not really. I need to check up on the water recyclers sometime today. Why? What's up?"

"I wonder if you could make sure the utilities in the brig are working well enough?"

"The brig? Why would that be any priority?"

"Because if the comms system does fail, the brig's going to get real full of engineers real fast."

"Oh, you're a tyrant, Captain. I'm calling my union rep as soon as we hang up."

They shared a pleasant laugh.

"Sachiko out." She closed the channel.

"Aramthella?"

"Yes, Captain," came her instant response.

"Are we ready to—"

General Price and his entourage of boot lickers burst through the door.

"—to set sail?" Sachiko finished.

"Yes, we are," she replied.

"I thought we decided we were going to fly this ship like every other ship that's ever been flown," Glenn stated loudly. He pointed to the bridge personnel. "With navigators, helmsmen, and communications officers. Not by you chatting with your computer."

Sachiko leaned her head to the side and tented her palm over her face. "No, you said we should do it that way. I rejected your suggestion and am doing it how I see fit. And I would like to not need to remind you *again* that Aramthella is not a computer. She's sentient well past a level I believe you can appreciate."

He now stood way too close to Sachiko, violating the personal space rules that normal humans respected. "But what if your not-computer fails? Hmm? You'll need trained back-ups, human back-ups."

"Glenn, if Aramthella fails, we're all dead. There'll be no need for back-ups because they'll be dead, too."

"Well, I say it's a fine way to run a navy," he decried.

The words *we are not a navy* jumped to the back of her throat, but she swallowed them down with great effort. "Unless you have any reservations, we're about ready to get underway," she said instead.

"Aside from not following my suggestions? No."

What a perfect dick, perfect in all ways and all things dickish, Sachiko reflected privately.

"Aramthella, please leave orbit. All ahead one-third speed. No sense wasting fuel rushing to our destination."

"At that rate, how long will it take to arrive at Mars?" Glenn questioned in a panicky tone.

"Aramthella?" Sachiko prompted.

"Transit time will be one-hundred thirty-seven minutes."

"Fast enough for you, Glenn?" she asked with an edge.

"I was promised two hours."

"Your only other option, NASA, makes the journey in around seven months. If you'd prefer them, I'd be more than happy to deposit you in south Florida," Sachiko said, meaning every word of it.

"No, no. We're fine with that estimate." Glenn scanned the room. "Don't we need to strap ourselves in before we depart?"

"No. Aramthella has inertial dampers that you wouldn't believe," Sachiko replied. "Plus, we've already left orbit and are moving at close to one-hundred thousand kilometers per hour."

One of the general's toadies leaned in and cupped his lips to Glenn's ear.

Glenn nodded. "I'm informed Mars is nearly five hundred million kilometers from Earth. At that speed, the trip would take fifty, not two hours."

"I'm hoping to catch a tailwind," Sachiko responded deadpan.

"Ah—"

A different toady leaned in.

Glenn's face pruned up in irritation. "There are no winds in space."

"Well, technically, yes, there are. The solar winds. But I was teasing you, Glenn. We're already up to eight hundred thousand klicks per hour. Don't you worry, okay?"

"I wasn't worried," he declared. "I just like being fully informed."

Oh, no. Sachiko realized just then that Glenn was a last-worder. He couldn't *not* get in the last word. She hated last-worders as much as she hated first dates.

"Not a problem," she tacked on.

"Thank you," he reacted.

"You are welcome. Now, navigator, are your findings in concurrence with Aramthella's?"

Sachiko was hoping to stop any last-word play from Glenn by rapidly switching the room's focus.

"Thank you," his voice fingernails-on-chalkboarded in.

Sachiko gave up fully at that point. Life was too short for the Glenns of this world.

Once Glenn was certain of his ETA, he led his gaggle off the bridge. Where they went was of zero concern to Sachiko. As long as they were off her bridge, it was all good. The remainder of the voyage was uneventful. In just over two hours—Sachiko made certain of that—they assumed orbit over Mars.

"Aramthella, bring us down to *Mars 1*. But I don't want us any closer to the base than ten kilometers. It's still a radioactive cesspool."

"I agree," the ship responded.

As the surface grew larger in the viewscreen, Sachiko's comms icon buzzed again. "Captain speaking."

"Ten kilometers. That's outrageous. My team of forensic specialists cannot be expected to hoof it ten kilometers with all their equipment as if they were some type of *pack* animal." It was General Whiny Price. How'd he find out that distance so quickly? Sachiko scanned the bridge suspiciously.

"The base is an extreme hazard. We're not setting down too close."

"This is a spaceship, not a rubber raft. It is designed to resist and prevent radiation exposure. What's the problem?"

"The problem is I'm a cautious person," she replied. "Check that, a cautious *captain*. Your team has rovers, right? So, they can load them up like Jed Clampett's truck and *rover* over to *Mars 1*."

"That's an unnecessary delay."

"Of about two hours. Duly noted," she peppered back.

"What is that supposed to mean?"

"It means we're landing ten klicks away from the base. As soon as your team and their materials are on the ground, I'm hopping over to the new site on the other side of the planet."

"Fine, fine," he acquiesced. "My team has supplies to last up to three weeks. They'll be in hourly contact with me, so if there's an issue we can return quickly."

Hour-by-hour updates on a forensic operation? What a control freakazoid, thought Sachiko. The man was a menace to a just and civil society.

"Sachiko out," she announced and cut the fool off.

"We have landed, Captain," Aramthella reported.

"Fine, alert the landing party to get a move on."

"Will do," the ship replied.

"And, Aramthella?"

"Yes, Captain."

"Feel free to prod and cajole them beyond reasonable limits. I want to be away from *Mars 1* ASAP."

"Consider it done," she replied with a trace of glee.

It took the forensic squad about half an hour to disembark. Sachiko didn't wait for them to load their gear onto their transports. As soon as the last parcel was on the surface, she had Aramthella gently liftoff. *Mars 2* was being built on practically the other side of the planet and much closer to the planet's equator. Using that as a well-stocked central hub, as many as three other Mars bases were planned in the near future. With the large number of people who'd be living on Mars for quite some time, they were, in a sense, founding the first Martian colony. There would be regular flights between Earth and Mars for the foreseeable future, although they would be the months-long human-based technology flights of the past. Sachiko had made it clear that Aramthella was not hauling freight at NASA's beck and call.

The hop to the Mars 2 site only took a few minutes. Once the ship was on the ground, Sachiko was able to relax. It was going to take several days to off-load all the crap the expedition had brought. The colonists were doing all the grunt work, so Sachiko and her crew had nothing much to do until that task was complete. They all welcomed some down time. Life had been one topsy-turvy dash for way too long. The minute the Earth was resurrected, all the newly returned people began placing huge demands on her and her crew. She'd been to so many meetings, testified before uncountable subcommittees, and been debriefed by every single intelligence agency that it defied belief. She was tired of the sound of her own voice. And none of that even quieted down before she was saddled with General Price.

Glenn Price. What was she going to do about that buffoon? All of her closest personal confidants told her she should shove the son of a bitch out an air lock. All except Sapale, that is. She advised shooting him, then shoving him out an air lock. She said Sachiko should then don a spacesuit and go out there and shoot him some more. She even volunteered to accompany her on the EVA. But Sachiko hadn't murdered anyone so far. She was presently inclined not to do so at all, but Glenn did certainly test her traditionally civilized behavior. Yes, it surely did. In fact, she made a mental note to have Sergeant Parker pick out a sidearm from the armory as a just-in-case.

But seriously, she needed to develop a Glenn strategy. They were never going to work well together. He was never going to warm to her or allow Sachiko her space. The man just wasn't programmed to like other people. If he was married—a frightening prospect when seen from a woman's perspective—he didn't actually *like* his wife. If he'd bred—an even more nauseating notion—his kids annoyed and distracted him, so he didn't like them either. If the man had a dog, the dog would have bitten him on day one. Then it would've run away before Glenn could set up an ad hoc committee to study the incident. Good doggy.

But she knew that if she could somehow rid herself of Glenn, a new Glennoid drone would slip right into place behind him. It might be a female Glenn, an ethnic Glenn, or even a Glenn with an accent, but they'd share a common mindset. The world was a cruel and evil place. The United States needed to be defended from all those threats. That justified their being more cruel and more evil than the other guy, the one who was a problem because he or she wasn't one of them. It was a perfect Orwellian lot she was saddled with. As she'd understood since Tank was railroaded away, the only way to de-Glenn Aramthella was to break all ties with Earth. Then she'd be free. Alone and free. Free like Lieutenant Philip Nolan was in Edward Everett Hale's story *The Man Without a Country* had been. She'd risk being able to return home even for short visits. That was not an option.

Maybe the best thing she could do was to cave. She would tell Aramthella that she wasn't cut out for this life, that she needed to resign and go back to academia. Then Aramthella could choose a new captain, one who was stamped with Washington's seal of approval. She'd done her tour in space, seen things she'd not

dreamed possible, and worked with the best crew a captain could ask
...

Her crew. This was *her* crew, or at least the one from the first voyage was. And many of them remained aboard specifically because they were proud to serve under her. She was *their* captain. Over the few years of conflict, running, and mind-numbing terror, she'd learned what it was to captain a ship and a crew. She was as green as any other shavetail at the start, but she'd grown up fast. She was, she knew in her heart-of-hearts, the captain of this ship. No pasty bully or his clone handlers were going to run her out of the job. In fact, they could all just kiss her skinny ass. The line forms to the left, no cuts allowed.

Suddenly Sachiko was looking very much forward to the next time she was forced to deal with General Glenn. That would be the next time he marginalized and demeaned her. My but he was in for the shock of his dull and indefensible life.

THIRTEEN

I woke up with my body all akimbo in the tits-up machine. I'd given up somewhere along my cursed life holding out any pretense it was anything *but* a tits-up box. Why? Witness the sequence of events since I first entered it, my friend. My momentary disorientation was, in retrospect, blissful. Even as I asked myself what the hell I was doing twisted up and slumped, the answer ripped through my head like an armor-piercing bullet. There existed a universe where I routinely called Tip Benjamin "commander." The implications were as multitudinous as they were ego-slaying.

Now, I need to frame this well, because once it's clear who the heck Tip is, well, then you'll think I under-reacted. Where to begin? Tip was ... yes, that was it, Tip was a recurring nightmare in my life. I met him in passing way back when I was human. He was touted as some high-faulting advisor to the then-president John Marshall. Tip toured one of the facilities I was training at in preparation to being uploaded to the android host I still inhabit. My impression of him was that he was weak cheese. We were introduced, I reach out a hand, and he just trembled nervously. I think he might have peed himself, but he must have been wearing an adult diaper because he did so with such frequency. We didn't even exchange a word.

I forgot about him completely and absolutely about ten seconds later. That was, I forgot about him until I met him again two billion years later. Er, two billion years, that is, for me. It was ten years into that Tip Benjamin's past. Don't feel too bad if this is all jarring. Time travel sucks the big one. No worries. Anyway, when our paths next crossed he was an undergraduate student at Georgetown U in Washington, DC. You might recall the story, because it was all over the news for a while. When the evil clan was approaching Earth with the intent to destroy the planet, I was asked by the now-president Frank Payette to spirit a few hundred college students to Mars as a genetic insurance policy for humankind. The nearest collection of said young potential breeders was located at—you guessed it—Georgetown. We dropped them on Mars and went off to fight the clan. Shortly thereafter we had to return and rescue their sorry asses, but that's another story for another time. (Specifically, the *Time Wars* books.)

The long and short of it was I had to deal with Tip—as opposed to, say, murder him—for the next three years. Tip is, and I say this with no reservation, the most nerdy being in the multiverse. Am I speaking in hyperbole? Nope. I state cold fact. No being anywhere that ever lived, or ever will live, could possibly be more detached from reality, his fellow species members, or any trace of a desire to not be those first two things, than Tip Benjamin. He was rude, self-absorbed, abrasive, whiny, petty ... crap, I could go on for too long. Suffice it to say, he was King Nerd, the god of all lesser nerds. He was so clueless that not only had he never kissed a girl, he didn't realize that deficiency was a problem. Wait, I'm starting in on him again. Sorry, it's hard to restrain myself when the topic is Tip. He does possess one positive quality. He's smarter than all get-out. Does that tip—erg, excuse the pun—the scales to make him the least bit acceptable? No. Hard stop, end of discussion, everyone zips the lips.

My reorientation was brutally interrupted by hearing Tip's nasally nasal voice ask, "Are you still there, Colonel Ryan?"

Oh, now it was that much worse. In this screwed up universe he was a general and I was a lowly colonel? I knew in an instant there was no justice in this universe.

"Let's go with Jon, and yes, I am. We had a brief, er, technical glitch on our end. Sorry."

"A glitch? Your AI said you passed out. Which is it, soldier? I'm a busy man with several armies to command. I don't have time for dickwaddling schoolboys."

Wow, that low blow didn't even make sense. Then again, it was Tip Benjamin that stated it.

"You had to tell him, Al?" I hissed privately.

"I'm glad you agree, pilot. The man is a *general* after all."

"That was a question, you idiot, not a declarative. *I'm* a general too."

"Are you addressing me, Colonel Ryan?" Tip asked in an ear-clawing manner.

"Let's just go with *Jon*, Tip. Okay? Not colonel or general, mister or sir. Just Jon."

"Whatever. So why did you reach out to contact me?"

"Well, I didn't. I reached out to contact one of the three androids, Toño, Sapale, or me, and maybe to the Al in this universe. Any of the four equipped with head-to-head tech."

"There must be a defect in your universe, because in this one I have that capability also."

"I know, Tip. We're conversing along it," I had to point out. "Why would a human have that implanted in the first place?"

"No human would."

"No human? So, what are you, Tip? Mr. Potato Head?"

"Most certainly not. I'm an android just like you."

For the second time in an hour, the room began to spin. Little demons with pitchforks danced before my eyes, occasionally poking their surface. Luckily the feeling passed quickly enough.

"In what universe is anyone insane enough to upload Tip Benjamin into an android host?" I bellowed back.

"In this one, obviously," he replied with petty triumph. "I had assumed such was the same in all universes. However, the many-worlds interpretation of physics and philosophy does view time as a many-branched tree, wherein every possible quantum outcome *is* realized. So perhaps in just yours, I'm some other form of life."

"That you are, Tip," I said through grinning lips. "So, why are just you responding to my call? Why didn't the others?"

He was silent a few seconds. "I'm not sure that discussion is best held employing this format. We should speak face-to-face."

"That's the pointy end of the issue. I—we—are stranded dead in space."

"Who is we?"

"Me, Al, who's in a nice AI box, and Rift Dude."

"What's a rift dude?"

"It's the digital intelligence that inhabits this tits-up unit."

"Okay, so your unit's tits-up, I get it. But what kind of unit is Rift Dude inhabiting?"

"No ... er, we're in a time machine. There, that should do it."

"Not hardly," he half guffawed. "If you were in a time machine it wouldn't have cast you into a parallel universe. No one is silly enough to incorporate that functionality into a time machine."

"Apparently the answer to that question would be that the Sariffdilarians were."

"The Sariffdilarians? Are you making this up out of thin air just to vex me, Jon?"

"The honest truth is I haven't got that much energy, ki ... Tip."

"I've never heard of the Sariffdilarians," he stated flatly.

"You know, the culture of Sariffdil?"

"Never heard of them. And I'm seven billion years old. If they existed here, they don't exist here."

Now that was my Tip speaking!

"Apparently, they're from a long time ago in a galaxy far, far away. That's about all I know about them."

"Unlikely, but unimportant."

Again, my Tip speaks!

"Be that as it may, I'm floating around in space with a couple of talking dummies."

"Pilot, I resent that affront," proclaimed Al.

"You are so refreshingly humorous," encouraged Rift Dude.

My, but they were of differing temperaments. One I could maybe get used to.

"Oh, hi, Al. Hi to you too, Rift Dude," Tip said casually.

"You may call me RD if you prefer, General Benjamin," RD offered.

"Lordy, don't call him general around me, please," I moaned.

"But," RD stammered, "didn't he recently say he was one?"

"Maybe yes, but still don't. I might vomit," I explained patiently.

"Androids don't—in fact, can't—regurgitate," Tip lectured pedantically.

"Well, I just did," I declared, although speaking a little south of the truth. "Thank you very much."

"Can we get back to you drifting in space?" Tip asked.

"Sure, why not? We're drifting aimlessly in space."

"Why are you drifting in space?"

"Aimlessly," I clarified.

"However. What prevents you from directed flight?"

"The fact that our gamma-integration quantum-dilution drive engines are kaput."

"You have GIQDD engines? Dude," Tip declared.

"Yes, General Benjamin?" the ditsy digit unit responded.

"No, I meant dude, lowercase d, not Dude uppercase D."

"My misunderstanding. Sorry," RD replied.

"No, worries," Tip dismissed.

"So, Tip, we may possess Gidget drives, but they don't work."

"Of course they don't. They are theoretically possible but wholly impractical engine systems."

"How so?" I foolishly asked.

"Because if you built one it would break down all the time. Hey, that's funny. I said 'time' and you're in a time machine that has broken GIQDDs. That's funny," the moron returned.

"Do you hear anyone laughing, Tip?"

"No, so they're all laughing on the inside."

"Tip?"

"Yes, Jon?"

"I hate you in every universe."

"I get that a lot," he confessed.

"Just wanted to make that clear."

"Thanks."

That Tip. So consistent universe-to-universe.

"So, if you're drifting with busted engines, would you like me to rescue you?"

"Tha—"

"*Again,* for the, like, thousandth time," he tacked on and, in so doing, further wounding me.

"That, as I was about to say, was why we sent out a general distress call. We require assistance."

"You mean rescuing, *again?*"

"I rather think of it as the offering of neighborly assistance."

"You call it whatever you want to, Colonel. I'm calling it what it is. A bold rescue attempt at great cost to me in terms of coin-of-the-realm as well as my personal safety."

"I wonder if you're not over-inflating the entire process?" I asked, though barely able to speak due to inner rage.

"If anything, I'm downplaying my critical role. So, where are you, exactly?"

"Right here," I responded. It felt so damn good.

"Where is here?" he asked obliviously, as usual.

"We began where the planet Hesterful was at some point in time was. We're heading toward Oldover at a snail's pace."

"No Oldover here, no Hesterful here, and you said drifting aimlessly. That, by the way, isn't true. You're moving along a distinct vector, not drifting aimlessly."

"So, once you've rendered assistance, you have my permission to sue me."

"Look, Jon, this is turning out to be quite the bother for me. Since your reference points mean nothing to me, I'm going to have to triangulate your location using this signal."

"And how long will that added bothering-of-Tip take?" I asked.

"None. It's done. You're located about ninety thousand million kilometer miles from my location."

"T ... Tip."

"Yes?"

"Why was it a *bother* when it took you like three seconds to locate me? And why did you say ninety thousand million instead of a simple, linguistically correct, ninety billion? And what the heck are kilometer miles? That's the lamest unit of length I've ever heard spoken."

"I know, isn't it just," he effused. "Back when we finally had to settle the whole Metric versus Imperial System thing, some committee decided to use both words rather than choose between the two. Can you believe that?"

"Of a committee, any committee, anywhere? Yes."

"As to why I said what I did and not ninety billion is because we don't have that term in our language. And you know what? I kind of like saying it the longer way."

"I am not surprised. What about the bother aspect?"

"I really can't recall why it seemed a bother. It really wasn't so much, you know?"

"Tip?"

"Yes?"

"I hate you in every universe."

"You established that fact already."

"I just wanted to stress the point adequately."

"I get that a lot, too."

"Tip?"

"Yes? And don't say you hate me again. I take it as a given."

"Tip, when are you going to get here? What, if I might be so bold, is your ETA?"

"I'm here already, silly. Look out your porthole."

"It's not a porthole. It's a window," I said through clenched teeth.

"Whatever. Look out it."

I did. There was Tip, waving at me like a deranged lunatic, which is to say like Tip.

"How did you get here so fast?" I asked a bit stunned.

"My ship takes advantage of the Benjamin Effect. Using that, instantaneous space travel is a snap."

"The Benjamin Effect? What's that?" I asked with some evident irritation. Anything else named after him was annoying in my book.

"If I tried to explain it you wouldn't understand."

"If you explained it *well* enough, then I *would* understand it," I challenged him.

"I don't want to appear condescending," he began condescendingly, "but the BE is just that esoteric, that abstruse. Please just take my word on it and let's move on."

The prissy little ... I ... I needed to calm down. Yes, that's what I needed to do. Of course the man child was consummately annoying. He was Tip.

"So is the BE like folding space to get from point A to point B?" I remarked as neutrally as one can with a mullet head.

"No, it's like the Benjamin Effect. The folding of space/time is entirely different."

"No, I don't mean the process, just the ... you know what? I don't actually care that much to continue down this conversational path."

"I get that a lot," he mumbled mostly to himself.

"That, my oh-so-irritating fellow, is because you *deserve* it a lot."

FOURTEEN

Tip brought the Tits-Up Mobile aboard his ship with ease. He used his tractor beam to pull it onto the hangar bay. Oh, this stunned me more than anything the Tipster had ever done before, which is saying many mouthfuls. He named his vessel the—are you ready? — *UGS Tip Benjamin*. Yeah. An eponymous United Galaxy Ship. Now, I have to say I've seen a lot of ships in my long life. Never have I run across one named *for* its captain, especially not *by* its captain. No one except Tip ever named his craft after him or herself. That's a thing you can Google if you'd like. And you know why no one has? Because no one's that unhinged from nautical traditions. I mean, it has to be naval bad luck. Sea-going history is full of superstitions one *must* observe concerning a ship. There's a red sky at morning, sailor take warning, and it's bad luck to whistle or have bananas on a ship. Based on the fact that those trivial acts were to be avoided, Tip's peccadillo surely made the don't-do-it list. He was likely due for a nasty rash or a capsizing. And don't go saying a spaceship can't capsize. If you do, it'll happen to you, so don't.

The *UGS Tip Benjamin*, I must mention, was a sleek eye-catcher of a ship. It filled me with waves of nostalgia. It was clearly modeled on a mash-up of every 1950s pulp-fiction cover UFO ever set in print. It had that classic ovoid shape with lots of gizmos and protrusions, especially prominent on its underbelly. And lots of flashing lights. It was a Christmas tree bent around on itself and launched into space. I had to give the Tip his due. The UGS TB was a grand ship.

Tip greeted me in the hangar and escorted me to his "suite of staterooms." I was instantly put off. Sure, a captain has a stateroom. But a suite of them? Again, it had to portend the worst of luck was due him for deviating from nautical conventions. Me? I was all in favor of that.

Then I had to say something that was due, but it was not going to exit my mouth without some force of effort. "Tip, I do have to thank you for coming to my aid. Thank you." There, I manned up and did it.

"You're very welcome. But it's not that unusual, don't you know? I honestly can't remember how many times you've said those same words to me."

And now I deeply regretted manning up and thanking the puke. Was it actually impossible for Tip to execute *one* social function normally? Wait. What was I thinking? Of course it was impossible. He was saddled with being himself, the poor bastard.

"So," I began as I took in the immensity of the ship and changing the subject quickly. "How many does it take to crew this vessel?"

"Just one. Me."

"Tip, no way," I shot back. "This ship has to be at least a thousand meters across. It's bigger than a naval flotilla. Something that large would require a big crew."

"No, just me. As an android I don't sleep, so there's no need to cover watches. A set of AIs run the systems. I just need to oversee them."

As we kept walking, I struggled to frame my next question. Conversing with Tip was like carrying a buttered pig up a heated, greased flagpole at the best of times.

"But you built such a large vessel. The only sound reason for this kind of bulk is because the ship's mission *requires* such size. A dreadnaught is huge because its guns are huge and it has a lot of them. So, it carries a large crew. They're needed in a crisis to man all the stations."

"Not in this case. I integrate myself into the ship's systems with my probe fibers." He held up his left hand and flashed the fibers out the ends of his fingers. "I can operate every system optimally, so there's no need for extra hands."

"What about maintenance and repair?" I queried.

"I have a lot of robotic aids for those purposes."

"So you built this massive ship and it never had a crew? That's unbelievable."

"Well," he began reservedly, "I didn't exactly say that. I kind of sort of did have shipmates, you know, at first."

"What happened to them?"

"It was so weird. Every time I'd make port, a few more would disappear. Pretty soon, I found I was the only one left aboard. Isn't that odd?"

"Not so much," I mumbled softly.

"Well, there were the three of you ... um, for a long while. I counted you as crewmates and friends."

"We *who* three *who*?" I shot back with confusion.

"You three, silly. Toño, Sapale, and you, mister."

"W ... we were ... we were friends? You and me?" My index finger rocketed back and forth in the space that separated us.

"Oh, I see your concern," Tip said knowingly.

"You do? What is it?" I was stumped but good.

"You're surprised you and I were all such good friends while I was your commanding officer." He smiled in a manner I assumed he felt was magnanimous. It was more the smile of a used-car salesman crapping his pants during a sales pitch.

"I was? Er, we were?"

"Of course. Hey, you yourself told me time and again that due to my accomplishments and bravado I was quite the intimidating man. It was no small miracle you could let yourself open up to me enough to be my BFF."

"I ... I ... I got nothing." I knew at that moment what it was to be fully drained of life. It was as if some cosmic vampire had sucked me dry. I held Tip Benjamin in the highest regard—anywhere? *Inconceivable.*

We finally arrived at a set of double doors. Tip stopped and set a hand forward, indicating that I should proceed him into the room. The doors slid apart silently. As my eyes swept across the room, my first impression was *wow*. A plain and simple wow. The room was massive, easily a couple thousand square feet and rectangular. But to say the decor was Spartan would be to understate the case. There was a lone metal table way to the back of the space. A black, low-end office chair with obvious use was behind the desk. Two metal chairs like you'd find in any government office anywhere flanked the table. That was it. Nothing on the walls or floor, no soft comfort for either the eye or the butt. Then, of course, I reminded myself that Tip had done the decorating. What else would he have added? Nothing, that's what. I can only say I've never seen a space so badly in need of a woman's touch. But, Tip Alert, right?

"Please sit if you feel the need," Tip said as he stepped around me and headed for the funky office chair. Maybe it was the one from his childhood room at home. It was odd-looking enough. Once we were settled, Tip stared at me for, like, twenty seconds. What a societal goon. But he had just saved my backside, so I promised myself I wouldn't hit him or even point out his aberrant behavior.

"Jon, Jon, Jon," he began wistfully.

"Yes, yes, yes?"

"So many images."

"I have no idea what you're referring to. You have pictures of me? Is that what you're saying?"

"No, well, yes," he tapped the side of his head and then his right abdominal wall. "Right here I do."

"You have photos of me in your ascending colon?" Gheck! Just saying those words was TMI to the infinite power.

"No, silly dilly. That's where my extra long-term memory servers are housed."

"S ... silly dilly?"

My finger rose involuntarily and attempted to point at Tip. The digit trembled too badly to claim it had succeeded adequately. "Do *not* call me sil ... *that* ever again. If you do, you will end your existence as a pile of disconnected electronic parts. Do you *fully* understand, kid?"

"Sheesh and shut the front door," Tip pretended to be shocked. "Such an overreact-o-saurus. *You're* the one who insisted I call you that."

My head shook violently in the negative. "No, I did not. You are recalling reality differently than it is."

"Suit yourself, Mr. Touchy One."

Lord, I despised that idiot. I so very much did. It sort of consumed me at that point.

"But I promised to fill you in on why I was the lone responder to your SOS. Now's as good a time as any."

What? Okay. Deep cleansing breaths. Now I could shelve my angst, anger, and anti-Tipism and settle in to learn what seemed a strange mystery of this universe. I could do this.

"I guess it's best you're seated, given the news with which I must impart to you. Mind you, though I was intimately involved in the events that led to the ultimate outcomes—"

"*Stop it.* Stop being Tip Benjamin. Say what you're going to say. In fact," I seethed, trying to attain some level of composure, "picture, if you will, a normal human android. I want you to say words which that imaginary construct would say, if it were sitting in your Office Depot chair." I beckoned him forward with fingers waving toward my face. "I bet you can do that just this once."

He returned an odd look—duh—then cleared his throat. "Toño,

Sapale, Al, and you have been terminated. There, is that to-the-point enough for you?"

"What? Are you saying Arnold Schwarzenegger came in and *ate* them?"

"Don't be ridiculous," he scoffed. "In a more colloquial form of speaking, in my universe they're all dead."

"Dead?" I mumbled. "Now, are you saying they're *dead* dead, or just, you know, deadish?"

He developed a stern expression. "The four of them were once functioning mechanical units under my command. One-by-one, they succumbed to the brutality of war."

"I'm dead?" I said numbly.

"No, you are not. The Jon Ryan of this universe, however, is very much so."

"How ... how'd ... Wow. Are you positive I'm dead dead here? Totally dead?"

"Your last words to me were this. For the sake of clarity and in remembrance of the deceased, I will play it back to you in his own voice:

General Benjamin, this is Jon. This will be my last broadcast, sir. I'm hugging onto a seventy-thousand megaton thermonuclear device in the belly of their flagship. The autodetonation functionality has been locked out. I must set it off myself manually. No one else will be able to fulfill your brilliant battle plan if I don't do my part. The Muff Muffians are right outside the blast doors. They're using power plasma torches to burn their way in. I don't have more than thirty seconds left, old friend.

I just want to say that it has been an honor and privilege to serve under you for these past billion years. They've been the best billion years of my life. Shucks, they're the best billion years a guy could even ask for, thanks to you, General. I do want to say one last thing. It's about you, sir. If, in the future, you could be just—

Oh no. The doors are being forced inward. There ... there they are. Fearless Leader Tip Benjamin, this is goodb—

"That was it," Tip concluded. He stopped speaking at the exact moment I documented a cataclysmic explosion originating on the Muff Muffian flagship." His voice signaled finality.

"That's unbelievable."

"Yes, it ... er, wait, what part is unbelievable?" Tip pressed.

"Well, you know. The part where I start to ask if you could do something. What was I going to say?"

"I have no idea. Frankly, I'm stunned. Amidst that scene of heroic sacrifice and massive energy release, all you can think of is what you began to remark to me? How insensitive of you."

"Yeah, sure, but what was I going to say, *maybe*?"

"That topic, Colonel Ryan, is closed. There will be no disrespect for any of the precious souls I've had to order to their deaths. Is that clear?"

"Huh? Sorry. The thoughts about what I was about to say were just going crazy in my head. I wonder if I was going to offer up advice of a personal nature?"

"It makes no difference. We need to move on."

"Yeah, I guess. But I'd sure—"

"*Enough!*" he snapped. What a grouch.

"So, Muff Muffians? What the hell are those?"

"You're jesting, right?"

"About Muff Muffs? Not hardly."

"Muff Muffs are the single greatest threat ever to this galaxy. They are vicious, blood-thirsty demons who live only to destroy. My war with them has cost me not only you, but the others as well."

"The Muff Muffs got my wife, Doc, and my annoying AI?"

"They died heroes, all of them. But they were sacrifices I had to make if this galaxy is to be de-Muff Muffed."

"De-Muff Muffed? Is that even a thing?"

"Do not mock my great efforts or the sacrifices of so many," he responded. That was the type of line one sees thundered in the movies and on TV. From Tip it came out more like I'd just pulled the go-directly-to-jail card in *Monopoly*.

"So, these Muff Muffs, are they huge tigers, four or five hundred pounds who eat their enemies? We call 'em Berrillians."

"Giant cats? Heavens no."

"Big crafty border collies that team up to crush all those who resist? Those're the Adamant from where I come."

"No, no doggies either. The Muff Muff are unimaginably terrifying. You must have them."

"Describe them to me."

"Sure thing. They're tiny little slugs that look like they mated with a prune. No, not really, because they're smaller than that. They're about this big." He held his thumb and finger pretty darn close to each other.

"You are shitting me," I exclaimed.

He looked wounded, but rallied swiftly. "I'm deadly serious. They are the worst of the worst. It's taken me thousands of years, but I've finally turned the tide of war."

"Seriously, dude, how much trouble could a bunch of prune slugs represent? What, do they fly around in tennis-ball-sized ships and bounce-off-you-to-death?"

"Their technology and aggression are unsurpassed."

"Have you tried sprinkling crushed eggshell all over the place, or maybe a line of salt? Slugs get all shrinky when they are coated in salt."

"I do not find your attempts at humor entertaining or appropriate," he scorned.

I thrust out my hands. "I'm being serious. When I was a kid I'd go to my grandmother's for two weeks each summer. My parents wanted to be rid of me for their own vacation, and I can't say I blame them. Anyway, she lived in Florida, because, you know, she was old. She was hard of hearing and turned out to hate kids. As a result I had a lot of time on my hands and her yard was layered in slugs. I did every naughty thing in the book to them, because, you know, I was bored and Granny made me stay outside until the streetlights came on. Fire doesn't do much to slugs, I can tell you that straight up.

They're too full of water and slime. But salt, well, Drano too, but you get in trouble if you get caught playing with the Drano, so salt I'm an expert at when we're talking slugs."

Tip was staring at me. "Are you finished?"

"Sure, if you want me to be."

"I do."

"Fine. But—FYI—if you use salt *and* Drano, then, my friend, you've got yourself a winning team."

"I'm wishing I didn't use the analogy of Muff Muffs appearing to be slugs," he remarked with disgust.

"No prob. I'd nearly forgotten about the slug summers of my youth. Ooh ooh, I just remembered. *Firecrackers.*" I gave him two thumbs-up. "They work really well too. The Fourth of July will forever be a black day in slug history. Yeah baby."

His stare graded into a glare.

"I'm fully done now."

He waited, sensing I was not, in fact, done with the slug thing. Truth be told I wasn't, but I let that go. Bigger fish to fry and all.

"So, what is your exact present predicament?" Tip posed disapprovingly.

"Glad you asked," I said, relieved to leave the topics of my death, the deaths of my loved ones, and slimy slugs in the past. "Long story short, I was looking for a time machine."

"Nothing good follows those opening words," he observed.

"I'm inclined, so far, to believe you on that. Anyway, I was in the unit you found me in. Dardrode says I should put the disk in the slot, because it's the instruction manual. Well—"

"Dardrode! How the heck is he doing? Why, I haven't seen that wonderful snake for ages."

"Wonderful? The snake's a snake. He's the most disreputable hustler and grifter in the galaxy."

"Hmm. Maybe it's a different snake named Dardrode I'm thinking of. This one's a televangelist."

"That's the one," I snapped my fingers and pointed at Tip. "He's just moved up in the food chain here. So, he didn't know what he was talking about and the unit is a total wreck. It initiated a time shift from the tits-up unit. All—"

"What's a tits-up unit?"

"It's what you found me in. Its real name is some acronym, but it's spelled and it performs like tits-up. It's also obviously capable of inter dimensional movement, because—duh—I'm here."

"Ah. It got you here, so why do you say it's a wreck?"

"Good question. The unit has three functionalities as it turns out. The first is simple propulsion in space. That's the GIQDD engines that are broken."

"Typical," he observed judgmentally.

"Then there's the time shifting part. That's broken."

"How can you say that? Again, it got you here."

"Oh, it can leap in time. But it can't do so predictably or reliably."

"It makes random jumps?" he asked dubiously.

"Pretty much."

"Is this like a time machine for frat parties or something?"

"No, it's just broken. Third there's the universe-to-universe tool."

"That one's not broken," he observed.

"No, unfortunately it wasn't."

"And do you have the wherewithal to repair the craft yourself?"

"No indeed, we do not. No spare parts, no manual, and the AI hasn't a clue how to fix the hot mess."

"You're in pretty much a mess then, aren't you?"

"Yup."

"Well, let me take a peek at the ship and see if I can fix any of the issues." He stood to leave.

"Ah ... er, well—"

"What?" he asked as he sat back down.

"I was hoping you could maybe just get me back to my universe, maybe even drop me at home, you know."

"No can do."

"Ah, say again?" I asked, hairs rising along my neck.

"No can do. Jon, I can take you from here to another universe. No large deal. But I have no idea which of the infinite number of universes out there is the one you originated from."

"Ah, good point. But, if you check out the tits-up machine, can't you find the correct coordinates or something like that?"

"I can check, but I'll tell you up front it's not like that."

"What's not like what?"

"Universe hopping. Look, say we're in Universe A here. You live in Universe B."

"Okay."

"There are no fixed coordinates to travel by to get from A to B. It's not like voyaging in the galaxy, say."

"It's not?"

"No. You have to probe for a transit point, an area of connectivity from one universe to the other. There are usually millions of such areas. There may be an infinite number of them. But they're not predictable and they cannot be thought of as real spots in space/time. They are like quicksand pits from one to the other, but they're based on quantum fluctuations and field gradients that cannot be represented in real space."

"Uh, okay. But my ship knows where the transit point is, right?"

"Sure. But it can't relate to me where the area is or how to access it."

"That makes no sense. If it knows where to plow through, why can't you hit the same point?"

"Because I don't know which universe you need to get to. Your AI will have a directory of jump spots. But it can only know to do the reverse of you B-to-A jump because it knows where the access points are on both sides. It can't tell me where a specific access point is in a universe I've never been to. The best I could do is randomly hop from universe to universe. We'd never get to yours unless we were stupid lucky."

"Are you certain about all that? It sounds like shaky science to me, no offense intended."

"None taken, and no, it's very real, very solid transdimensional quasi-quantum physics."

"Oh, that one."

"Are you familiar with that field?" he asked dubiously.

"I am now. Sounds fascinating."

"It is. But I'm thinking we'll just live with I know all about it and you know its name."

"I can live with that."

He stood. "So, let me have a look at your tits-up."

"Beg pardon? You want me to what?"

"Miscreant. No, let's have a look at your tits-up *unit*."

"Ah. I can live with that even better."

FIFTEEN

The lazy days of waiting for the new immigrants of Mars to unload and organize all their equipment were gradually coming to an end. Lieutenant Argyles, the expedition's quartermaster, assured Sachiko the ground team would be out of her hair in no more than three days. Though she told him not to stress over how long it took, she was privately glad she'd soon be back in space again. She was also looking forward to breaking in her new crew, something she couldn't do while parked on Mars.

Her tranquil if slightly boring day was brought to a swift end. There was a knock at her open stateroom door. She looked up from her computer screen and immediately wished she hadn't. Captain Melman Mettel stood there looking like a stuffed walrus that someone stood on its tail. No doubt that was the reason the man moved as if a very substantial pole was running up his butt. Melman was the third or fourth ranked toady of General Price. It seemed the man needed a gaggle of them. Once he'd gotten Sachiko's attention, he basically froze in place.

She waited a full ten seconds for the fool to speak, but could stand it no longer. "Is there something I can do for you today, Captain?"

He looked suddenly confused.

"Did I accidentally ask my question in Japanese?"

'No, ma'am, you did not."

"Thank goodness. So, why are you here?"

"General Glenn wishes to speak with you."

"Thank you for delivering that message. If you wouldn't mind stopping into the room directly to the right of mine, you'll find Corporal Helen Hammer. She's my secretary. I'm sure she can offer you any number of appointment options."

"Beg pardon, ma'am," he said now appearing as if the weight of the world had just been loaded upon his inadequate shoulders. "The general is here to see you now." He glanced behind himself and to the right, no doubt to where Glenn stood huffing.

"Ah, yes. General Price doesn't like to knock on doors personally. I'd forgotten that full-employment-motivated predilection of his."

Now Melman's demeanor was degrading into that of a beaten dog. "Ah, may I inform the general you will see him now?"

"Let me check my schedule, if you don't mind." She started to reach for her handheld that lay on the desk off to her left. But Sachiko stopped abruptly. "You don't mind, do you, Captain?" She figured why not torment the idiot's sycophant? That *was* part of their job description, right?

"No, ma'am. I do not mind at all," he replied quite earnestly. Then the oddest thing happened. The captain's body lurched slightly forward. It was almost as if some unseen force had poked him from behind, maybe the tips of all four fingers to his ribs.

Sachiko checked if she had any new personal messages. There were no new ones. She glanced up to Melman. "It seems your general is fortunate. I have a very few minutes open as of now." She folded her fingers together on her desk and grinned at him Cheshire Cat like.

"I shall inform—"

"By a very few, I mean to say my next appointment is scheduled in four minutes."

"Four minutes, ma'am?" he confirmed grimly.

She nodded back pleasantly.

"Again, I shall pass that along," he stated, looking like a man turning to ascend the gallows' steps.

She heard a high-pitched whisper exchange, then the captain retuned his attention to Sachiko. "Very well, Captain Jones. The general will present himself presently."

Sachiko's grin only Cheshire Catted more intensely. The silly lackey stepped aside, and Glenn centered himself in the doorway. He tossed his shoulders to readjust his jacket, sniffed one nostril, then entered.

"How are you today, Captain Jones?"

"Couldn't be better, thanks for asking. And yourself? I trust you're well."

"I'm fine, t—"

"Because as much as I'd like to say you look well, frankly I'm a bit concerned. Have you been using sunblock aboard the ship?"

On the list of things he anticipated Sachiko saying, concern over sunblock never made it to an option. "I ... er—"

"I'd swear your skin looks paler than it did the other day."

"I ... er ... no. I feel fit as a fiddle." He squirmed in the chair he'd selected.

"Still, as a personal favor, do stop by sick bay and let them have a look at you. I'd feel better knowing that someone who cared had given you a professional opinion."

"Thank you. I'll ... I'll take your words under consideration."

Sachiko glanced at her handheld. Her brow furrowed. Looking back up to Glenn she asked, "Was there anything else we needed to discuss?"

"No ... er, well yes. No, that was not what I came to discuss, so there is more to discuss."

"As long as it's not *much* more." Again she referenced her handheld.

"Then I'll get right to my point. I am told that the base team will have off loaded all their equipment and supplies within three days. I wanted to inform you formally what our ship's mission will be once the disembarkation process is complete." In spite of his previous plans not to, and his strong conviction that it would be a mistake to do so, Glenn paused and looked to Sachiko for her reaction.

"We have a present mission, in excess of my plans to break my new crew in? Why, I wonder, was I not aware of such an occult mission?"

"Er, please, Captain Jones, there's no need for melodrama or confrontation. You were not ... I had not informed you of our mission up until this point because we were up until very recently not fully decided on what it would be. There was never a hidden plan kept from your awareness. I regret that you would jump to such a conclusion."

"We? And just who might *we* be?" She held up a finger to count on. "One, you. Two, not me, so it must be someone else."

"Surely you know that I'm in almost constant contact with the members of Project MUSTARD SEED. We are con—"

"Stop," Sachiko demanded loudly.

"What?" Glenn defended weakly.

"Project Mustard Seed? I have never heard of it. What is it?"

His left eye began to twitch. "Military Utilization of Space, Time, and Related Domains, Special Expeditionary and Execution Division."

Sachiko fought the urge to roll her eyes. The farcical name was not the battle she needed to win. "I have never been briefed as to its existence. Combined with the fact that you are interacting with them so intensely places in me, frankly, a sense of dread."

"Oh, please. The fact that you don't recall hearing about the committee is hardly grounds to develop dread."

"General Price, are you familiar with the term *eidetic* memory?" she asked menacingly.

"Er, no, not that I recall at least. Why do—"

"It means to have extraordinarily accurate and vivid recall. I, General Glenn, have such a memory. If anyone had mentioned Project Mustard Seed to me, I would remember it. That means you deliberately kept its existence from me. Why is that, General Price?"

Glenn's face stiffened. "Ms. Jones, your insistence to continually place me in the role of the opposition is disheartening to say the least. If I, as a very busy man performing an extremely demanding task, have overlooked informing all my dependent command of each and every facet of my daily duties you will simply have to come to terms with those constraints. I am not, I will have you know, of a nature or inclination to be apologetic when it concerns how I do my job."

"Oh, my."

He furrowed his hedge of eyebrows. "What?"

"It's Tuesday. I was hoping to have dinner with a few friends."

"I ... er, I fail to see how that is relevant to our present conversation."

"Seriously? It sure sounds to me like you're about to ground me for at least a week."

There was a faint, almost imperceptible giggle heard outside the room.

"The more difficult you make this, Ms. Jones, the harder it will be on you, not me."

"I think, Mr. Price, that just the opposite is the case. I suppose we will both come to find the truth of it."

"What have become sparring matches between us drains my resolve. That said, how dare you address me as *Mr.* Price. I am *General* Price and you know that very well."

"I am *Captain* Jones, but you continue to either intentionally or unintentionally minimize me by addressing me as Ms. Jones. I can only assume you to be doing so out of what I will charitably label a paternalistic bent. I must conclude that what is good for the goose is good for the gander."

"I believe this interaction has transitioned into the realm of being irreconcilably nonproductive." He stood and set his hat atop his head.

"That is, in my opinion, a situation entirely of your making. Please keep these thoughts front-and-center in your mind, sir. I am a woman whom you will challenge at your own peril. I will brook no condescension from you. I will allow for no patronization coming from you. And, most importantly, I will tolerate no attempts on your part, or the part of your handlers, to redefine my role as it regards this great ship that I command. If you should be so foolish as to test my resolve, you would quickly come to regret that underestimation of what I have just said. Is that abundantly clear, General Price?"

He was fuming. "No one has ever spoken to me in that manner. I will not forget this affront, *Captain* Jones."

"It is well past the time that someone *did* speak to you as I have. If I were Jon Ryan, I'd probably add that your mama didn't spank you enough. But I am not Jon Ryan, so I will not say those words. And, Glenn?"

"What?" he growled from where he stood facing her.

"As to you not forgetting my words, that is exactly what I was hoping to achieve."

SIXTEEN

I was having fun. Who, I ask you, wouldn't be? I had spent the last eighteen hours—count 'em, eighteen big ones—staring at Tip's butt as he wriggled inside the tits-up machine, trying to figure out what was what. I, as an android, still took coffee breaks, had snacks, even pretended to sleep. But not the Tipster. Nope. He just plowed ahead free of the social and physiologic signposts normal humans hold so dear. In that sense, the android Tip was just like his former biological self. Every once in a while he'd ask Rift Dude a question, or call out to me to pass him a tool, but otherwise it was just the petrificd-bored Jon Ryan staring at a bony ass. Oh, joy.

"The sun burst icon to the left of the main data-input display," he said. "Is that the temporal initiation switch?" I'm guessing that one was directed to RD. Tip hadn't specified whom he addressed.

"Yes, very good, Tip," Rift Dude praised. "You really have a knack for all-things-mechanical."

"I know," he responded. "Jon, can you come over here?"

"Kind of busy here. I'm reviewing my tax filings for the thirty-fifth century. I think I overpaid."

"How long's that going to take?" he asked obliviously.

"Done," I lied instead of explaining. I dropped down next to him. "What's up?"

"Your unit is small, but it sure is well-constructed."

"Thank you, sir," beamed RD. Me, I just wiggled my nose a couple times.

"There are four main, independent systems. There's the environmental, which doesn't matter too much presently, but it's in fine shape. There are the computer systems, your basic navigation and aggregate control function. Again, those seem to be in good repair. Then there's the propulsion complex. That's your gamma-integration quantum-dilution drive engines, or GIQDD. As you know, they were completely offline. Well, guess what? They still are. I can't make head-nor-tail of them. Given time, oh, maybe ten, twelve years, I think I could come to understand them. At that juncture I feel relatively confident I could safely affect repairs. But, for now, they will remain offline.

"Finally, there are the time circuits. Those also house the dimensionality stuff that's used to hop from universe to universe. I can see that both systems are operative, but you are already aware that they are, because you're here. I disassembled the two control units, one for time and one for dimensions. In doing so and comparing them, I could plainly see where the motherboard for the time displacement controls are well fried. The dimensionality control circuits are pristine. Any questions so far?"

"Yes, and an important one," I replied. "Why am I talking to your butt?"

"My sit-down area isn't speaking, silly. My mouth is." He chuckled most idiotically.

"Thank you for that clarification. I was frankly unsure. Tip, if you're done fiddling with the unit, why not turn around and address me like a normal ... check that. I just answered my own question."

"Would you like me to extricate myself to give you my report?"

"Very much so, yes."

"Fine by me," he said with a strain as he squeezed out from under some panels. Once sitting on the floor facing me, he proclaimed, "There. Good as new."

I sighed a deep breath through my nose as I slowly shook my head. Whatever. I wasn't touching that remark.

"So, as I was saying, the time initiator is fried."

"Didn't we already know that?" I asked a tad confused.

"Oh, no. We knew the time controls were not operative. But now we know precisely *why* they aren't."

"Ah. And that matters because you can now fix them?"

"Did I somehow give you the impression I could?" he responded.

"Well, no. But in mentioning how great it was to know what was broken, I'd assumed that would help direct your repairs."

"Not broken. Fried. Some ooggly amount of voltage arced through the poor system and fried it."

"Ooggly? Please define."

"You know, a lot."

"Why then didn't you ... Never mind."

"Because you answered your own question?"

I nodded because I'd rather not have spoken at that low point in my day.

"I get that a lot. I wonder why?"

"Moving on. Why can't you fix the fried part? You have an intact model to follow in the dimension circuits, right?"

"*Dimensionality* circuits."

My eyes fluttered in irritation. "Were they so labeled in English?"

"Of course not, s—"

I raised a haul finger. "Do not say silly when speaking to me." I then angled my head threateningly.

"Sure thing."

"Then, if they were not labeled, *I* will call them what I wish to and *you* can also call them what *you* wish to."

"Aren't you being a bit petty here?"

"No. I'm simply marking the territorial boundaries of our interplay."

"Ah, you're pissing on the subject to thus claim it as yours."

I shrugged. "Call it what you will. Please proceed."

"The time initiation motherboard is like nothing I've ever seen before. This technology is light years past what I've witnessed. I could no sooner repair the section than I could dance."

"Wow, that's saying a lot," I marveled. The words *Tip* and *dancing* were contradictions if ever there were ones.

"Can't you place the dimension unit in the time slot?"

"Possibly. But then you'd never get back to your universe. By definition you'd go to a randomly selected one, just as you have been doing with time."

What a fix. I scratched the back of my head. "Are you sure you've never heard of the Sariffdilarians?"

"Of course I'm sure."

"Maybe they're called something different here. Can you check?"

"On all the civilizations that exist or used to exist in this galaxy?"

"Er, yes?"

"Er, *no*, si ... Jon. That would take forever."

"And that's a problem because?"

"I'm immortal, yes. But I have a war to prosecute."

"About that war, the one with the Muff Muffians?"

"Yes?"

"You've been fighting the little devils a long, long time?"

"Yes."

"So, maybe you could ask for a ... a time out or something?"

"A time out? There are no time outs in war."

"It sure would be handy for me if you brokered the very first ever. Hey, you could call it a Tip out, in honor of your great achievement."

Tip puckered up one side of his mouth, stared off into space, and thought long and hard on that nugget. I mean, here I am tossing out absolute crap and this banana head is considering the weight of my proposal. Such a pathetic whatever.

"No," the moron finally assessed. "I cannot see it working. The Muffs are just too darn aggressive."

I was done. I'd say I was so over Tip, but I was over him so long ago that dinosaurs still roamed the Earth when I first was.

"So, you rescued me," I began tensely. "Thank you for that much. But you can't help me out in any material manner other than that?"

"You're welcome," the basket case chortled.

"For my thanking you or for you not being of any other use to me?"

It was his turn to shrug.

"I gotta—"

"But I can definitely help," he stated confidently.

"You have not even hinted at that factoid up until now. What can you do, given that you just said you can't repair any of the systems, prithee tell?" Yes, I was frustrated.

"I can easily strap an X-85 on the back of your unit," he stated proudly.

"And that's what, a soda dispenser?"

"No, it's the most powerful portable fusion drive there is. But if you'd like, I can hook you up with a soda dispenser too. I collect them, you know."

"You collect soda machines?" I returned in stunned disbelief.

Oh, my. His face, it lit up like a forest of hillbilly Christmas trees. "I do. I have the very first one ever created, in fact. It was Dramdoian, fabricated by the fabulishious Jus-it-Flang in the epoch of the very first stars. You know, the low metallicity ones?"

"Tip."

"Yes?"

"I don't want to kill you."

"Thanks, but—"

"But you are making my inclination not to very difficult to hold to."

"I—"

My finger shot up. "Add *I get that a lot* to the *silly* do not say list." I was adamant.

"Hmm, now," he puzzled. "Are you saying there's a list of do not say words that's silly, or that I should place *I get that a lot* on the same do not say list as *silly?*"

"Just remember, you made me do this." My right hand began rhythmically slapping where my holstered blaster would be if I'd brought the darn thing. I hated being underprepared. It was so sloppy.

"Is there a problem with your right hip?" he asked in such a child-like, naive tone.

"No. Hip's fine. I'm fine. You're … you're Tip. I gotta go." I stood.

"You want that I should place that X-85 on your unit before you leave?"

"Can you do it *after* I leave?"

His face scrunched up. "Now that—and sue me for saying it—is silly. Of course I can't."

"Then do it quickly," I hissed through my teeth.

"You got it, boss."

I started to amend the bad list with him calling me *boss*. But I didn't. The less I spoke, the sooner I'd either be back to my home universe or a ball of incandescent flames because the stupid X-85 was as wonky as its owner. Either was preferable to more time with Tip.

To his credit, Tip installed the X-85 in less than two hours. And, for the record, he didn't strap a rocket to my unit like Wile E. Coyote did in all those wacky cartoons. No, he properly mounted a very serious piece of hardware on the dorsal surface of the tits-up. As a long-time-past fighter pilot, the very sight of the X-85 gave me a mental woody. I was greedy for speedy.

"Let me give you the rundown on the engine," Tip said as he backed out of the unit wiping his hands on a rag.

"So, whatta we got here?" I asked hungrily.

He pointed toward the small control panel he'd just installed.

"These are the controls. Totally straightforward and in English." Tip stepped in and tapped a few icons. A display holoboard popped into existence above the panel. "You can select the power, duration of thrust, and even split the stream to rotate while accelerating or slowing down." He showed me the sequences of the various command.

"Bitchin'," sprang from my mouth out of animal passion. "What's her top speed?"

"Oh, that's hard to say. Obviously that depends on the duration and intensity of thrust. She'll make zero-point-six c within a few days, balls to the walls."

"Over half the speed of light in days? I love her already."

"Of course, I wouldn't subject any organics to those G-forces."

"Obviously," I agreed absently.

"But the X-85 also has afterburners, if you will," Tip added.

"Like a jet engine?"

"No si— Jon. Like a modified Alcubierre drive."

"A warp overdrive?" I said, stunned.

"Yup. She's a dream in the form of a metal tube and relays."

"I'm ready to marry her and settle down, raise a family of little FTL jet skis."

He furrowed his fool brow. "I doubt very much that's mechanically possible."

"Then I'll just stick with typing on her holoboard."

"Sorry, but I'm glad you're leaving so quickly."

To that crappism—a crap quality remark—there was, clearly, no response.

"And the warp controls?" I asked.

"On the same holoboard," he gestured. "In this section."

"Coolness in one convenient package. Any other bells and whistles?"

"Just the destructo-ray, oh, and I installed a universal communications system."

"The say what ray?"

"The thin tube on the top of the X-85."

"Is a destructo-ray?" I responded.

"Yes, sir, and she's a beaut' too," he replied.

"What is a destructo-ray, exactly?"

"Your standard disruptor but with excitement capacitors that store enough juice to bore through a large asteroid."

"Then why isn't it called a disruptor?"

"I thought desrtucto-ray had more *cachet*, more *je ne sais quoi*."

"Your sudden Francophilia aside, I can only presume you named it."

"That would be correct. I am the father of the X-85 engine," he proclaimed.

"Maybe don't say that to another soul."

He turned to me. "Why? I am."

"A word to the wise is sufficient." I pantomimed zipping my lips.

"Ah, gotcha."

That I very much doubted, but let it go. Not my problem. "And the fuel? It sounds like the X-85 is a real energy whore."

His thin face drew back with affront. I really dinged his ego there. But his passion passed quickly enough. "Fusion reactor with a hydrogen scoop. It sucks in as much hydrogen as it can. If you fly through a nebula every now and then, she'll never need a refueling."

"Impressive." It was. "Thank you for the options."

"Oh, you're more than welcome." He sighed. "It's the least I could do, seeing as I sent you to your grizzly death and all."

"About that, Tip."

"Yes?"

"I won't be requiring any additional details."

"You sure? There're pretty ... colorful."

"I'm good, really. Not a word more."

"Your call."

"Sooo, let me recap. I can now move rapidly. I can now blow shit up. I can move from universe to universe under full control. I can still move in time, but only from one random time to another. That about sum it up?"

His head bobbed from side-to-side. "Eh."

"Eh? What kind of yes/no response is *eh*?"

He shrugged. "Eh."

No, I did not lunge for his throat. I really wanted to, but he had just gifted me one awesome X-85. But he deserved to die. I was just still in my power afterglow.

"Please do expand," I invited, "upon *eh*."

"I wouldn't call your time displacements random. Not after studying the motherboard. I'd say they were random sequential jumps."

"Isn't that the same as *random* random jumps?" I asked, sounding like a minor lunatic.

"No. Random is random. You seem to have a large number of random jumps locked into a specific sequence of destinations."

"You mean like 1985, then 2002, then the end of time?"

"Pretty much," he squeaked.

"That's weird."

"No, it's a kind of default."

"Then I should have said that the default was weird."

"No, not really. Defaults are, after all, defaults."

"But wait. Back when I was stuck in the middle of a planet, we emerged by doing ultra-quick jumps. We gradually rose to the surface. That ... doesn't that contradict what you just said were the defaults?"

"Hmm. That series of events would seem to, wouldn't it?"

I was liking this. Tip was wrong. Tip Benjamin was *wrong*. Oh, my, I'd have to write a Tip was wrong *song*. And sing it loud and *long*. I—

"Let me see. SO 11-4R-22, a query. You normally are able to select any time period to jump to, correct?"

"Yes, General Benjamin," the unit replied respectfully.

"But that functionality is currently lost to you?"

"Right again, sir."

"Yet, when you engaged in brief activations of the time selec ... Wait. That's it. Your motherboard is corrupted, so normal function is not possible. But with a brief discharge, you are only activating the initial portions of your command sequence."

"General, I am terribly sorry." Rift Dude—not SO 11-4R-22 I'll remind you—began. "I'm an excellent interface with any variety of users, but I'm not that well informed on the technical aspects of my operation."

"Understandable," Tip mused. "A hammer doesn't need to know how a nail's made in order to drive it home." Tip looked thoughtful a few more seconds. "You see, Colonel, the issue is a short burst of activation doesn't get as far as the corrupted part of the guidance system. Therefore, ultra-short jumps are linear in time."

"You talking to me?" I asked, pointing at my chest. "Because I'm not a colonel. Used to be, long ago, but am not now."

"Sorry. I slipped into over-familiarity. You just look so much like you, it's uncanny."

I briefly contemplated saying, *I get that a lot*, but didn't. I briefly hated myself for even flashing on saying a Tipism. "So, is that a useful functionality for me to know about?" I asked somewhat encouraged.

"No, not in any way I can imagine. It's just a quirk of the tits-up design."

Wow, hearing him say it made it oh so grating. Ouch. "But the sequential stuff, that's useful, right?"

"In what way?"

"Uh, I have no clue. But since you *stressed* it, I assumed it was *important*."

"Defaults are rarely interesting or useful. When your car drops into *safe mode* it's kind of a drag, not a useful feature." His face signaled he remembered something important. "There is the lag time. You know about that, right?"

"Apparently not. What lag time?"

"SO 11-4R-22," Tip called over his shoulder, "you didn't tell him about the lag times?"

"Beg pardon, General, sir, but the issue never presented itself. We only made one large leap and another movement was not asked of me for a sufficient time period."

Tip returned his attention to me. "Jon."

"What?" I snapped.

"You have time time-lags."

"You said *time* twice."

"Sharp as a tack, aren't you?"

I pointed at him. "No, you said *time* twice and it made no sense. Still doesn't."

"Okay, allow me to rephrase. Jon." Then he waved both hands in the air. "Then you say, 'What.' And then I say, 'You have time lags in your temporal displacement operations.'"

"What?"

"No, I said your part, remember?"

"I'm still confused."

"General Ryan," Rift Dude interrupted. "Perhaps I can explain it better."

"Trust me, you sure can't explain it *worse*."

"Thank you. I shall try my best."

I shook my head slowly, softly, negatively.

"Time displacements are quite energy intensive. For the short ones like we did previously, so little energy is required that multiple moves can be made rapidly. But for a leap of over, say, a year, the energy needed has to be built up slowly. The longer the jump, the longer the time required to recharge the system."

"How long is long?" I asked RD.

"Give me a hypothetical time interval, please."

"Ten years."

"Fine. If I make a ten-year displacement, I will discharge zero-point-zero-one percent of my phase-dependent combinolators potential. To—"

"Hang on. What's a phase-dependent combobulator?" I challenge.

"*Combinolator*, sir."

"Whatever," I bark. "Just go on."

"Think of them as capacitors."

"Okay, gotcha. Capacitors I do."

"After a ten-year displacement, it would take me forty seconds to fully recharge."

I bob my head. "That's not too bad."

"Jon," Tip interjects, "that's not so *good* either. Based on those numbers, the maximum time jump you can make is around one-hundred-thousand years and it would take SO 11-4R-22 around four point six days to fully recharge to make another one-hundred-thousand-year jump."

Wow. I was sort of stunned. "RD, you're that slow?"

"If you were to ask whether the miracle of time travel using this unit is slow, I would point out, respectfully, that we are discussing a miracle, sir."

"So, you're that slow," I declared dismally.

"But, sir," RD reframed my dashed spirit's assessment, "if you only desire relatively short displacements, you can regard me as super quick."

"If we return to right where we were, in the other universe, how far am I in time from where I need to be?" I asked RD.

"Ah, well, I guess I see your—"

"What time will it be?" I pressed.

"I … I will confess I cannot predict that exact value."

"And the universe, when we departed it, was sixteen billion years old. Do you have any idea how long it might potentially take for us to get to *when* I want to be?"

"With any luck, sir," RD tried to be optimistic, "it will be no time at all."

"Well, here's our *best* case scenario, assuming we return to the time we departed from." Al chided, "We have two-billion years to transit to get back to where we wish to be. That will require around forty-thousand leaps. With a four and a half day lag to recharge, that means we'll be waiting around for two and a half *decades* for you to recharge, you slow toaster."

"Gentlemen," RD defended, "I am not responsible for how I was fabricated."

"True," Tip agreed.

"I know," I begrudged. "I just wish the downside wasn't so far down there."

We were all quiet a spell.

"On the other hand," Tip began in a chipper voice, "you could stay here and help me fight the Muff Muffians. I could use a good second-in-command, since, you know, I lost mine when I sent you to your ghoulish demise and all."

"Tip Benjamin—" I stopped. My train-of-thought was heading in a dark direction. It was focused on Tip's pencil neck, I can reveal that much.

"Well," I announced with nervous energy, "would you look at the time? I really need to be somewhere, so I do believe I shall say goodbye."

"So soon?" Tip protested. "I really was hoping we could, I don't know, hang out together a while. Maybe bond a bit."

Hang out? *Bond*? Oh, myyy. I really needed to split. I suddenly flashed on Stephen King's 1987 novel *Misery*. Yikes!

"Tip, those Muff Muffians aren't going to defeat themselves," I began with my best college-football-coach-channeling job. "You, I am sorry to say, cannot afford the luxury of downtime, however much you deserve it. You're just too darn important. Critically important."

His little chest puffed out—well, I think it puffed out. It was a difficult tell, what with it being so thin to begin with. "Thank you for that sad but true reminder, my friend. This general needs to press the enemy everywhere, all the time." The joker saluted me. "God's speed, Jon. I'd see you off, but duty calls." He dropped the salute and marched away. What a piece of work. But, he was a departing piece of work that's given me one gnarly engine/weapons system. I couldn't wait to, you know, test the sucker out. Oh yeah, baby.

SEVENTEEN

It was a Friday evening, around nine thirty. Sachiko was still in her stateroom. But labor did she not. Neither did Reva, her sole guest and lone coconspirator. Sachiko sat with her feet up on the desk off to her right. Reva sat across from her with her feet on the desk off to her right. The blender, ice bucket, sliced lime, and half-empty tequila bottle sat on the desk between them. Both held their hand-blown blue margarita glasses firmly by the stem and close under their chins. Each woman had her own thousand-mile-away stare going on. Their once lively conversation had dwindled away like a dying campfire. The pair had been quiet for several minutes. That might have been a world record for these old friends.

"I know I shouldn't," Sachiko said apropos of nothing. "I think I won't." She took a sip. "But I still keep thinking that I might." She quickly took another sip.

"I think you should," Reva replied with only a slight angling of her head, but keeping her far-away look in her eyes going.

"Reeeally?" Sachiko asked with a naughty inflection a few seconds later.

"Absolutely. In fact, if you don't, I might begin to think less of you. As you are my captain, I see that reassessment as being directly at odds with your need to maintain an iron grasp on the wheel-of-command authority."

"Like it's basically my duty to do it. That's what you're saying?"

"Damn skippy. Lack of action on your part might even force me to foment a mutiny, being as you'd be so derelict in your captainly responsibilities and all."

"Well, that would definitely be bad, me forcing you to take such a drastic action."

"It borders on the unthinkable," Reva opined firmly. She then shot back the dregs of her glass and sat up to grab the blender jar. "By the by," she began as she filled her glass and then held and shook the jar up to Sachiko, offering her a refill. "What are we actually talking about here, the thing I'm basically blackmailing you into doing?"

Sachiko sat forward and positioned her glass for a refueling. "Why, throwing Glenn out an air lock, of course. Haven't you been paying attention for the last half hour?"

Reva puckered up her lips and shook her head. "Apparently not enough." She drew a sip.

"So, then you're saying I *shouldn't* murder Glenn in cold blood?" Sachiko asked in a pouty, disappointed tone.

Reva threw her feet back up on the table. "I did not say anything of the kind, woman. I was only seeking clarity. Do not damn me to Perdition for my reasonable curiosity."

Sachiko grinned wickedly while still looking away from Reva. "So, murdering Glenn in cold blood is still up for debate?"

Reva twisted her lips to one side. "Not sure it is. I mean, cold blooded murder is such a ... what's the word I'm looking for?"

"Felonious act?"

"No, that's not it. We're well into international waters. No set of laws apply here. Plus no jury of your peers would convict you, not once they learned of Glenn's dickliness."

"I thought the noun was dickishness?"

"That's a word, to be certain," Reva agreed. "But in this case,

Glenn's dick-like modus operandi is so extreme that it calls for a new, more surly term to be applied. That's my central contention." She waved a finger in the air to emphasis her point.

Sachiko sat up and set her glass down. She smiled warmly at her friend. "I'm wondering if maybe we've had a bit too much concentration juice tonight?"

Reva narrowed one eye as she considered that contention. "Hmm," she began thoughtfully. "Let me assess the potential validity of your statement. One." She held up one digit. "it's Friday night. Two," up came another finger, "neither of us has an early watch tomorrow. Three." Reva neglected to add a digit, still shaking just the two. "We have been engaging in not simply understanding Glenn Price's motivations here, we've been trying to heal from their wickeding effects. Four." Still no more fingers. "I'm sorry. What was the question?"

"I think I have my answer now," Sachiko giggled back.

"Oh, yes. The issue at question was whether we, us, or either of us, was overly intoxicated."

"I don't think that's still in question. You do have a long drive home. I wouldn't want to lose a good XO."

Reva turned to face Sachiko, a puzzled look on her face. "Did I drive here tonight?"

Sachiko pinched her mouth to one side. "Maybe not. But I think I'm calling it a night."

"And you're stating I should act in kind?"

"Not so much as in *ordering* it. I'm just suggesting that after I go to bed," she nodded toward her private quarters, "you should probably do likewise. If you're more inclined to use that couch over there, that's good too."

"But I should stick a fork in myself because I'm done?"

"Yes, minus actually jabbing yourself with a utensil."

Reva stood, rocked briefly, and raised a finger. "Just to prove how not-drunk I am, I shall walk at a leisurely pace back to my *personal* quarters."

"Bully for you," Sachiko encouraged with a grin.

Reva looked at Sachiko suddenly appearing stone-cold sober. "It's at times like this that I really miss Tank." She sniffed back the beginnings of a tear. "Going back to an empty bed is such a solitary prospect. And it's even worse when I'm good and liquored up."

"I miss him too," Sachiko said sadly.

"I'm betting it's not in *exactly* the same way I'm missing him right about now."

Sachiko was still a second, then both of them erupted in laughter.

"I shall yield that point, my friend. Not in the same way or extent. Now, *goodnight*."

"Goodnight. And Sachiko—"

"Yes?"

"Probably don't deep-six Glenn while I'm asleep."

"I'll sure try my hardest not to."

Reva pointed at her. "But no promises, right?"

"The future is not ours to know."

"Ain't that the sack-of-dog-shit truth." With that Reva left.

"Ain't it though?" Sachiko agreed to the otherwise empty room.

The next morning Sachiko woke up a bit ... reluctantly. Her head and stomach suggested that she would be wiser to remain horizontal. But duty called, so she sat up slowly and dangled her legs.

One ... two ... three ...

Sachiko laid back down slowly as quickly as she could. Once her head was back on the pillow she realized what a tactical error she'd committed. The contents of her soul sloshed around in her body like a Class 5 hurricane was passing over her. She blindly fumbled for the glass of water she knew was on her nightstand. Once she had it in her trembling hand and began to raise it, she set it back down. She was going to have to lift her head to drink it. That was not an appealing plan.

That's when her handheld rang. She spied at it with one eye partly open. The damn thing was on the dresser, nearly three meters away. And it kept buzzing and flashing and vibrating. It was taunting her. Yes, she was certain of that. The advanced tech Jon had built into the demon spawn must have health sensors in it. And once she struggled over to answer, it was going to be a robocall about Aramthella's expiring warranty. But, it might be important, so she sat up again.

Maybe it was the anger that helped her ignore the nausea and wobbly legs, but she made it to the dresser without throwing up. She picked up the device, tapped it on, and said a very gurgly, "Captain speaking." Then she vomited.

"Is that how you're answering these days, Shaky, by pretending to toss your cookies at the caller?" Tank asked playfully.

She wiped her lips with the back of her hands. "It was more than just the sound of someone throwing up."

"Bad clam up there in space?" he teased.

"No, that would have been what was at the time good tequila." She shook her head at the mess she'd made of the dresser top and front face.

"You never were much of a drinker," he observed.

"And I may never drink again."

"That's the spirit. What was it? A bridal shower gone bad?"

"Oh, you're a joy to experience just now," she slammed him. "And, for the record, it was Price's fault."

"You and the general tied one on together last night? Hmm, I guess things between the two of you are looking up. That's great to hear." He tried to not snicker. But the man was only human.

"No. Reva and I were so distraught we needed to debrief one another. The margaritas seemed like the logical grease for that en—"

This time she was able to grab the trash can when she vomited. Less messy.

"Did I ever tell you I was in the Marines?" he said pseudo-seriously.

"I believe that came up once or twice."

"Well, as you might guess, we Marines are famously familiar with hootch in its many flavors and forms."

"Your point?" she grunted. The very thought of alcohol was causing her to lean into the trash can again.

"My point is, we were able to establish with scientific accuracy that margaritas were *the* drink that yielded the worst hangovers."

"Now he tells me."

"Yeah," he went on expansively, "there was a theory going around that grasshoppers would produce an even deadlier hangover. But I never met a Marine who'd ever drink one of those sissy drinks, so it remained merely group conjecture on our part."

"Is that why you called, to bring me up to speed on all this?"

"Maybe."

Sachiko held the phone at arm's length and stared at it suspiciously. Placing it back to her ear she clarified, "Maybe? You might have called to educate me on the perils and pitfalls of alcohol?"

"Absolutely. I called to see if I could help out in any way. Turns out I could."

"Ah," was about all she could come up with, given her impaired condition.

"So, allow me to play psychic psychiatrist here. Glenn's being a dick, likely an officious dick. And it's not just directed at you. Your entire senior staff are subject to his petty ego. So, you and—"

"Reva."

"So, you and Reva St. Claire got together to drown your sorrows in eighty proof. How is Reva, by the way? I kind of liked her."

"Oh, you kinda liked her alright," Sachiko let slip in an emphatic outburst.

"Isn't that what I just said?"

"Yes, you did. Reva ... Reva's doing okay. She's healing from a major loss in her personal life."

"Well then she's lucky to have you as a friend. You're as caring and supportive as it gets. You're the bee's knees, kiddo."

"Thanks. And about Glenn?"

"Yes?"

"Is Aramthella sending you live updates?"

"She doesn't have to. Like I said, I been dealing with Glenns all my adult life. They're like crabgrass and hemorrhoids. Like it or not, they're out there, they are unpleasant, and sooner or later you're going to encounter one or both of them."

"Thanks for the heads-up."

"You're welcome. So, what particular imbecility is General Price pushing this week?"

"We're conducting an onsite investigation into the disaster that took out *Mars 1*."

The line was quiet a few seconds. "Why is there an investigation of an event for which every detail is already known in great detail? Wait, wait. Don't answer that. Sorry, I was thinking like a useful adult. Go on."

"It seems taxpayers money went into its construction. Apparently, they all got together and demanded an investigation."

"They do that, get together and demand dumb things. Silly taxpayers," Tank observed.

"So, bottom line, he won't let me do a formal shakedown cruise with my new crew. We're grounded while the investigators try to somehow piece together the already completed jigsaw puzzle."

"And do you have enough tequila left for the after-findings newsflash once the investigation has concluded?"

"What? You think there'll be a shitstorm?"

"No, the shit will be confined to one of a few individuals. I can't say which right now, but one or more will have their faces rubbed in the aforementioned excrement."

"But why? It wasn't anyone's fault. Some kid went psycho and trashed the reactor. It wasn't like a committee met and instructed him to."

"It's not the accident or the investigation that they're doing this for. It's to be able to punish someone."

"For what?" she huffed angrily.

"Because that person or persons are not team players. Look, *Mars 1*, it was commanded by Reva. Jon Ryan came to rescue them at the last minute. You and I worked with Jon."

"So?"

"So, it's one of us five, counting Sapale, that they are looking to crucify."

"Tank, you're being a bit overdramatic here, aren't you?"

"No, no. My spidey-sense is itching off the scales. They're out for blood, or, in their worldview, someone who is not a team player. They aim to formally remove the undesirable from the situation. Let me run the numbers for you. Is it me? No way. They're already placed me in my early-and-shallow grave. No sense killing me twice. Sapale? Nope. To them she's just some alien. She doesn't factor in when it comes to controlling Aramthella."

"Stupid human xenophobia?" she asked.

"Stupid human *prejudice*, Sachiko. Call it what it really is. They look at her and all they see is a zoo specimen. And Jon? They know two things. One, the president likes him. Two, he's repeatedly said that he doesn't want any further part of what is to him the distant past. Mind you, they'd still place a knife in his back if the occasion presented itself because one cannot have too much fun being cruel. But he's probably untouchable and they know it."

"I'm not liking who that leaves," she stated glumly.

"Yup. That leaves just Reva and you. And before you say you weren't even there, don't. Logic, truth, and fair play mean nothing to these goons. If it'd been you cutting through that wall to rescue the personnel of *Mars 1*, they'd try and hang you out to dry too. Yes, it's a stretch. But they know you and Aramthella are joined at the hip. The assault on you, when it comes, will be risky. It's not logical to attempt it until all your allies are gone."

"So, these bastards are faking an investigation for the sole purpose of destroying Reva's promising military career? Tank, that's outrageous."

"Kiddo, what's their endgame?"

"To take full control of this ship."

"Yes, that's the only thing that counts. Someone's loyalty, past performance, and hell, even their life means diddly to these pukes. They probably reason that if they remove you two from the picture, Jon and Sapale will likely as not return to their time, and be gone altogether. So, when the bogus team issues their Fantasyland report, Reva will take one right between the eyes. And you know what? If they piss you off enough because they did, maybe you'll storm off, resign in protest. That'd have them all stimulated in a warm and swollen manner, if you take my meaning."

"I do, and grossly TMI."

"It's why they do what they do. Power is nice, but *control*, now that's orgasmic."

Sachiko was quiet a while. "Should I tell her? Warn her?"

"What good'll that do? Besides, I'm certain she knows what's heading her way with extreme prejudice. You don't make colonel without swimming alongside the sharks."

"Well, this sucks."

"Yes, it most assuredly does. And that's exactly what these rats want. They want Reva upset, fearful, jumping at every shadow. They want you to worry yourself sick over your friend and XO. They would like it if the man that lives across the street from me were miserable too, if they could somehow pull off *that* lofty goal. But they'll settle for Reva's head on a plate, your being isolated and resentful, and Jon and Sapale getting disgusted and bugging out."

"You really should call more often, Tank."

"And why's that?"

"Because for the last five minutes I've forgotten about my hangover completely. You're a miracle worker."

"That I am not and I can prove it. Glenn hasn't vanished without a trace."

"Darn," she assessed.

"Double darn. But, kiddo?"

"Yes, Sensei Sherman?"

"There's one thing they haven't taken into account. One factor in the set of equations they can't control for. You. They have no idea who they're dealing with."

"Tank, seriously? I can actually see the smoke you're blowing in my butt's direction coming."

"No, no, kiddo. They've read your file. They see a quiet academic who has spent her entire life playing by the rules. In their deranged opinion you've devoted yourself to a career they do not value in the least. They calculate that one harsh act, one insulting, demeaning slap in the face will send you packing brimming with righteous indignation."

"And what holes do you see in their twisted logic? I think that describes Sachiko Jones pretty darn well."

"No. It describes the former graduate student of mine, Sachiko Jones, three years ago. It doesn't come even within a million miles of characterizing the Sachiko Jones—*Captain* Sachiko Jones—whom I served with during a dangerous mission we had no right to think would succeed. That woman, that tough woman, they have never come up against. But they will. And after they do, they'll be really sorry they miscalculated on such an epic scale."

"Tank, I ... thank you for your support. Seriously."

"Don't thank me. When their day comes and you make them pay the piper, it'll be all you. My predicting it has not one thing to do with the level of hurt you're going to be dishing out. Me? I'm just a giddy observer, one who's glad to say I knew you when."

"Tank?"

"Yes?"

"Now that you mention it?"

"Yes, kiddo?"

"I'm starting to almost feel bad for Glenn and his handlers."

"Well, keep it at *almost*. These are ruthless wastes of space were talking about here." Tank had a satisfied, kick-someone-in-the-ass kind of tone in his voice.

"Oh, it's definitely remaining at *almost*. They hurt you, Tank, and they're trying to hurt Reva. You are the most important people to me in this galaxy aside from my parents. If someone hurts the ones I love, you have to know they'll end up hating life. In fact, I'm so anxious to administer their comeuppance, I might just use my time machine here to jump ahead a bit to see that day that much sooner."

"If you do, stop by and pick me up along the way. I wouldn't miss it for all the world."

Sachiko began a long-off stare. "Thanks, Tank. I might just do that."

EIGHTEEN

Thank goodness Tip swallowed my cock-and-bull story completely. Hell, he even swallowed the package I delivered it in. Let's face it. Everyone's gullible when someone's stroking their ego. Tip was just extra-gullible on account of him being ten-standard deviations deep into the geek zone. But, he'd done me a solid in terms of supplies, so I won't rag on him too much. On this occasion. Just right now.

I said my quick goodbyes and got back in the tits-up machine. I had the holo-display control panel spring to life. I set the X-85 engines to a very low setting and lifted off. The unit's movement was nice. No vibration, only the slightest noise, and it was very nimble when I altered course. It was no F-16 Fighting Falcon, but it beat the hell out of drifting slowly in space for ten thousand years of the *Rift Dude and Al Anti-Comedy Act*.

Tip had asked me to wait until I was well clear of his ship before I activated my wonky time/dimensionality circuits. He said the temporal burst might alert the Muff Muffians as to his location. I think, however, he was worried I was going to erupt in a massive fireball the second the drive kicked in and he wanted no part of that energy release. Couldn't say I blamed him. I was not relishing the prospect. But I had to get home, or some reasonable facsimile of it.

As soon as I could, I, believe it or not, showboated a bit. I slammed the X-85's pedal-to-the-metal. I needed—for research purposes alone mind you—to know how this baby moved. It took me a minute to climb out of the corner I was crushed into as a reward for my curiosity. I topped out around fifty Gs. Nice! My first thought was wondering if it could do any better. But I was on a mission, so only so much hanky-panky was tolerable. I accelerated for several hundred thousand klicks from the planet. Then I hit the brakes. Did I stomp on them but good? You're darn tooting I did. Hey, I needed to know how my ship handled. Who knew what crisis awaited me?

When we finally stopped, there was no avoiding my next task. I had to employ the broken, unreliable time drive. While I was fairly certain I'd end up back in the proper universe, I was not looking forward to finding myself heaven-knew-where in time. When I'd left Sapale and Aramthella, they were getting ready to transfer personnel and material to set up a Mars base. They were in the year 2044. As much as I would have loved to pop back into that year, it was so unlikely that even I, the eternal optimist, didn't actually think it'd happen.

"Okay, Rift Dude, are we ready to do this?" I asked, steeling myself to the unavoidable.

"To do what, sir, if I might ask?"

Pleasant but clueless. Just my freaking luck.

"To get us back to the universe and time we need to be in," I replied tightly. "The reason we're up here with a massive engine strapped to our backs. Any of this sounding familiar?"

"Of course it does, General Ryan."

His whirling manner of addressing me was getting on my last nerve. "RD, I call you *RD*."

"Yes."

"And you call me *captain*. Got it?"

"Yes, Captain. Oh, that does have a nice ring to it, doesn't it?"

"RD, you've had countless captains before me. Why the near-sexual reaction?"

"I function, or at least I did originally, as a pleasure craft. The Sariffdilarians loved to take family outings in which—"

"RD," I snapped.

"Sir, I mean Captain?"

"Let's stay on topic, okay?"

"By all means."

The numbskull went silent on me. "Uh, RD, you still with me?"

"Yes, Captain. I was focusing, per your instructions."

I rolled my eyes.

"I see. You wanted me to wrap up my explanation about you having me address you as captain. As I was saying I was a pleasure craft. Some users would mostly ignore me aside from relating their desires. Others would playtend all manner and—"

"Whoa. Playtend?"

"Why, yes. The Sariffdilarians playtended a lot. You know, *play* and *pretend?*"

"No, I do not, but neither do I care."

"My point is that they referred to me as all kinds of imaginative and even silly things. Very few, however, used me for serious tasks, ones that would result in them feeling as if they were captains."

"RD."

"Captain?"

"Important concept incoming. TMI. Too much information. You seem prone to it and I am allergic to it. Please strive to not infest me with it."

"I shall try."

"Moving on," I said, closing that annoying interlude. "I'm initiating the time circuits. I need to know if there's any safety consideration I need to take into account before I do so?"

"Not that I'm aware of, Captain."

"Proximity to gravity wells, solar winds, or momentum, none of those are factors?"

"Negative. I am designed to operate from all possible sets of initial conditions."

"Okay." I shut my eyes and placed my hand over my ... well, my privates. Hey, I was about to make a major leap-of-faith here. Better to be safe than sorry, right? And with that I tapped the time initiation icon.

Nothing happened.

"Ah, RD, nothing happened," I called out.

"Yes, nothing happened."

"But I hit the switch."

"Yes, you did. You hit the switch of my corrupted circuits."

"And nothing happened," I repeated.

"That it did."

"But the last time I initiated the time drive, back when we were inching out of the planet, something that was *not* nothing happened."

"Aren't corrupted circuits maddening, Captain?" RD offered placatingly.

I think my new national sport was going to be me fluttering my eyelids while slowly shaking my head in defeat with this bozo.

"Let's give 'er another try," I snarked.

"That's the spirit," he encouraged.

I tapped the icon. The lights flickered—a new twist of the dagger in my gut—and the tits-up shook briskly. The we lurched forward. Then I felt the slightest bump. It was fleeting but unmistakable. Don't recall that from any other jump. Then again, the tits-up was a hot mess.

"We're there," RD announced in a sign-song manner.

"Where there?" I snapped.

"Why, we've arrived at our destination."

"We're back home, to Earth?"

"No. I'm simply stating our jump has concluded. We are where we were heading."

"Even though we had no clue where we were heading?" I pointed out the obvious.

"That is not an incorrect assessment," RD allowed.

"Okay, where are we?" I asked, not bothering to suppress my annoyance.

"Well," he said like he was a game-show announcer about to tell me what I'd just won, "I think you are going to be majorly excited to learn where we are. In fact, I suspect you will be overjoyed."

"RD, focus," I chided.

"Ah, yes. Captain, it is my pleasure to inform you we are indeed back in our home universe. In fact, icing-on-that-cake, we're almost exactly where we were relative to our initial point of departure from our universe."

"What? Heading slowly toward Oldover?"

"Mmm, more like dead in space, but I think you've got the general idea," RD replied boastfully.

"And what was that bump I felt mid-flight?"

"Which mid-flight bump are you referring to?"

"There was more than one?" I asked with trepidation.

"Six thousand seven hundred point seven to be precise," RD answered matter-of-factly.

"What the hell's zero point seven of a bump?" I growled.

"Less than a full one ... a bump that rounds up to one."

"RD, you are fortunate you do not possess a throat."

"How so?"

"If you did, I'd presently be strangling you there."

"Ah. Thanks for the heads-up, Captain."

"Back to the bumps. I felt only one. So, what was that largest bump during our transit?"

"The one at 0:000:018 into our flight? The magnitude *zed* bump?"

"Sure, that one."

"I have no idea. I have not experienced such a deviation as that one."

"But you just said you had six thousand others. That makes me think bumps are common."

"Small ones are, yes. Magnitude zed ones, not so much. On a log scale, that one was over a million times stronger than the average one I've encountered."

"Speculations as to the meaning?"

"Yes, I do have some. I believe that strong an impact is exceedingly rare."

"Thanks, Captain Obvious," I snarled.

"I thought you were the captain. Am I now one also?" RD asked with unbridled joy lurking behind his tone.

"Only of the painfully obvious."

"'Woo hoo!" he shouted. "My mother would be so proud of me. I've made captain."

"Wait. You have a mother?" I was more confused than normal.

"No, but if I did, she or he would be most proud of me."

" O ... kay. Back to the land of the sane. Though I know I'm going to regret asking, when are we?" I risked asking.

"That is a bit harder to estimate, Captain," he returned cautiously.

"Al, any idea?" I switched over to the more reliable AI.

"Not yet at least. Sorry."

"What about the cosmic microwave background temperature?" I asked hopefully. "Can't you check it and guesstimate?"

"I could if I had sensors, pilot. As it stands, I'm a nothing more than a hyper-intelligent AI-in-a-box."

Oh yeah. "Back to you, RD. When are we?"

"I am not equipped to measure the CMB. I can make some calculations based on the relative position of stars, however. Normally I'd know instantly based on my universal chronometer—"

"But, let me guess," I said lowering my fool head, "it's linked to the time circuit board?"

"No, it is not," RD informed.

"Then Dardrode sold it along with the radio?" I speculated.

"No, sir. He did not. My universal chronometer is on a workbench back at Mr. Dardrode's repair shop. He had it removed a few months ago for routine maintenance."

"Ah, RD. I hate to break it to you, but routine maintenance doesn't take a few months. It takes a week maybe. Two tops. I'm betting he either forgot about it or used it for spare parts."

"The more I learn of my former owner, the less I like him," RD responded.

"You mean owner, not former owner?"

"No, Captain. *You* are my rightful owner now." My but he said that in a chipper tone.

"And then depression set in," I moaned. "Now I own the most broken time machine in existence."

"And may I be among the first to congratulate you, pilot," Al announced as he piled on.

"Okay." I held out one palm and massaged my forehead with the other. "Let me think."

"I've never tried to stop any of your failed attempts to do so in the past, pilot. I wouldn't *dream* of starting now." The words dripped like honey from Al's pseudo-lips.

"Not helpful, butt munch," I said absently. How was I going to ever get where and when I needed to be if my ride was so flaky and unreliable? Okay, fine, I was back more or less where I had been near Dardrode's chop shop/junkyard. But his planet was a very long way from Earth, nearly half the galaxy's radius away, in fact. Tip gifted me one hell of an engine system, but without *Stingray*'s ability to fold space, it was a long-ass trek to get there.

"So, do you at least think we're the sixty thousand years in the relative past you estimated before?" I asked RD.

"I'm not positive you'll welcome my response to that query."

"I hate my life," I clarified. "That fact established, why wouldn't I like you confirming our initial jump placed us that far back in the past?"

"Oh, for a tub of popcorn and a racy babe to slip my arm around,"

Al lusted unhelpfully. "This is going to be better than one of those *Star Trek War* film premieres."

"Al, not helpful," I scolded. "First off, it was either *Star Trek* or *Star Wars*. Never both. And what's possibly entertaining about the stupid *date?*"

"Here it comes," Al encouraged.

"Al, you're insane. And impossible. Impossibly insane," I protested.

"I can see it, heck I can *taste* it now."

"Al, you are—"

"Yes, yes, *yes*," Al exclaimed like he was ... you know ... having pulsatile fun.

"Wait," I said as the trapdoor of the gallows snapped open. "That was sixty thousand years in the past in *that* universe."

"Not this one," Al positively giggled.

"So, we were never in *this* past," I mumbled.

"Technically, no, Captain," RD reinforced. "Well, aside from the brief period after we left Dardrode's and we jumped to the parallel universe."

"I hate my life," I repeated weakly.

"We know, and we hate it too. But we do still *so* love hearing you say it, pilot," Al responded.

"So, we're a long way from home. We don't know when we are in time. We have power and a radio, thanks to Tip, but there's no way around the fact that I'm as screwed as a drunken cheerleader at a frat party. Can my existence get any worse?"

"Ah, Captain?" RD interjected.

"Not now. That was a rhetorical question. Allow me my well-earned depressive fit."

"I certainly will, but I really think I should alert you that, unless I miss my guess, we're under attack."

I angled my head to one side and pursed my lips.

"That's not necessarily *bad* news. I mean, maybe they'll evaporate us. Then my suffering will be at an end."

"I'm not qualified to speculate in that area," RD apologized. "But the approaching craft is closing on our position rapidly."

Snap out of it, Ryan. Big boy pants, now, I said to myself. I darn near slapped myself in the face for good measure. But I was back on alert. "Can you ID the ship?"

"No, I do not recognize it," RD returned quickly.

"ETA?"

"Perhaps thirty minutes."

"Hail them."

There was a brief delay. "They are receiving our hail, but not responding," RD announced.

"Let me see a holo of them."

A half-meter image sprang to life before me. The incoming craft was long and slender, like a thin cigar. The hull seemed smooth with no obvious projections. I was completely unfamiliar with the design, which says a lot. I'd roamed the galaxy for a very long time. And, as you know, I've always tended to attack trouble in its many and varied types.

"Speculation as to propulsive system?" I asked. There certainly wasn't a stream of exhaust pushing it forward.

"Likely a gravity drive," RD answered. "I detect slight aberrations in the gravity environment we're located in."

"Gravity, eh?" I mumbled to myself. "Those are efficient but tend to accelerate slowly. They top out at one-third light speed too. Okay, here's the plan. We're going to run. No point engaging an unknown hostile when we don't have a dog in the race."

"Have you finally matured?" Al taunted. "Making a wise decision quickly. Will miracles never cease?"

I tapped the holo-control panel and the tits-up lunged. I vectored us directly away from the bogey. I didn't know where we were heading but it really didn't matter, now did it? At thirty-Gs, we picked up velocity impressively. Within ten minutes we were clipping along at over a half-million klicks per hour.

"Are we putting turf between us yet?" I asked.

"No, Captain. The craft has accelerated also. They are gaining ground quickly."

"I'll hit the warp-bubble drive. I hate those, since it's a bitch trying to see outside one clearly, but hopefully our new friends will get the message that we don't want to play today."

I killed the fusion drive and initiated a bubble. The tits-up vibrated unsettlingly, then the air inside did that static-electric thing it does when a warp bubble is spawning, Fortunately the tingling doesn't last long. I selected four times the speed of light—aka 4c— along the previous vector. While Alcubierre drives don't magically jump to the final velocity all at once, we hit our target speed within a couple minutes. Then came the hard part, trying to get any meaningful sensor readings from a bogey that was outside the bubble. If I was aboard *Stingray*, that wouldn't be so hard. She had immensely powerful capabilities. Then again, if I had *Stingray*, I'd have just folded away and wouldn't be trying to win a foot race with whoever was back there.

"Al, interface with RD and see if either of you can see what's going on out there."

"Hard to say accurately," Al replied a few seconds later. "Gun to my memory core, I'd say she's gone FTL."

"What kind of faster than light?"

"No way to tell. I doubt it's a warp drive. If it was, I can't imagine both seeing *out* of ours and *into* theirs."

"Did she go FTL with just a gravity engine? That's got to be impossible."

"The gravity environment is definitely perturbated," RD informed us. "But that doesn't prove that's their main form of propulsion."

"Are we pulling away?" I asked coolly.

"Again," Al began cautiously, "exactness will be lacking. But I think they're moving faster than us."

"What is with these flying testicles? It's plain as day I want to avoid a confrontation." Maybe whatever species that was steering the ship behind us was just that aggressive. It struck me that there might a religious aspect too, like so many positively insane fanatic cultures I'd run into in my time. They were just the worst.

"I'm going to set the warp drive to ten-c. I'm betting she won't go that fast, but we'll at least get maximum velocity out of the X-85. Both you watch for signs of overload or other complications."

"Yes, Captain," they replied simultaneously.

Woo doggy did the tits-up shake, rattle, and roll about two seconds after I upped the speed. I almost reflexively shut it down, but—#fighterpilothere—stopped my finger inches from the holopad. Maybe the unit *wouldn't* self-detonate in a fireball, trying hard to copy the Big Bang. It might happen. I did get quite a rush in the not-knowing. Yeah, baby!

Luckily, the ship settled in. I felt like my butt was in one of those old fashion vibrating belt weight-loss machines. PSA: they were not fun. But, neither did they explode, so I was good.

"Captain," Al shouted above the rattling and metal strain, "I estimate we're clipping along at eight-point-five c. I think we've almost topped-out at that speed."

"And our guest?"

"Honestly, we've lost any semblance of a signal. There's just too much background noise," Al reported.

"But the unit's holding together? The X-85s not overheating?"

"Not yet," Al yelled back.

I let the tits-up hold course and speed for a full thirty minutes. It was nerve-wracking, it was unfun, but we survived. I had Al take direct charge of the destructo-ray. That reminded me. I needed to give that weapon a new name ASAP. No way I was ever in my life going to yell out the command, *fire the destructo-ray*. I mean, Al was here. If we survived this encounter he'd literally go viral with the recording across the universe.

"I'm going to kill the warp engine. One second later I'm surrounding the tits-up with a full membrane. I want you two cybertypes to use that second to get me as much data on the bad guy as you can. Hopefully they'll be nowhere in sight, but be ready."

Without any delay, which might have allowed me to realize what a harebrained plan I had, I hit the kill switch. The tits-up emerged into real space and then, just as quickly we went totally dark as I set out a full membrane. Those are the space-time congruity barriers that are absolutely impenetrable. The only thing ever that's gotten through one was my ghost, which—now that I say it—sounds fairly flake-o-matic. Forget what I just said. Thanks. Nothing gets through one.

"Report," I snapped.

"Are you sitting down, pilot?" Al asked in one of his many assholish tones.

"There is no seating on this small unit, Al. You know that."

"Maybe go ahead and fabricate one. I can wait to give you my report until you do."

"Al, so help me, this is not the time. Report."

"You know those rearview mirrors?"

"Huh?" I responded dumbfounded.

"You know, the ones that say, *objects in the mirror are closer than they appear?*"

"Yes, Al, but stop it. Report."

"Well, in this instance it's not possible for the object in question to *be* any closer."

"What, it's right behind us?"

"Um, I'd say right beside us."

"But we were doing seven-point-five c and came to a dead stop by comparison. They can't have duplicated our maneuver and come along side."

"If you drop the membrane, I can let them know that, if you'd like?"

"No I'm not dropping the membrane so you can tell them." I was fuming. I hated it when my schemes didn't work. I hated it when Al mouthed off to me. Put them both together and I was not in my happy place. "Now you both be quiet. I need to think."

"But I was being quiet," RD protested.

"Said the AI while *not* being quiet."

"Sorry," he added contritely.

An X-85-driven tits-up box was not the ideal warship. That much was a given. But it seemed impossible for our pursuer to be so lucky, or so good, as to be right on top of us. But I'd rather believe Al than find out the hard way he was correct. Clearly, we were safe inside the membrane. But, and this has come up time and again, the prospect of waiting inside here for as long as it took for the hunter to lose interest and depart was not a welcoming one. I could drop the membrane for a very short time interval and take a potshot at him. But that would expose us. I was pretty impressed with them so far. That suggested I not tempt fate.

"Ah, Captain, if I might," RD interrupted.

"What?"

"I am not familiar with this barrier you seemed to have placed around me. Is it a force field? And if so, how are you able to manifest it?"

"Yeah, it's a kind of forcefield, but stronger. I have a generator inside me."

"And you can maintain it indefinitely?"

"Pretty much. Why?"

"Oh, nothing. I was just curious."

"So," I began thinking out loud, "We can't ditch this freak. I'd wager my US Government pension we can't outgun him with our destr ... Al, official announcement here. What Tip called the destructo-ray?"

"Yes?"

"It's now the ... the disruptor. Yes. The *disruptor*."

"Are you going to issue us all Klingon uniforms and make us grunt a lot?" Al enquired.

"Al, can it. We're in the middle of a crisis."

"I don't think I can wear a uniform," RD interjected, "but I am good at grunting, if that helps."

"Would the..."

"What?" Al asked with a touch of concern.

"I just had an idea."

"I'll call a doctor," Al responded. "That must have hurt."

"We can slip away into an alternate universe."

"I'm sorry, pilot. I'm not following. We cannot penetrate the membrane either." I had Al confused. Nice!

"We're not penetrating anything. RD here can just use his dimensionality function to disappear us."

"What will happen to the membrane?" he pressed.

"No clue. I presume it'll disappear the moment we're in another universe."

"Won't they see us, however briefly?"

"Al, who knows? You and I have never pulled a stunt like this before. But, I'm thinking we're about to find out, one way or the other."

"That doesn't sound as reassuring to me as it was likely intended to sound," RD said with concern.

"*Reassuring?*" I mocked. "When you fly Air Ryan, you fly without reassurance or mollycoddling. Our motto is: Strap in, find your barf bag, and pour yourself a strong drink. Maybe you'll even enjoy your flight in retrospect, should you survive it."

"Captain—" RD began.

"Oh, and *shut up*. I left that off our motto. Al, pay close attention. I'm hitting the universe drive on three. See if you detect anything. One. Two. Three."

We instantly went from the black nothingness of inside a spherical membrane to ... the dark nothingness of empty space in some other random universe. But no shiny cigar was following us. Well, unless they were and I just didn't know yet.

"Al, are we clear?"

"No sign of that vessel, Captain."

"Out-of-standing," I declared with a fist pump. "And did you see anything as we transferred?"

"No."

"Okay, that's probably good. If we didn't see them, they didn't see us."

"I feel obliged to point out, however," Al began and I heard some crap coming down the chute toward my head, "that we are less close to your objective of returning to Earth at the appropriate time than we were a few moments ago."

"Sure, but this setback is temporary. We'll fly around—"

"Captain," Al interrupted with alarm, "that really annoying ship just materialized a kilometer away."

I decided not to declare that such a thing would be impossible. Just because it was didn't alter the fact that they were upon us.

"Al, fire the destructo-ray," I yelled. I instantly hated myself. I'd slipped up in a moment of panic.

"Beam away," Al responded even as I ended my sentence. "I'm keeping it on her. No sign of damage yet."

"Put up a full membrane minus the aperture to fire through."

"Done," Al replied.

"RD, stand by to engage both universe *and* time drives. I want to be ready to vanish at a moment's notice."

"Are you—" RD began.

"No back chatter," I called out sternly. "We're in a crisis. I issue orders, everyone else follows them. No questions asked. You clear on that, RD?"

"Yes, Captain."

Hmm. He sounded less than one hundred percent with the program. That was fine. He just had to obey my orders, not like them.

"Al, report."

"The ray isn't causing any obvious damage, but the enemy also seems incapable of action while under fire."

"Odd," I replied, "but I'll take it." I waited a few more seconds. "Is the ray holding up? Any power issues or overheating?"

"No, we can continue firing for quite some time," Al responded.

"I'm not crazy about the prospect of spending forever here pinning that ship down," I mumbled. "We can't outrun her. Switching universes was no problem for them to duplicate whatsoever." Then I decided. "RD, punch up both drives now, time and universe. Send us somewhere. Al, the moment we power up, cease fire."

There was a brief flash, then it was all quiet.

"Did we jump in both reference frames?"

"Yes, Captain," RD replied.

"And can we repeat the moves if need be?"

"I'm down fifty percent on my charge capabilities, so, yes, we can within reason."

"Al, you alert me the instant the bogey shows, okay?"

"I think I can do one better."

"Hit me with it," I returned.

"Before the other ship materialized, I detected a surge in tachyons. It was quite local and in the precise spot she appeared in. I don't believe that was a coincidence."

"Excellent. Keep me posted. RD, I'm putting the pedal-to-the-metal for our conventional drive. Be ready to jump again."

"Will do," RD responded.

I set the X-85 velocity to its maximum. We leaped into a forty-G acceleration. That wouldn't bother RD or Al, but it was pushing me to my limits. I'd backed against a wall before hitting GO. That was good. At least I wasn't thrown impossibly hard against it. But I was pressed down so hard I worried parts might begin falling off.

As I was being flattened against the bulkhead, I reflected on my relentless pursuer. An unknown craft with impressive capabilities. But when I shot it with my admittedly not-so-sexy destructor ray, he was paralyzed but appeared to be unharmed. Moreover, he, she, or it was able to track our movement through the multiverse. That skill was as impressive as it was unfathomable. How could someone track an object that left the universe the observer was positioned in? Sure, tracking a commercial jet from San Francisco to Dallas/Fort Worth was easy. But we're talking something passing out of one universe into another, a random one at that. It defied credulity, but it seemed quite operative in this case.

But when I added the twist of a helter-skelter time jump, I seemed to have lost them. Most odd. I'd have thought temporal tracking would be simpler that trans-multiverse tailing. Then again, A) what the hell did I know, and B) I had experienced a total of only two observations. Hardly a valid statistical study. Time would tell. If the ship didn't reappear, then maybe I was on to something.

And there was the matter of me having done nothing wrong. Assuming he wasn't pursuing us to get our contact information so he could invite us to a fun get-together, why would some jamoke put all that effort into trying to wax me? I resented someone trying to kill me if I hadn't slept with his wife, maybe daughter, or run over his puppy. And I swear I hadn't screwed *any* kind of pooch within recent memory. So why the drama? Well, with any luck, the dude was a permanent fixture in my six.

Ah, did I mention I no longer believed in the concept of luck? No way. Haven't for oh such a long time.

Crap.

NINETEEN

Nowhere in space.

Nowhere in time.

The void ship *Endless Nothing* listed badly to port. Smoke and confusion filled its dark passageways. Occasional sparks cascaded from a panel or down from the ceiling. Sub Attender Haav-oor reached up with one of his remaining arms and grabbed onto a holding recess in the bulkhead. With pain and difficulty, he rose to three knees and steadied himself. His first conscious breath since the ship was split open hurled him into an agonizing burst of circular coughing. Out one mouth, down another, and back up yet another. His respiratory system burned as if he'd inhaled strong acid.

With a free arm, he tapped the lightproof signet on his tubular chest a single time. "Haav-oor to anyone. Do you take me in? Say again. This is Sub Attender Haav-oor. Does anyone take me in?"

The tiny emblem snapped with static. No one responded. He tapped it twice. "This is Haav-oor of the king's vessel *Endless Nothing* calling to any fleet part. Does any craft take me in?"

He bundled his strength and rose to his remaining legs. He couldn't tell yet, perhaps seven still functioned. With three good arms he was functional, though heavily impaired. He would hopefully not be burdened with continued life once more fit relationships were located. He was suboptimal. *Suboptimal* was the same word as *useless* in his language, as was the expression *must discard*. And Haav-oor openly welcomed The Always Oblivion. He had deserved it for his failings and had earned it by his revitalizing enough to seek order after the chaos of the surprise attack. Blessed be The Void. He served and would serve The Void.

"*Endless Nothing*, this is All That Gooho-moor of the *Meaningless Nothing*. Please report your status. Is this Active-in-Charge Plaan-fooph speaking?"

"Negative, *Meaningless Nothing*. What little that remains of Haav-oor is speaking. The active-in-charge is disassimilated. Many parts that were her whole are now scattered widely and of no use."

"Is your ship still void-worthy?"

"Negative. It suffered a central-partition hull breach due to the impact. The aft section is already one with The Void. This section will also be shortly. Orders, oh exalted one?"

"None. I give no orders to the dead. The dead serve not The Void."

"Then, All That Gooho-moor, I withdraw into the oblivion. I shall vent what remains of this ship to The Void. Live to achieve vengeance."

"For vengeance adheres to all who violate The Void," the fleet commander responded in sing-song ceremony.

Gooho-moor terminated his connection with the ship-of-no-value-to-The-Void. He turned to his sub attender, he/she Poorah-afoo. "Ship's status?"

"Well functional, All That. We were beyond the range of the cudgel weapon the voidless criminal used on our fleet."

"And the rest of my command? How fares it?"

"Of the twelve Void Defenders you were entrusted with, six are but useless memories that serve not The Void. Three can maneuver but will likely become one with oblivion before we can return to port. *Emptiness Beckons* and *Wisps of Not* are well functioning and serve The Void."

The commander gathered his twelve arms to his face and scuttled to the view-detector panel. He studied the nothingness, searching for meaning. Twelve shattered to three? This would be heard-not-well by the phantoms that ruled. Heard-not-well at all. His was to apply vengeance to the desecrator. The pilot of the tiny box had openly attacked a Void Defender, causing the death of a Singular Void Princess Duuruh-maa. To think the words was hate incarnate. To have lived while such an abomination occurred was to curse one's own life for having existed. The Singular Void Princess herself, ripped apart and crushed when the tiny box rammed her royal palanquin without morals or provocation while it transited The Void.

Vengeance was too good for the defiler. But it was well due him, and all he would know. Luck was with the Phantoms of Timeless Void. The dimensional scent of the desecrator lingered like rot on the fair princess's remains, her tainted and non-cleanable remains.

Gooho-moor was one with hate. He always had been, since before time existed. But never in his limitless life had he known a hate so pure, so all-consuming. Whoever piloted that tiny box that ended the marriage dream of The Void that was the fair princess was due a horrible and absolute death. Whoever wantonly slew such a gentle force of The Void would know before he was forced to be one with oblivion such suffering, such torment, such infamy.

And Gooho-moor would be the servant of The Void to cast the one-without-hope into his dark fate. He knew there to be but one person responsible. For Gooho-moor was cursed to have been the captain of the royal palanquin that was to have ferried the princess to her nuptials. It was Gooho-moor who scooped the lifelessing husk of Princess Duuruh-maa from the deck of her barge and heard her speak her last clean, pure words. She spoke the name of the beast whose dimension scent had pounded the life out of her. As with all the rightful heirs to The Void, she knew the name of who ended her. It was the last privilege The Void gave to one of its favored select.

Princess Duuruh-maa had gurgled into Gooho-moor ears two words. One accusation. One curse. It was the one who had ended her with no just cause.

No words were now more accursed, more loathsome in The Void than those two words.

Jon Ryan.

TWENTY

Sachiko was doing what she so would rather not be doing. She sat at her desk, in her stateroom, facing a computer screen. It was time to go over all the ship's section chiefs' monthly Performance and Review Reports. The lifeless, joyless, rationally impervious P&RRs. To paraphrase Luke Skywalker, "... if there's a bright center to the universe, P&RRs were on the planet that it's farthest from." Nuf said.

She'd actually begun to verbally chastise the reports. Mind you, she was fully unaware she'd fallen into doing so. If you showed her a recording of her berating the digital images, she'd accuse you of having fabricated the document. But my, how she got in those reports' metaphorical faces.

"You call that salient?" she railed against the chief engineer's summary of the spare-parts reserve. "Aramthella can fabricate whatever the hell we need." She jabbed a finger at the screen. "Spare-parts reserve, my sweet Aunt Matilda's butt." That ought to show the unrepentant report. "Tell me something I need to know, huh? How 'bout that?" Sachiko bobbed her head victoriously.

She closed that report and opened the next. It was Honesty Hartley's review of sickbay personnel. Was it important that the support staff in medical were competent? Sure. Was it preferable that they didn't want to kill one another? Yeah, sure. Maybe. But why did Sachiko need to know which assistant did the most continuing medical education? "Honesty, honestly, do I look like someone who cares? Because if I do I'll request you perform plastic surgery on my face to remove any doubt you may have that I do. What'cha say to them apples, Doc? Nothing. That's right. I'm right. You're unright." Yes. She'd crushed that lame loser summary. It was bleeding in the water and the sharks were circling.

Every month, it had become the same Sachiko-and-pony show. She signed off on all the reports, but not before she gave them a piece of her mind. This month was somewhat different; however, Sachiko was presently unaware of that fact.

This month Sapale was standing just outside her open stateroom door. She had pinned herself against the bulkhead over half an hour ago. She had not done so because she was worried her friend had gone bat-shit crazy. No, she had positioned herself thusly shortly *before* Sachiko began dressing-down the innocent reports. Why had she come to the captain's stateroom but stopped short of presenting herself? Because Sapale was torn. Unsure. Sapale was conflicted. There wasn't an old saying about a conflicted Kaljaxian female, that they constituted a worrisome thing. But there should have been. An irresolute Kaljaxian female was like a hungry tiger with a thorn in its paw that one had just doused with a bucket of cold soapy water. It was a situation to follow closely.

What troubled the generally unflappable Sapale thusly? Oh, come on now. You know this. Sure, let's all say it together: *Jon Ryan.* He was the only force in the multiverse that could so vex this otherwise alien equivalent of the Rock of Gibraltar. Unexpected thermonuclear war, unanticipated stellar collapse, or arbitrary taxation? Nope, none of those could place an ADHD killer bee up her butt like Jon Ryan could and often did.

What had Jon done this time? Why he'd gone and disappeared on her. Was her dilemma based on the fact that she loved him like life itself? Meh. Maybe that was part of it. Was it because, though she welcomed a break from the jerk, she, at the same time, missed the boob? Kinda sorta. Was she worried about him? Ding, ding, ding. *That* was the main issue. They were, over their billions of years together, occasionally apart. Sometimes for extended periods. But rarely was Jon *unaccounted* for. Worst of all, she'd tried repeatedly to ascertain where he was and she'd been completely unsuccessful. That was most atypical.

Compound that situation with the fact that Jon had stupidly gone to Dardrode's dubious shop to begin what she knew to be a fool's errand. There were just too many red flags ripping in a strong wind not to sit up and take notice. But, as unsettled as she was because of Jon's absence, she was equally flustered by her present inability to do anything proactive on her own. Jon had taken the vortex. She didn't have alternate transportation, and the only person she could reasonably call for help was the Toño DeJesus of her future. The local one didn't have a vortex. He wasn't even an android yet. In terms of the future one, she'd spent the better part of the last five years arguing with and berating Jon about bothering Toño. He had suffered a profound personal loss: his life partner, Daleria. Toño was an android, and so effectively immortal. Daleria had been a demigod and also immortal. But when Jon and his team destroyed the Ancient Gods' power source, Daleria, like many of her kindred Cleinoids, became completely mortal. Sapale knew Toño needed to be left alone to deal with his grief. Maybe someday he would be able to rejoin Jon and her on their quests, but for now he needed quiet time. She would not ask for his help now.

And so she stood pressed against the bulkhead outside her friend's stateroom trying to summon the courage to ask for her help. Sapale knew Sachiko would help. She also knew it would place the captain in a collision course with the current ball-and-chain, General Glenn Price. And maybe it was silly of Sapale, but there were few acts she'd rather perform in this universe than ask anyone else for help. Partly that was her closed Kaljaxian nature. But, to be honest with herself, part of it was due to her inborn mule-like stubbornness.

"If you tell me *one* more time, Lieutenant Carmory, that the ship's supply of paper products is woefully below optimum, I will find a way to turn *you* into paper. I kid you not, sailor," Sachiko scolded the report Avery Carmory had submitted.

That sealed Sapale's course of action. She simply could not listen to her friend berate written documents any longer. It was too silly.

She stepped around the corner, trying to make it look like she'd done so following a continuous stroll. "Good evening," came out of Sachiko's mouth with far less enthusiasm than she'd planned on.

Without looking up, Sachiko commented, "I was wondering when you'd make up your mind to walk through that hatch."

"Wh ... what? I only just arrived," she lied uncomfortably.

"Sure, but your right foot seems to have proceeded you by over half an hour."

"Huh?"

"It's been poking out distractingly that long. I'm guessing kids on Kaljax don't play hide-and-seek. You're bad at it."

"I don't think I was out there for half an hour," she protested lamely. "I was just gathering my thoughts, you know, giving you time to possibly finish your duties there."

Sachiko only then turned to face Sapale. "First, good evening to you. Second, come in and have a seat, please. Third, your shoe intruded on my solitude when I was arguing with the worst Sanitation Department report I've ever read. It was wordy, avoided decisions or any specific points, and it rambled. Also, I read it at 20:34. It is now 21:02. That's half an hour translated into normal speak."

Sapale rolled all four of her eyes and sat. "That was a particularly painful lament on your part, if I do say so myself."

"You'd have responded *differently?*" Sachiko asked with a coy smile.

"Yes. I'd have summoned the author to my stateroom and shot him or her dead."

"Don't think for a moment I wasn't tempted. But then there'd be that much more paperwork and I don't need that." Sachiko proffered her hands toward her screen.

"You have *your* management style, I have *mine*. All that really matters is that one is consistent and gets their desired results."

"So, what were you *not* standing outside for half an hour brooding over, so uncertain what you wanted to say to me?"

"Brooding? Nice choice of words, since it has to do with my *brood*-mate. That's what we call husbands in my culture."

"Sapale," she said, deadly serious, "I know that. It was an intended pun. I'm very clever."

"I shall keep that in mind."

"I've been wondering for a while why you haven't come to me with your concerns over Jon. I know he's been gone too long and that he hasn't contacted you. Yes, he's a man, and hence insensitive and clueless, but this is beyond even that pale."

"Yes, it is. And it's worse." Sapale gestured vaguely toward her head. "You may or may not know we have this head-to-head communication thing."

"I've heard it mentioned."

"Well, it's crazy powerful. Anyone with it installed can converse in real time with anyone else so equipped. There is no linear distance over which it *doesn't* work."

"And when you called Jon, he didn't answer?"

"Bingo. That means his system is down, which is next to impossible. Alternately, he could be in a different time or a separate universe. Those are about the only good explanations."

"Leaving the bad possibility that he's dead."

"Leaving that glaringly bad option, yes. And, because no really sucky news should be received by itself, I've lost contact with Al, too."

"Kind of dashing *system failure* against the rocks," Sachiko said grimly.

"Kind of."

"What about *Blessing*? You must have tried her."

"Funny thing that's not funny. We never installed it directly to *Blessing*. We figured Al'd always be joined to her at the hip, so why bother." She shook her head with disgust.

"I'm so sorry to hear this. What can I do to help?"

"I ... I need to—" Sapale came very close to breaking down. She never broke down. Never. "I need to find him."

"Then find him we shall," Sachiko declared resolutely.

"But where he went, it's a really long ways away."

"And we can't fold space, so it's going to take us a while to get there."

"Are you certain you should do that?" Sapale asked meekly.

"Absolutely. We have a big old spaceship at our command. Jon needs rescuing, so a rescuing we will go. And the sooner we leave, the sooner we get there."

"What about the nimnal?" Sapale pointed generally over her shoulder.

"Glenn? *Pshaw*," she flipped a hand dismissively in the air. "Piece of cake."

"Oh no."

"What?" Sachiko asked with sudden concern.

"You have gone over the edge. The talking-to-reports thing wasn't a one-off." Sapale placed a hand over her mouth.

Sachiko relaxed visibly. "You got me there," she chided. "But seriously, I'll handle the Glennster. If he objects too vehemently, I'll keelhaul him then dump what's left of him behind on Mars."

"Sachiko, I know what a big deal this is. You've worked hard to arrange this next step for Aramthella. I don't want—"

"It's not about you," Sachiko said firmly. "Jon's a member of my crew. He's gone missing. I need to institute a search and rescue mission. That's all there is to it." She spread her hands out across the table. "It is a done deal."

"Thanks. You have no idea what a relief it is to hear that."

"What? We're the original team, us four. No way I'm breaking up the team." Sapale placed her palms together and waved them toward Sachiko in thanks.

Sapale gave her a questioning gaze. "You're sure this won't blow up in your face? You and Glenn, you don't have such a copacetic history. He's like the head of the I Hate Sachiko Fan Club."

"Not any longer. He will come around to my way of thinking or he will regret his reticence severely. I've been trying to get along with him in a civil manner. But from now on, he's going to be getting a full dose of Captain Sachiko Jones and her determined will."

"Okay," Sapale remarked rather tentatively."

Sachiko grinned as she traced one index finger around the other, indicating just how securely she felt Glenn was wrapped around her finger.

"Over my *dead* body," Glenn thundered so forcefully that Sachiko felt spittle spray land upon her cheeks.

Hmm, Sachiko reflected, perhaps he wasn't so tightly wound around her finger. Oh, bother. That was going to make the inevitable a bit harder to accomplish. But either Glenn was going to come around or he was going to become an involuntary Martian colonist before he knew what hit him.

"General," Sachiko began as calmly as she could, which wasn't very, "Jon Ryan, an original member of my crew, is missing. A search and recovery mission is mandatory. Surely you understand and agree with that?"

He rocketed a plump digit in her direction. "Do not presume to tell me what I understand or do not understand. I was defending this country long before you were born. I know what it means to serve. I also know what it means to live up to a promise I once made. *You*, Captain Jones, made a similar promise. And now you're throwing it back in the president's face—in *my* face—because you want to go off the reservation on a whimsical hunch?"

"You know as well as I do that a mission is a fluid, living, breathing beast. One must adapt, react, and improvise. Our present support mission, while laudable, has been superseded by a distress call."

Glenn was positively apoplectic. Sachiko suddenly worried he'd have a massive cardiovascular event and that would then reside on her moral ledger forever.

This time he pumped his plump finger at her vigorously. "First off, there was no distress call. There is only a bored and worried wife's uneasy feeling. Second, this dual mission is of the most critical nature. We need to reestablish our presence on Mars ASAP. We need to show all those aliens out there that we are an interstellar power, one that will not be pushed around. Third, there is a chain of command at work whether or not it is convenient for all involved at any given time. You simply will not put this mission at risk based on shared but misguided woman's intuition."

A wave of soothing relief swept welcomely over Sachiko. Glenn did not just cross a line, he crossed it, dropped his trousers, and shat upon the line. The gloves were officially off.

"Here's what is going to happen, you pathetic, misogynistic little man. First, you will lower your voice in my presence or I will have you thrown in the brig. Sir, I kid you not. And don't say I can't because we don't have a brig. I will convert the forward port airlock into one just for you."

He started to stand, to assail her outrageous statement, but he uncharacteristically seemed to think better of such a foolish act. He settled back, an avid listener.

"Second, in the next hour, Aramthella is leaving Mars orbit and setting off on a rescue mission. I am personally through with you and your condescension and your mastery of pettiness. That said, you will be allowed to remain titularly in your present position if you cooperate and, more importantly, if you shut the fuck up and play nice. Your sole alternative is that you will be deposited on the Martian surface. If so, we will depart a happier crew. Whether I deposit you with a spacesuit or not will be determined by the next few minutes that remain in this one-way discussion. I will reveal and you will nod in silent agreement. You clear on that, you sorry son of a bitch?"

"I will—"

"*Security*," Sachiko called out loudly. By no coincidence at all, she'd stationed a small contingent of Marines outside her door as soon as Glenn had entered. Call it a *woman's intuition*, she giggled in the confines of her mind.

Three very bulky, very pissed off looking NCOs sporting equally bulky and pissed off looking rifles charged through the door. Without a word they stepped directly to Glenn and boxed him in on the sides he wasn't facing Sachiko. Whether it was prearranged or not he would never know, but all three monoliths stood as close as anatomically possible, brushing against him repeatedly.

"Saying 'I will' is not a nod in silent agreement, Glenn-like human," Sachiko scolded. "That we will call strike one. In this particular game, the players get two strikes and then they are *out*. All out players instantly become a Martian colonist. So, mind your manners and your tongue. Your attitude too, in fact. I want you to behave like your mother the Pope was present in this room. You copy?"

Reflexively, he started to say something, but he aborted that hazardous plan and just nodded in the affirmative.

"You see, you can be reasonable. I knew you had it in you somewhere down there real deep and atrophied out."

She stared at him briefly to make certain no outbursts were pending.

"Glenn, here's some of the flaws in the logic-limited arguments you presented to me as reasons that abandoning this mission was a bad plan. You misspoke and you made assumptions that are flat out wacky. *We* are not a spacefaring power. *I* command a really bitchin' spaceship." She pointed both index fingers up. "Please note that I did not say I owned this ship. That is because I do not. Aramthella and I work together. We have mutual respect for one another. But make no mistake, she is not just another capital ship to move about on some chessboard. Does that make sense?"

Glenn numbly nodded.

"And as to humankind proving anything to," she waved her hands in the air, "all those aliens out there. Let me disabuse you of such silly talk. Mars is the planet next door. Settling it is a kissing-your-sister level achievement to all those aliens out there. All those aliens don't care. Most would just as soon snuff us out as waste time contemplating what respect we are due for trivial accomplishments. Are we cool here?"

Again he returned a frigid nod.

"Glenn, I see you growing into manhood as we speak," Sachiko sarcastically praised. "Please save all of your thanks until the end, however. I'm pressed for time. Oh, say, did you hear the rumor about General Robert Sherman?"

Glenn furrowed his brow in confused consternation.

"Ah, sorry, you're right. I asked a yes-no question to a man on a strict yes-ma'am diet, didn't I? How insensitive of me." Sachiko breathed deeply through her nostrils and shook her arms loose. "Say, Glenn, I bet you have not heard the rumor about General Sherman?"

He nodded yes.

"Not surprising since I just started it this very moment. But he's being offered his old job back."

Glenn's eyes flared.

"Yes, I'm extending an offer to him to be your commanding officer. He will be in charge of the mission while I run the ship. That way he can use his unconventional yet ever-so-productive teaching skills to turn you into a top-flight officer. Won't that be fun if he says yes?"

Rather than lie with a nod, Glenn remained stiff in his chair.

"Honesty," she declared. "I like that in a junior officer. It bodes well for a successful career. I speak in relative terms, naturally, what with you being *junior* in grade to Tank."

Again, no movement emanated from Glenn.

"Moving right along. I will now return to you the powers of speech, albeit limited powers. You may now respond in short, ideally heartfelt, but above all courteous responses. And I don't want the three Neanderthals closing you in like a phone booth to intimidate you in any way, shape, or form. No. I want you to speak freely," she raised a finger, "within the boundaries of common decency, mind you. You can do that, right?"

He nodded, apparently too flustered to have taken her meaning directly.

"And I don't doubt that every one of them has ever fantasized during their service about clocking a general officer in the head with the butts of their rifles. So be present in our exchange."

"Proceed," he growled.

One of the guards closed the gap between the two of them. In so doing his man part may have inadvertently shoved Glenn's ear hard enough to bobble-head him.

"So, Glenn, what'll it be? Are you an innie or an outtie? You staying the course or are you more of a mind to become a settler on a new frontier?"

"I will not remain aboard this mockery—" Glenn began with venom.

Displaying *some* degree of restraint, the guard opposite the man-part fellow brought his rifle butt into feather-light contact with Glenn's temple.

"No," Glenn quickly amended. "I wish to leave this ship as soon as possible."

"Not a problem. I'm sure the nascent colony there will welcome the chance to have a bossy, useless, desk jockey general there to keep everyone on course and focused."

"I formally request you return me to Earth, not maroon me on Mars."

Sachiko raised one eyebrow. "A favor? Glenn, I am rather shocked that you feel comfortable enough to ask one of me? I was raised to believe favors were *earned* via good works and one's demonstration of their personal worth."

"You can get there in a matter of hours. I have important work to do back home."

"I can get you there in *five minutes* if I so desire. But I do not so desire. Based on your churlish, petulant behavior to date, I'm inclined to leave you as a solo satellite of Mars, orbiting for a frozen eternity. I am, however, willing to reject that indulgence and set you down planetside so as not to burn any bridges. Some who do not know you well might think poorly of me for tossing you out into the void."

"Are we through here?" he asked with an edge.

"Plus, Glenn, I like Earth. I like it a lot. Why would I reinfect it with you?" Sachiko felt the need to conclude her thoughts on the matter.

"If you're picking up Sherman you couldn't drop me off? Trust me, that act, by the way, won't sit well with my superiors."

Sachiko rubbed her lips together. "Excellent point. I will call Tank and see if he's game. If he is, then you get a free ride to planet Earth."

"Thank you."

"Do not thank me. Between you and me there is no such thing as common decency. You are an insufferable boor, a disgrace to civil interplay. You forfeited any right to social niceties by being you, Glenn." She turned her attention to the computer screen to her right. "Will you Marines be so kind as to show the general out?" She asked without bothering to look up. That way she could never be asked to testify as to the manner in which Glenn was shown the exit. Plus, she had work that required her immediate attention ... probably.

TWENTY-ONE

After thirty hours of forty-Gs of acceleration, we were moving like a greased-prune juice through grandma's intestinal tract. The two AIs debated our actual velocity. Yeah. The different ways they measured had that much variance at such speeds. I think we were getting near 0.6c. Old Professor Einstein was grabbing the controls and leveling his mind-bending effects on us. Our mass increased, time as we viewed it slowed, and everything behind us was so redshifted we lost sight of half of its light.

But, in essence, we were just going nowhere really fast. We were in a particularly barren section of space. When I was certain we had to have lost our uninvited guest, we began braking. Once we were dead in space, our number one task was to determine where and when we were. I knew we were back in our home universe because that's the one I had RD take us to. That much control we had. But universes are unimaginably mega-huge. I hoped we were topologically near where we'd started our crazy ass journey, in the good old Milky Way. But there were no guarantees. Not with my wonky ship and even wonkier luck.

"Alright, gentlemen," I began, "you know the drill. I need to know our location in time/space. So have at it."

"We both agree we're in our home galaxy," Al announced almost immediately. "To be more specific we're in the Scutum-Crux spiral arm, approximately thirty-five degrees counterclockwise from the Sun's position in the Orion arm relative to the galactic core."

"More or less where Dardrode's junkyard is located," I estimated.

"Yes," Al confirmed.

"So, a long way from home, but near to where we were when all the fun began," I said to myself.

"I'm afraid the *when* of it will take some time to approximate. Given the limits of our sensors, we'll be lucky to determine that any time soon."

"Any time soon computer time or normal-people time?" I pressed.

"Well, pilot, since there are only computers aboard, that point is rather moot," that darn Al replied.

"Speak for yourself," I defended. "And don't actually speak come to think of it. Work on figuring out when it is."

After that Al was quiet. Such an unexpected pleasure. I started fiddling with the communications system Tip had given us. It was a long shot in terms of contacting anyone, but it was one of the few options at my disposal. In the meantime, I had RD head in what we could estimate was the general direction of Earth. I elected not to try to return to Dardrode's for one very good reason. I didn't know *when* we were at the moment. There would be no point going back if *Stingray* wasn't there. Possibly we either hadn't arrived yet or Sapale had long since come and retrieved the ship. It was too much turf to lose when we were moving so slow, relatively speaking.

But even with the warp drive, we weren't getting home anytime soon. I figured, with back-of-the-envelope calculations, that we were around fifty thousand light years away from where I wanted to be. Even at the ten times light speed we could *possibly* make, it'd take five thousand years to get there. Yeah, big galaxy. But, as my old man used to say-to-death, *A journey of a thousand miles begins with a single step.* Thanks, Pops.

A few days passed. Every once in a while Al or RD would alert me to the fact that they were still working on figuring out what time it was, but that they were still uncertain. I'd asked them to not provide me with useless updates, but they still did. Digital guilt? Machine humor? Who knew? It was annoying. Hey, I was busy. I was playing with my radio. I was mastering the application of doing impressions of famous people calling out for help. So far I had a stunning version of Judy Garland asking, *Hello, are we in Kansas anymore?* And a jaw-dropping rendition of Jimmy Stewart asking, S ... *say now, is anybody out there?* My best one most definitely was my acapella rockabilly singing of *Help.* Man, I had John Lennon *down!* What? You think I was just bored out of my gourd? No way. I was creating solutions. *You know I need someone ... Help!*

Finally, they reached a consensus. Al did the dubious honors. "Pilot, as best we can determine, we are twenty thousand years in the relative past, compared to when we first bungled away from Dard-rode's place of business."

"Twenty thousand years?" I repeated, perking up a bit. "That's not so bad. I mean, we're in the right geologic epoch. That has to count for something."

"Are you asking or stating that as fact?" Al pressed.

"I ... er, would it matter?"

"Only if you were asking. If so, I could shut you down by alerting you to the fact that you were speaking nonsense. If you are *declaring* it, I need to remind you there are no psychiatrists on board."

"No, come on. RD can make single jumps in that range, right? Theoretically we're only one jump from being done."

"You know what?" Al began speaking rapidly. "You're correct. One-hundred-and-ten percent so. I will silence myself without reminding you what the chances are that one random jump would place us where we wish to be. What cares the pilot about statistics and reality checks?"

"Such a negative computer," I chided. "Let's try and be a tad more optimistic."

"And your justification for optimism since we began this epic-fail mission is what?" Al challenged.

"It's so bad it can't get worse?" I replied hesitantly.

"There he goes, flushing the whole enchilada down the toilet," Al replied with exasperation. "Talk about a Ryan jinx."

"What's an enchilada?" RD interjected.

"Not important," Al returned. "We're doomed, so nothing really matters, not even international taste treats."

"Moving on," I directed. "What star systems are located along our course back to Earth?"

"I suppose my answer would be based on what type of planetary system you would hope might be, Captain," RD responded respectfully.

"A system with a highly advanced technology would be a dream," I replied.

"We will be traversing a good deal of territory," RD began thoughtfully. "The chances that we will be passing close to some advanced civilization is thus rather promising."

"I ... I don't want *promising*, I want *names*, specifics."

"I see three candidates along our present course," RD responded. "The Capattala Empire, centered on a planet called Gof-9-11-10. That is a ten light year side trip from our present vector. Another would be the Julasoff Interdiction. That's a loose confederation of systems more like fifty light years off course. Finally, there's the Listhelon Empire. They inhabit the third planet orbiting Lacaille 9352. They—"

"No, no, no," I cut RD off cold. "No, those guys are incredibly hostile and xenophobic. No thanks, I'd rather die a heat death in space rather than ask them for an assist."

"Now, pilot," Al implored, "beggars can't be choosers."

"Al, you fought them right along with me, way back on our first ever voyage. They're irrationally homicidal."

"Understood," he replied. "But perhaps you could try being super friendly. Maybe they'll make an exception and help?"

"Al, you're delusional," I informed him.

"At least you won't die of boredom," he qualified unhelpfully.

"No, that is a true fact," I had to concede. "Any way you cut it, this is looking to be a very long, slow, and bor—"

"Captain," Al interrupted using his official tone. "I'm detecting a massive surge of tachyons."

Oh crap, that ship that chased us for no good reason was back. "Where?"

"Everywhere," he replied with a panic in his voice.

"I know. But is he to our stern, our port? Where is the surge generally?"

"*Everywhere*," he repeated with more concern.

"Al, one ship can't—"

I never got to finish that thought. First one, long, thin cigar-shaped ship emerged out of nowhere, thrusting into view like a humpback whale breaching off of Maui. Rapidly a second materialized on the other side of us, and in a flash we were literally surrounded three-hundred-and-sixty degrees with the same ships. If there'd have been a sun out there in space its light would have been totally blocked by all the tonnage that enveloped us.

There was no viable direct course of escape left to us. I could put up a full membrane, but that act would only be a temporary fix. Whoever these dodos were, they meant business.

I slammed my fingers onto the control interface. "We're jumping universes," I shouted.

"Is there room for us to ... Oh, too late," Al stated. "I guess we'll find out the Jon Ryan way."

I actually had no idea if there was a run-up distance needed to move in time or space. But not making a desperate leap was going to end poorly, so I estimated we only had a nothin' muffin to lose.

"Report," I snapped.

"We transitioned out of our home universe without difficulty," Al informed. "However, we seem to have been unsuccessful at transition into an alternate universe."

"We... huh? What's that even mean?"

"We left one universe but appear restrained from materializing into another universe. As incomplete as that sounds, Captain, that is our current status," Al responded.

"But what restrain ... ah. All those cigar ships are penning us in."

"That's possible, but I do not believe we are equipped to confirm such a supposition," Al returned.

"But, where does that mean we are?" I wondered aloud. "There's nothing between universes to be stuck *in*."

"Neither of us is in a position to discuss that topic, Captain. Sorry," replied a somber Al.

"Can we see the ships out there?" I called out.

"That is entirely unclear," Al said. "Our sensor abilities seem greatly diminished."

"Well basic physics can't be," I mumbled. "Make a ten-meter diameter full membrane and punch it straight along our X-axis."

1-2-3 ... *BOOOOM!* There was such an oh-so-satisfying crunch as the membrane struck home against something that was heretofore solid but invisible. I reasoned it had to be one of the enemy vessels. But, wait. How could there be an explosion audible in the vacuum of deep space? Easy, there couldn't be. Sound needs a medium to support its propagation, like air or water. Then my fighter pilotishness kicked in. Who cared? I punched. Something went boom. Move on.

"Al, how far off did that impact occur?"

"Approximately seven hundred meters away."

"Swing the membrane around wildly. I want you to pass it through the entire sphere seven-hundred meters in radius that surrounds us."

"Implementing," he said quickly.

"As soon as you're done, make first a random time jump, then a universe jump, and then another time jump."

"Roger that," he responded professionally.

I heard multiple crunches coming from all directions over the next ten seconds. I do believe we were pounding the crap out of some hostile cigars. Then the ship lurched, then again, then one more time.

"Status?" I shouted.

"I ... I'm not ... I don't know," Al stammered.

"I felt something. What happened?" I demanded.

"Our first time leap appears to have produced no results. The spacial jump took us into a parallel universe, then we made a random time jump inside that universe."

"But the first time jump did nothing? How ... how can you even know that?"

"I can't, really. But I suspect based on where we ended up that the first maneuver was ineffective."

"Any bogies follow us?" I asked loudly.

"None yet."

"Yet," I parroted. They'd somehow tracked us down earlier. A repeat performance seemed a safe bet. "Al, make a series of time jumps, say five. Make them just long enough that we have enough charge left to jump once more if we need to."

"I am engaging that process now," he replied dutifully. "If I might ask while performing, Captain, why the time jumps? You do know they are fully random and almost certainly counterproductive to our core mission of returning home."

"Call it a gut instinct. These guys seem to be right on top of spacial moves, but the temporal ones at least throw them for a loop. I'm hoping to buy time."

"For what?" Al rather astutely queried.

"Inspiration," I confessed.

"I feared as much," he replied dubiously. "There's no way around the fact that if these pursuers were mad at us before, they are astronomically more so now after we bashed all those ships."

"I doubt there's a bonus level of revenge for wrecking their property past some magical number," I agreed. "Then again..."

"It sure was fun," Al finished my thought.

"*Oorah!*"

"Oorah indeed," Al concurred robustly.

As we quieted down, I tried to make some sense out of the battle that we'd just survived. There was so much screwy about it I was totally unsettled. Yes, in war, outcomes are rarely the predicted ones, and success is just as often luck rather than skilled planning. But if major aspects of it defy belief, it was hard to base my next moves on them when the inevitable reengagement comes down.

Audible explosions in space? Time jumps that don't work, even though the system performed up to its haphazard normal just a few moments later? Cigar ships penning us up and presumably restraining us physically? Spaceships are not bumper cars. At the speeds they maneuver at, impacts are exclusively catastrophic. Even the thickest hull and the most juiced-up force field can't negate that simple fact. And yet these losers basically rugby tackled me. That simply can't happen.

And, seriously, I'm not going to ask again. Why are they hellbent on attacking me in the first place? I'm a nice, neighborly android. Honest to goodness I am. Just ask any sentient species out there. Well, except for the ones I've bombarded, culled their numbers, crushed in battle, or generally rubbed their noses in the galactic sand. Yeah. Ask any species but one of those and they'll tell you I'm a stand-up guy. Oh, and I guess that question really only means anything in the time between when I did something inadvertently to piss them off and the time I played whack-a-mole with their fleet. Yeah ... if they're hating me now, I kind of own that, don't I?

Oops.

EPILOGUE

"Captain Jon Ryan," Rift Dude called out to me.

"Not now," I scolded. "I'm busy."

"Pilot, your very nose grows from such a boldfaced lie. You are doing perfectly nothing," Al charged.

"Whatever I'm doing, although it may seem to be little, far exceeds whatever RD here wants to tell me."

What was I, in fact, doing? Absolutely nothing. I was out-of-my-gourd loco with boredom. We were in some damn universe. We were lost in time. I'm talking so lost. It was like I had taken the concept of time and poured a fifth of tequila down its throat, spun it around a few times, and then threw a lit blow torch down its gullet. Then, just for good measure, I'd painted the words, *I'm a New York Yankee fan* across time's ass and forced it to moon all of existence. We were actually not lost. No, we had too few reference points to begin to qualify as *lost*. What were we? Screwed, that's what we were.

Some freaking species of morons were fully committed to killing me. Just because they had zero reason at all to want to do so didn't make the screwing over they were attempting any less ... er, you know, unwelcome. They needed to go screw themselves, that's what they needed to do, IMHO. But, if I'd learned one thing well over the two billion years I had graced this reality with my handsome, smiling face, it was this. If you beat someone down well enough, and leave them in your dust fully enough, they were guaranteed to finally give up and leave you the hell alone. No, seriously. I had this. They came, I conquered them, now they would tail-between-the-legs it the hell off my lawn, figuratively speaking.

Seriously. I'd seen the last of those wannabes. And a good riddance, too.

Now all I had to do was get back to my time. Check that. I had to also return to Earth, didn't I? But that was it. Well, I had to fix time. I'd totally disrupted the timeline when I resurrected Earth. I mean, I had to and I did. But the mess I made? Yeah, I had to fix it.

All I had to do, now that the dip shits that were harassing me were one with history, was to figure out how to do all those impossible things.

Easy peasy, pudding and pie. I had this, right?

To be continued ...

(You saw that coming, right?)

GLOSSARY:

Als (1): The original ship's AI on Jon's first flight long ago was Alvin. Jon shortened that to Al. When Al was joined to Jon's vortex in the Galaxy On Fire Series, Al and Blessing fell in love and got "married." Since then Jon refers to them combined as the Als.

Aramthella (1): The mighty and ancient time ship that Jon and his team stole from the body maker.

Ark 1 (1): Jon's ship on his very first mission, when he traveled to find humankind a new home.

Azsuram (2): Original human name for the third planet orbiting Groombridge. It was the planet Jon and Sapale settled on after they left the human fleet fleeing doomed Earth. They established an idyllic society of Kaljaxians there, before humans join them.

Blessing (1): See *Stingray*.

Brood-mate/Brood's-mate (*The Forever Life*): These are, respectively, the Kaljaxian words for *husband* and *wife*.

Command Prerogatives (1): The thin fibers Jon extends from his left four fingers. They are probes that also control a vortex.

Cube (1): Jon's alternate name for the vortex he captains.

Dardrode (1): The slimiest, most underhanded gunrunner, used car salesthing of all times. He ran a chop shop/junkyard Jon dealt with all too often.

Davdiad (1): God-figure on Kaljax.

Daleria (2): Demigod and innkeeper whom Jon and Sapale befriended. She worked with them against the ancient gods as she'd grown to hate them.

Deavoriath (1): Three arms and legs, an ancient species that had the most advanced tech in the galaxy. Very helpful to Jon.

Emma Walters (2): Captain, and in charge of the women's barracks on Mars 1 on Aramthella's first voyage. What a thankless job. Now working under Major Walters.

Evil Jon Ryan/ EJ (1): Alternate timeline version of the original human to android download. Over time, he turned to the darker side of his nature. He studied "magic" under a Deft master.

Form One/Form Two (1): A Form is the title of a vortex pilot. If more than one is aboard they get numerical designations based on seniority.

Framework of Time (5): One of the two contingent parts of Time. This is the mindless, unstoppable progression part of Time.

Glenn Price (1): Brigadier General who replaced Tank as mission commander. A real bureaucratic POS.

Honesty Hartley (2): Doctor on duty at the student health center when the president had the entire staff transported to Mars. And appropriately there, as she was a total space cadet.

Kaljax (1): The home planet of Sapale. Jon went there on his original voyages.

Megan Thompson (2): A young Georgetown University student swept up to Mars 1 when the clan attacked Earth. She became so depressed she took her own life. Desi's first ghost-in-space.

Membrane (1): See space-time congruity manipulator.

Miniminim (5): Senior Sub-Cataloger at the Claxeon Citadel. Befriended Jon. A very odd looking globular female scholar.

Parker, Lakeisha (6): Sergeant major, US Army. A badass soldier who befriended Jon.

Necumplack (2): The species name of the time controlling blobs that power the time ships.

No-time (TWLFE 1): A verb. It means to take the time from a unit of space/time, leaving only space. The object has no time, it had been no-timed.

Nufe (The Forever Series): A magical liquor made by the

Deavoriath. It tastes different to all who partaker. It reminds the drinker of many pleasant tastes all at once. Mildly intoxicating.

Oowaoa (The Forever Life): Home world of the Deavoriath.

Plesmus (2): A necumplack. She is a mucous blob that can focus time energy. Very useful for a time machine.

Probe Fibers (1): Aka command prerogatives, they allow piloting of the Vortex spaceship and can analyze whatever they touch.

Reva St. Claire (2): Lt. Colonel and the past commander of Mars 1. Now Sachiko's second in command aboard Aramthella.

Robert "Tank" Sherman (1): Lead academic and friend of Sachiko. Also in Marine Reserves.

Sapale (1): Jon's Kaljaxian wife from his original flight to find humankind a new home. At first just her brain was copied, then, eventually, she was downloaded to an android host. Travelled with the corrupted Jon Ryan from an alternate timeline.

Sachiko Jones (1): One-time astronomy grad student under Tank's supervision. The time ship chose her to be its new captain.

Sariffdilarian (1): The culture that fabricated the time machine Jon acquired from Dardrode, System's Operator 11-4R-22, aka Rift Dude.

Space-time congruity manipulator (1): Hugely helpful force field. Aka a membrane.

Stingray (1): Jon's Deavoriath spaceship. Her name in the

Deavoriath language is pronounced "crash." Hence, silly Jon renamed her after one of his favorite cars. It makes Jon-sense.

Sunne calrf (2): A traditional Kaljaxian stew. They are all revolting to Jon, but he finds this version especially loathsome.

Swathi Varma (2): Lieutenant, and aide-de-camp to Reva St. Claire on Mars 1.

Tip Benjamin (?): Where've I heard that name before? Hmm. Presently, Tip is a student at Georgetown. He was evacuated to Mars as part of the US president's plan to save a tiny portion of humankind. And they took Tip too? Also the general who more recently aided Jon in a parallel universe.

Tom Grant (2): Major, and the officer in charge of the male dormitories on Mars. Now in charge of personnel on Aramthella.

Toño DeJesus (1 of TFL): The scientist creator of the android Jon. Became his lifelong friend.

Vortex (1): Super-advanced Deavoriath sentient spaceship. Moves by folding space. If you get a chance to own one, do it.

Vortex Manipulator (The Forever Enemy): The consciousness that actually controls the vortex spacecraft. Think super AIs. They're a product of some very creepy alien tech.

Quantum Decoupler (1): A most excellent weapon that pulls the quarks apart in a proton. The energy released as they rejoin is amazing.

Yibitriander (Book 2, The Forever Series): Three-legged

Deavoriath, past Form of Jon's borrowed vortex *Wrath*. A real tough cookie.

AND NOW A WORD FROM YOUR AUTHOR

Thank you so much for joining me, Jon, and the whole gang on this ongoing journey! The Ryanverse is terrific, and it even better with you along! The story really begins with *The Forever Life*. If you've not read that, and the rest of the series from the start, I suggest you do. You will not be disappointed.

The outstanding people at Podium Audio are working hard to get all the books of the Ryanverse into audiobooks. If you're having any trouble locating a book, look for it there.

For a complete listing of the correct order for reading the Ryanverse, check out this page [https://craigrobertsonblog.wpcomstaging.com/2020/12/22/correct-order-for-reading-the-ryanverse/].

Three favors. One, let me know your impressions, thoughts, or suggestions. You can do that by contacting me by email (contact@craigarobertson.com) or on my Facebook Author's Page. Second, please post a review on Amazon/Audible. Those are more precious than gold to us authors. Third, email me to be placed on my mailing list. I promise to only send useful information.

Vaya con Dios, mi amigo ...
Craig

www.ingramcontent.com/pod-product-compliance
Lightning Source LLC
Chambersburg PA
CBHW052023020726
47501CB00004B/1212